"I'LL SEND SOMEONE BACK FOR YOU," SHE SAID.

Range, his hand wrapped around the saddle horn, smiled. "I don't think so," he said, and shoving her foot from his stirrup, swung up behind her.

Candace felt his body settle in behind hers, his thighs molding to the back of her own. She felt his breath on her cheek, his hand resting on her leg as he held the reins.

Range knew the moment he'd swung his leg over the saddle and slid down onto it that he'd made a mistake. A groan of despair nearly ripped from his throat as his body pressed against hers, but he managed to stifle it, and silently curse himself for an idiot a half-dozen times.

With each step Satan took, Candace's hips swayed against him, unintentionally teasing his self control. The soft waves of her hair brushed against his stubbled cheek. The fragrance of her lilac scent swirled around him, and the aching need to touch her further, to wrap his arms around her and lose himself within her embrace was almost more than he could bear.

BOOK YOUR PLACE ON OUR WEBSITE AND MAKE THE READING CONNECTION!

We've created a customized website just for our very special readers, where you can get the inside scoop on everything that's going on with Zebra, Pinnacle and Kensington books.

When you come online, you'll have the exciting opportunity to:

- View covers of upcoming books
- Read sample chapters
- Learn about our future publishing schedule (listed by publication month *and author*)
- Find out when your favorite authors will be visiting a city near you
- Search for and order backlist books from our online catalog
- Check out author bios and background information
- Send e-mail to your favorite authors
- Meet the Kensington staff online
- Join us in weekly chats with authors, readers and other guests
- Get writing guidelines
- AND MUCH MORE!

**Visit our website at
http://www.zebrabooks.com**

SILVER LININGS

Cheryl Biggs

Zebra Books
Kensington Publishing Corp.

http://www.zebrabooks.com

ZEBRA BOOKS are published by

Kensington Publishing Corp.
850 Third Avenue
New York, NY 10022

Copyright © 1998 by Cheryl Biggs

Zebra and the Z logo Reg. U.S. Pat. & TM Off.

First Printing: June, 1998
10 9 8 7 6 5 4 3 2 1

Printed in the United States of America

Prologue

"You will not leave."

The thundering voice and the loud crash that followed jerked six-year-old Nicky awake. He bolted upright in bed, frightened and disoriented.

His mother screamed.

Another crash.

Throwing back the covers, Nicky forced his trembling legs to move and jumped from the bed. He ran across the dark bedroom to the door, opening it just a crack, but enough so that he could see out.

The pale glow of a lamp in the front parlor spilled into the empty hall and through his doorway.

He crept from his room and down the hall. At the doorway leading to the front parlor, he paused, hugging the door frame and peeking around it.

His mother stood across the room, in profile to him. Her dark hair, which was always pinned up neatly in a bun, flowed down her back and over her shoulders as she clung to the back of a chair.

"You're not leaving, you hear me? You and that brat of yours aren't going anywhere."

Nicholaus cringed as a huge, burly fist suddenly swung into view.

His mother screamed.

The fist slammed into her face.

Her arms flew up, her legs buckled, and she fell awkwardly into a nearby table.

"Mama!" Nicky screamed, and bolted from his hiding place.

"No. Nicky, go back," Allison said. She struggled to her feet as blood streamed from an ugly gash on her temple.

He stopped halfway to her and looked at the man who'd hit his mother. The lamp was at his back now, turning him to a huge, black silhouette. Nicky cringed.

Allison turned toward the man. "You won't get away with this," she said.

He laughed, and before she could react, he lunged forward and struck her again.

"Run, Nicky," Allison screamed, as she tried to get to her feet. "Run."

"You ungrateful whore. Ain't no one going anywhere." He stomped toward her.

Terror nearly choked Nicky, but his limbs were paralyzed by fear.

Allison screamed at him again. "Run, baby."

Tears filled Nicky's eyes. "Mama," he cried.

Allison clawed her way across the floor to him, struggling to her feet at the same time. She shooed him before her down the hall. "Run," she gasped weakly.

He ran into his bedroom, but when he turned to look back at her, she wasn't there. Nicky ran back to the door. "Mama," he cried, seeing her slumped to her knees on the floor in the hall, her shoulder against the wall the only thing holding her up. "Come on. Mama."

She pushed at him weakly. "Go, baby, run," she gasped, then sank to the floor. Her sightless eyes stared up at the ceiling.

Nicholaus trembled violently. Blood covered one side of her head, her shoulder, and was slowly forming a large pool on the floor, creeping toward his bare toes.

Heavy footsteps thumped on the plank floor. "Allison!"

Nicholaus ran into his room and slammed the door shut, throwing its bolt lock.

Almost instantly a foot crashed against the door. "Open this damned door, you good-for-nothing brat."

Nicky grabbed his shoes, the shirt and pants that his mother had laid on the foot of the bed for his use in the morning, and sprinted for the open window. He scrambled through it just as his bedroom door splintered open behind him.

Chapter 1

Everything seemed suddenly and unnaturally quiet.

Range swung off his saddle. Even though to anyone watching his posture would seem relaxed, he was acutely alert to everything around him. He had to be. There were too many people who wanted him dead.

Several men quickly disappeared from the chairs they'd occupied in front of the hotel, retreating inside. A woman hurriedly scooted her children into a store at the far end of the block, the closed sign going up in the window the moment the door shut behind her.

Range noted the movements, and at the same time ignored them. They were normal occurences whenever he rode into town. He didn't like it, had never gotten used to it, but he couldn't blame them. His reputation preceded him wherever he went, and it wasn't a good one, though there was a lot more attributed to him than he was actually responsible for.

He'd been picking up his mail here, however, for the

past six months, and had thought that the people of Pine Grove would have gotten used to seeing him come by occasionally. Obviously that wasn't the case.

He tied his horse to the rack in front of the general store, then stepped up and onto the boardwalk. The solidly muscled black gelding whinnied softly behind him, then shook his head, sending dust-covered tendrils of black mane slicing through the air.

The ride had been a hard one, the job in Kansas having taken a bit longer than he'd planned, and garnered him more trouble than he'd expected. But he was more than good at covering his trail, so he didn't expect the marshal to appear on his heels anytime soon.

Range removed his hat, wiped his forehead against the black sleeve of his shirt, slapped the Stetson against his thigh to rid the hat of the dust it had collected on the trail, then resettled it onto his head.

Before entering the store, he paused and casually looked around. He was always cautious, always wary. It's what had kept him alive. Doors suddenly closed, and window curtains dropped back into place. The sun beat down mercilessly on the small Texas town and surrounding countryside, as if attempting to bake everything in sight. Even a group of young boys who'd been playing stickball down the street had wilted under the heat's assault and taken refuge in the shade of the livery's overhanging roof.

Range felt the back of his shirt stick to his flesh and rolled his shoulders in an attempt to escape the damp, clinging fabric as much as to ease the tension that had knotted itself there during his ride. His hands dropped automatically to hover beside the pair of guns that hung low on his hips, as his gaze continued to move slowly over the street, lightly scanning every building and wagon, piercing the shadows, missing nothing that could be a potential threat. Finally satisfied that fear rather than challenge was the heaviest thing in the air, he turned toward the open door of the general store. The spurs that clung to the back of his boots jingled softly with each step. *The music of death,* someone had said to him once, after watching and listening to him walk into the street to face off with another man. The conchos that lined the outer seams of the black leather chaparrals that hugged his legs caught the sunlight and threw it, in a burst of silver, at the general store's window.

The store's clerk saw him enter and immediately turned away from the customer he'd been helping. He grabbed a packet of papers from a nearby shelf and slid it across the counter toward Range as he approached. "Been gone longer this time," the clerk said cordially. He fidgeted with the gold-rimmed spectacles that perched on his long, beaklike nose, as if he couldn't quite get them properly in place.

"Yeah." Range shuffled through the stack of mail. He didn't believe in small talk—with anyone—and engaged in it as little as possible. Too many times things got said that shouldn't, and that could lead a man into trouble. Especially a man who lived by his guns.

"Need any supplies?"

"Cartridges," Range mumbled. "Coffee. And some tobacco." He pulled one envelope out and tossed the others back on the counter. It wasn't a letter, but a telegram. He unfolded it and, as habit dictated, glanced at the name of the person who'd sent it before reading the message. It had been a long time since anything had shocked him, but the name he stared at now did. His heart seemed to stand still as the blood in his veins chilled. He forced his eyes to release their hold on the name at the bottom of the page and read the message. "Son of a bitch," he muttered softly, when he finished. "Son of a god-damned bitch."

"Well, I never!"

Range glanced over his shoulder at the older woman who'd responded to his muttered curse. He tipped his hat toward her. "Pardon, ma'am," he said, his voice suddenly a deep, velvetlike drawl. "Didn't see you there."

With a scathing glance, she sniffed her rejection of his apology. "I'll come back later," she snipped, and bustled her way out of the store, slamming the door behind her.

Range refolded the telegram and shoved it into a pocket of his vest, then turned back to the clerk.

"Sorry about her," the clerk said.

"Doesn't matter. I need to send an answer to this."

The man nodded, and, after rummaging about beneath the counter, produced a piece of paper and quill, and looked up expectantly at Range.

"To the Rolling M Ranch," he said, "Tombstone, Arizona. On my way."

Chapter 2

He was no more than a shadow on the horizon, a specter of black moving easily toward her. Candace took a step back, as if by retreating into the shade of the veranda's overhanging roof she could remove herself from view. It was an unusual thing for her to do, and she didn't understand what made her do it now. Fear had never been a natural part of her nature, but she told herself—even as she stepped into the shadows—that it wasn't fear that motivated her, merely caution.

Yet even that reaction lacked conviction and explanation, so she made no more effort to understand her puzzling response to the sight of the approaching figure, but merely resigned herself to accept it. For now.

Horse and rider moved easily down the entry drive, neither hurrying nor hesitating, seemingly oblivious of the Rolling M's wranglers at work in the nearby corrals, and the dry, crackling afternoon heat that hung on the quiet, still air like a smothering blanket of flame.

The horse's black coat glistened in reflection of the bright sun overhead, causing ripples of silver light to dance over and around muscles that flexed and pulled taut with each rise and fall of the animal's powerful legs. Tiny clouds of dust rose in the air behind the horse each time its hooves met the ground, and the occasional swish of his long, black tail looked more like fluttering threads of ebony silk than mere horse hair.

Candace felt an unexplanable shiver of anticipation slither over her flesh as she watched horse and rider draw nearer. Nothing about the man seemed familiar, which heightened her suspicion that he was a stranger.

There was an arrogance in the movement of both man and beast, a subtle aura of insolence that at once drew attention and challenged it. They moved with a fluid grace that made them one with each other, yet gave the impression that neither were master of the other. As they drew steadily closer, Candace could see that the rider was dressed entirely in black. The sight impressed her as ominous, and she had a feeling that was exactly what it was intended to do, the feeling he wanted to instill in others.

Apprehension gripped every cell of her body now, every fibre and muscle. She had no idea who this stranger was, but she sensed that his arrival on the Rolling M was no accident, and this was no innocent visit. A few months ago she wouldn't have bothered to care, wouldn't even have wondered at a stranger's arrival, but things had changed. There'd been too many accidents recently, too many comments that could mean other than what their words conveyed, and the tension that had settled over the household, increasing with each accident, each veiled insinuation, had gotten to the point lately that it was almost palpable.

At first she'd thought it was just her, but she didn't think that any longer. Candace's fingers curled around the fabric of her riding skirt and balled it within her fists. What she did think, without even knowing why, was that this man was a gunman, a hired killer, and that sent a shudder skipping up her spine that was as cold as ice.

Range saw the woman on the porch watching him. The sight dredged up memories he hadn't wanted to think about now. A shot of melancholy suddenly ripped through him, so unexpected, so fierce, it was like a bullet tearing through his flesh and nearly knocking him from his seat.

He'd waited years for this opportunity, had hoped and prayed for it, and never really expected it to present itself, so that lately he'd been thinking about just coming here anyway. But his waiting had paid off, and now that it had, he knew he had to take extra precautions, measure each step, each word, and turn his back on no one.

He shifted slightly in his seat, feeling the comfortable weight of his guns resting on each thigh. It had taken over two decades, but he was finally back. The time had come at long last to uncover the truth, and mete out the revenge that was so long overdue.

The woman, however, could present an unexpected pleasure, or problem. He'd know which soon enough.

Candace absently brushed a lock of long, blond hair from her shoulder and, forcing her hands to release their near-death grip on the folds of her skirt, she crossed her arms beneath her breasts. The movement caused the open collar of her white blouse to shift slightly askew. She took another step back, further into the shadows. The heel of her riding boot scraped against the rough plank wall of the house. There was no further retreat unless she went inside.

She had just returned from a morning ride to Gates End, the ranch where she'd grown up, and was still clad in a riding skirt. Unacceptable attire, in Garth's opinion, to greet guests, but she knew instinctively that this man wasn't a guest.

Part of her wanted to run into the house, to give in to the unreasonable fear. Another part of her insisted she remain where she stood and satisfy her curiosity, or merely reassure herself that she was wrong.

She swallowed hard, her throat parched from her long ride and the dry heat.

He was close enough now so that she could see his face. It could have been termed an attractive one, rugged lines and smooth features resonating strength and virility, except for the fact that it appeared no warmth of spirit or soul dwelt behind the handsomely cut features. He was still at least thirty feet away, yet even at this distance she formed the impression that his eyes were almost as black as the clothes he wore. The notion was deepened by the dark shadow that hung over the upper portion of his face, created by the brim of a black Stetson riding low on his forehead.

She knew he was looking at her, scrutinizing her as carefully and thoroughly as she was him, yet something—some undefinable urge she did not understand—held her on the porch, refusing to let her turn away and retreat to the safety of the house.

Garth wouldn't like her standing there, watching the stranger approach, wouldn't like the fact that she wasn't dressed for callers, but she didn't care. Not anymore.

She felt the stranger's eyes move over her slowly, blatantly, the stroke of his gaze like fire to her flesh. Candace shivered, seeing a picture of them in her mind, like a reflection, that she knew wasn't true, yet was too clear to deny. It was as if he was actually touching her, his eyes able to see past the thin folds of the muslin day blouse she wore, beyond the heavier threads of her riding skirt, and through the sheer fabric of her camisole and pantalettes. In her mind she stood naked before him and couldn't move, couldn't turn away, or even take a breath.

Suddenly, out of the corner of her eye, Candace saw movement near the barn. With an effort that took all of her resolve, she turned to see her husband walking toward the rider, whose approach remained insolently slow. Unexpected callers were rare to the Rolling M, but she sensed—especially now, seeing Garth rather than their foreman moving to greet him—that this caller had been expected. She turned her gaze back to the stranger and watched as he reined his horse in near the training corral.

Garth was still several yards away.

The stranger swung a leg over his saddle and dismounted, a movement Candace found as smooth and symmetrical as that of a panther slipping quietly, stealthily, from the leafy boughs of a tree.

But even though his movements seemed casual and easy, she sensed that he was more alert to everyone and everything around him than any man she'd ever encountered. She watched Garth close the distance between himself and the man in black, then pause before him. He said something she couldn't hear and offered his hand.

Range Connor stared down at Garth Murdock's hand. He'd prefer to shoot it off rather than shake it, but that was something he had to keep to himself. He reluctantly grasped the man's hand with his own gloved one, thankful the black leather prevented their flesh from actually touching.

Garth wasted no time in getting down to business, but Range had known he wouldn't.

Candace frowned. Something was wrong. She could feel it in the air . . . in her bones . . . in her heart. The feeling intensified as she watched. The stranger stood with his thumbs tucked into the front of his low slung gunbelt and nodded his head occasionally. Garth, shorter, stockier, and much older than the man in black, did most of the talking and gestured continually with his hands, as he always did.

She tried to fight back her anxiety and tell herself she was imagining things, simply fearing trouble where there was none. But as much as she tried, she couldn't quite convince herself that there was nothing to be concerned about. Garth wasn't a man who normally stood around talking to drifters—or anybody else for that matter—which reinforced her suspicion that Garth had been expecting his arrival.

That in itself was unusual and unsettling, since Garth hated company and rarely invited or welcomed anyone to the Rolling M.

At that moment the stranger shifted his weight, and the small silver conchos attached to the outer seams of his leather leggings caught the sunlight.

Candace's gaze darted downward, drawn by the sparkling silver. Her eyes suddenly paused as they moved over the gunbelt settled low on his hips. His holsters were secured snugly to long, lean thighs, and nestled within the gun belt's cylinders of leather were a pair of Colt .45s. The same calibre gun that her brother had always carried. The same as the one she'd secretly bought two months ago—just in case—and kept hidden beneath the camisoles and stockings tucked into a drawer of her dressing table.

She wondered suddenly if, unlike either hers or Brandon's gun, the wooden handles of the stranger's weapons were notched. One cut for every man he'd killed. She'd heard that some hired gunmen did that. Her gaze shot up to his face and, as the unconscious thought became a conscious one, she shivered, as if the cold surrounding him had reached out to touch her. At that moment Candace knew, unexplainably, that she was right about him.

The door beside her opened and Jesse Murdock, Garth's younger brother, stepped from inside the house onto the veranda. "Who's that?" he asked, staring at the stranger, his tone snarly and tinged with liquor.

She shrugged, not wanting to talk.

Jesse muttered a curse beneath his breath, then stepped from the porch and approached Garth and the stranger.

Candace continued to watch the men, but most of her concentration was centered on the stranger. Unsure why, she felt certain he was a man other men would fear, but he would be comfortable anywhere, sure in his skill and the danger it threatened. He would stand apart from other men always, watching them, assessing them, even as they watched and assessed him. But he would do it out of arrogance and confidence. They would do it out of fear.

Range felt her gaze on his back, but didn't turn. His business was with Garth, and that came first. If there were pleasures to be had here that he hadn't expected, those could wait until later.

Candace saw Garth suddenly jab a thumb toward the house, as if in emphasis of something he'd said, and the three men turned toward her. With her heart suddenly pounding erratically, she hurriedly stepped into the house, welcoming the coolness of its shadowed interior.

"Hey, sis, what's the matter?"

Candace stopped in the middle of the dining room on her way to the kitchen and looked at her twenty-year-old brother. He turned his wheelchair away from the table and glanced up at her. A frown creased his brow.

She stared down at him for a long moment before answering, but her gaze fixed only on his face, and she refused to let it drop lower, to his legs . . . useless limbs that were slowly wasting away.

With her blond hair and dark blue eyes, Candace knew she took after their mother, but Brandon and Brianne, twins several years younger than herself, took after their late father. Their hair was the deep, rich brown of newly turned earth, their eyes a blend of pale blue and gray. And where her features were rounded, full, and, as her mother used to describe, sassy . . . just like her personality, their features were thin, straight, and classically aquiline.

Several sharp sounds echoed from the kitchen, the clatter of a pan being set in the dry sink, a heavy platter on the counter, an oven door swinging shut. The kitchen was Brianne's favorite place in the house and cooking her favorite thing to do, luckily for Candace, since she hated to cook, thus wasn't very good at it. She glanced at the table. Her brother had been working on his figures again, preparing for the day when he would inherit Gates End, their father's ranch. They still had another two weeks to wait until Brandon would turn twenty-one—but with each passing day, Candace became more frightened that her brother would never reach that birthday, and the sprawling adobe house and rolling hills of Gates End would never again be theirs.

Brandon pushed his wheelchair toward Candace. The movement caught her attention and jerked her mind from its unpleasant thoughts.

"Candace," his eyes narrowed when she didn't answer, "what's wrong?"

She forced a smile to her lips. He had enough to worry about, and so did she, without her conjuring up trouble that probably didn't exist. "Nothing," she said, and widened the smile, praying it didn't look as fake as it felt. She started to move past him, to enter the kitchen, and placed a hand lightly on his shoulder. "Someone is here to see Garth and I thought it better to come inside, that's all. Especially since I'm not dressed for company."

He caught her by the wrist and twisted around to look up at her before she could walk away. "It's not like you to hide from something, Candace. Or give a care how you're dressed." His tone was instantly riddled with suspicion, his eyes hard. "Who's here?"

She shrugged out of his grasp. "I don't know, Brandon, really. Just a stranger. I didn't like the look of him, that's all. He makes me nervous."

Brandon jerked his chair around and rolled toward the window.

Candace felt her heart constrict with a surge of sympathy she knew she could never allow her brother to see. Only a year ago he had been a vital, strong young man, always laughing and joking, lighthearted to a fault and looking forward to the future as if it were a magical kingdom he couldn't wait to explore. Now, because of a saddle cinch that broke at the wrong moment, he was a cripple, and though the Brandon she'd known was still there, buried deep, only resurfacing occasionally, the one most people saw nowadays was a Brandon full of hatred, anger, and bitterness.

But she couldn't blame him.

Pulling back the curtain that hung over the window, Brandon stared out at the stranger approaching the house with Garth and Jesse. "If I had to bet my money, I'd bet that he's a hired gun."

Candace felt a cold chill sweep over her at Brandon's confirmation of what she'd already suspected. No, what she'd already known. She shook her head, wanting, needing, to deny the fact. "That doesn't make sense. Why would Garth hire a professional gunman, and why would he greet him as if he were an old friend?"

"Maybe he is," Brandon said, his tone one of sneering contempt. "A man like Garth Murdock probably knows every undesirable piece of garbage between here and the North Pole. Maybe beyond."

Candace shook her head. "No, Jesse would have known him then, and he didn't."

"Then Garth probably hired him."

"But why? Hatchabee and the others don't want a gun-fight. They're ranchers, not killers. And anyway, there's more than enough water for everyone." Candace stared across the room at her brother, unable to believe they were even having this conversation.

Brandon dropped the lace panel, slapped a hand against one of the chair's wheels, and whirled away from the window to face her. "Maybe your husband isn't going to give them a choice. That's more his style, isn't it? Takes what he wants and the hell with everybody else."

"No, I can't believe Garth would do something like that." She stared at Brandon. "There has to be another reason that man's here."

Brandon grinned, but there was no warmth or humor in the curve of his lips or the words he spoke: "Well, maybe my beloved brother-in-law has finally decided to stop rely-ing on accidents in his effort to get rid of me and has brought in someone to do the job right."

Candace stiffened. Too many things had happened in the past year that might or might not have been accidental, and all to Brandon. He was convinced Garth was behind them all, but she wasn't ready to believe that. Not that she actually loved Garth Murdock, but the thought of him purposely trying to kill Brandon was just too horrendous, too evil, for her to accept. "That's not true," she said softly. "It can't be. That cinch breaking was an accident." Her gaze met his. "It could have happened to any of us."

"But it didn't happen to any of us, Candace," Brandon snapped. "It happened to me . . . because it was supposed to happen to me. Only I was supposed to break my damned neck and die, which probably would have been a hell of a lot better than this." He slammed a fist down on the arm of the wheelchair as he glared at her, then spun around and looked back through the window. "I've become very accident-prone since my last birthday, wouldn't you say, sis? I somehow find my way in front of a stampede, my horse throws a shoe and falls, throwing me, only days after he'd been freshly shod, a rattler decides to take over my bed, and my saddle cinch breaks." He glanced over his shoulder, his eyes narrowing slightly as he looked back at her, as if challenging her to deny the truth of his words. "I don't know what the hell Garth's up to this time, Candace, but if it has anything to do with me, you, or Brianne, he won't live long enough to see his plans through this time, I promise you that."

"Brandon, please don't talk that way about Garth," Brianne said softly, walking into the room from the kitchen. A lock of her long hair had worked its way loose from the ribbon she had used to tie it at her nape, and she reached up to tuck it back in place. She was a mirror image of Brandon, though her features were more delicate and softer, almost fragile. "You know if he hears you it'll just set off his temper. Anyway, if it wasn't for him the Lord only knows what would have happened to us after Papa died."

Brandon's eyes shone with the anger that had been steadily mounting in him ever since the day Doc Swaydon had told him he'd never walk again. He laughed hatefully. "Well, let's see, Bri," he sneered, "if it wasn't for Garth Murdock our sister wouldn't be saddled with a husband old enough to be her father who not only can't give her any children, he can't even make love to her."

"Brandon!" Candace snapped. "That's enough."

"And you," he continued, glaring at Brianne and ignoring Candace's reproach, "wouldn't have to slave in the kitchen every day like a servant, or be forced to sneak around in order to see Wade Hawkins while good ol' Garth sets about making arrangements to marry you off to some ancient banker friend of his." He slammed his hand on the arm of his chair. "And I sure as hell wouldn't be sitting in this damned wheelchair."

Brianne gasped and stared at him. "Oh, Brandon, you can't really think . . . I mean . . ." She looked at Candace, her eyes brimming with unshed tears.

Snorting softly, Brandon jerked around and looked back out through the window. "Crying isn't going to do any of us any good, Brianne. Especially now."

Candace hated the way things had changed since Brandon's accident, but as much as he believed Garth was capable of treachery and murder, and responsible for the accidents he'd suffered in the past year, she still had her doubts. Though truthfully, they weren't as strong as they used to be.

Garth Murdock was a well-respected businessman, and as far as she knew he was certainly not in need of money. But she couldn't deny that she was having a hard time convincing herself that all of Brandon's accidents had been accidents. And since the law dictated that she and Brianne couldn't inherit Gates End, that meant no one would benefit from Brandon's death but Garth, which left her without a reasonable argument against Brandon's logic.

"So, what's for supper, Bri?"

Candace fairly cringed at hearing Karalynne's voice. Six months ago Jesse had met Karalynne when her acting troupe passed through Tombstone, stopping to play the Birdcage on their way. Like a besotted twit, Jesse had talked her into leaving the troupe and brought her to live at the Rolling M. But he had yet to marry her, so there was some hope at least that they'd all wake up one day and she'd be gone. Candace wouldn't care except that Karalynne expected to be waited on constantly, refused to help with the chores, whined about everything, and ran around the house most of the time half-naked, clad only in her underthings and a very sheer, lace-trimmed wrap.

She turned as the woman entered the room, her red gown swaying about her legs, dark hair done in a cascade of curls that fell over one shoulder, and the gown's deeply cut decolletage revealing more breast than any woman should reveal outside of the bawdiest of saloons.

"We have company, Karalynne," Brandon said, "why don't you get out of your night clothes now and put something decent on? Or are you looking to snare yourself another fool?"

"Why, you little—"

Suddenly the front door opened.

Chapter 3

Garth stepped into the room first, smiling at Candace. "We've got company for dinner, Candace," he said, removing his hat and settling it on the hook of a hat tree that stood by the door. "Know I didn't give you any warning. Is it going to be a problem?"

"Of course not," she replied, glancing at her sister for confirmation.

Brianne nodded, and Candace felt a sweep of relief. She turned back to Garth. He'd aged considerably in the seven years she'd been his wife. He was fifty now, his black hair was heavily streaked with gray, and his body was growing thick. Handsome could never be a word applied in description of Garth Murdock. Stable, responsible, healthy, strong. Those words a person could use. But a woman would never describe him as good-looking.

"The more the merrier, right, Candace?" Jesse quipped, moving around Garth and flopping down on a chair. He smiled up at her and Candace found herself marveling, not for the first time, that Garth and Jesse really were brothers. They were as much alike as night and day, their personalities and temperament exactly the opposite of each other. Jesse was tall, lanky, and lean, and even though he was only five years Garth's junior, his hair was still dark. And with his sharply cut features and whiskey brown eyes, women could definitely describe him as handsome, in a roguish sort of way.

She'd even thought so for a while, in spite of their difference in ages, and before she'd married Garth. But that had been a long time ago, before she realized that though Jesse might look good enough to turn a woman's head, his personality was sorely lacking.

"Where's Karalynne?" he barked, looking around, then pointing his gaze toward the kitchen, as if he actually expected her to be in there.

"Oh, she was out here whining a few minutes ago, but she went back to her room to primp some more," Brandon sneered. "That's all Karalynne ever does, except sleep and eat. And of course . . . whatever." He shrugged and sent Jesse a snide smile, leaving the innuendo hanging in the air between them like a challenge.

"Brandon, please," Candace said, her tone sharp.

The stranger stepped through the doorway and moved to stand to one side of Garth and Jesse, though he removed neither his hat nor his guns, as most people did when they entered a home. He seemed to issue a darkness that swelled around him and instantly threatened to engulf the room.

Candace felt her pulses race. She had been right. His eyes were black—as black as an Arizona desert beneath a moonless sky, and just as cold.

"As cold-blooded as a rattler with a chill."

She'd once heard someone say that in reference to a hired gun and now, looking at this man, she understood what the words meant. Her hands curled into fists at her side, though half-hidden by the folds of her brown riding skirt. She felt ready for a fight, and didn't know why. At the same time she realized that, in spite of the several days' growth of beard evident on his face, the hardness of his features, and chilling iciness of his gaze, she hadn't seen a man as handsome as him in a very long time . . . if ever.

His hard, black gaze moved over her, lingering momentarily, studying her rather than flirting with her, then it swept away, and moved over Brianne just as impassively before settling on Brandon, and repeating the process.

She saw his interest in the wheelchair, but was surprised at seeing a flash of sympathy sparkle in those cold killer eyes. As swiftly as it had appeared, however, it was gone, leaving her uncertain that she'd really seen it at all. He turned toward her again, meeting her gaze, and she felt the breath catch in her throat, fear hammer at her heart. It was as if she were looking into a void . . . a cavern of dark, emotionless, macabre nothingness.

Garth removed his gun belt and hung it on the rack beside the door. "Candace," he said, breaking the silence that had befallen the room, "this is Range Connor. I've hired him to watch out for our interests in this water rights dispute we're involved in with Hatchabee and the others."

She stared at the stranger. Range Connor. His name repeated in her mind over and over like an ominous, dark echo. A cold shiver snaked its way up her back, a slow, frosty chill that seemed to curl around each vertebrae, penetrate the density of each bone, and instill ice particles within the very blood that rushed through her veins. There probably wasn't a man or woman west of the Mississippi who hadn't heard of Range Connor. He was a man whose most renowned talent was his skill with a deadly weapon, and it didn't necessarily have to be a gun, though that was usually the case. She remembered having heard once that he was credited with having killed more men than a person could count using all their fingers and toes. His reputation was that he hired his gun out to those who needed someone killed and didn't want to do it themselves, and gave no more thought to the who and whys of a situation than if he was merely going out to chop down a tree.

Some men swore he was spawned by the devil. Others claimed he **was** the devil.

Looking at him now, close up, dressed head to foot in black, with eyes whose ebony color rivaled the very darkness of the night and sent a shiver racing over her flesh, Candace felt certain that whatever the truth about Range Connor was, he was definitely at least related to the Devil.

What business did he have at the Rolling M? The unsettling thought nagged at her, but she pushed her apprehension aside and forced herself to smile.

Garth turned to Range. "Connor, this is my wife, Candace."

She saw the slight rise of one dark brow and the assessing look that came into his eyes, followed by the one she was so familiar with, the one that flashed into most strangers' eyes when they discovered she was Garth Murdock's wife rather than his daughter: *Why would a woman marry a man who was at least twice her age?*

Candace drew back her shoulders. She didn't answer that question for other people, and she wasn't about to answer it for him.

"It's a pleasure to meet you, Mr. Connor." She hoped her tone didn't attest to the fact that meeting him, and worrying about why he was present at all, was about the most *un*pleasant thing she'd had to endure lately. "We'll be ready to dine in just a few moments."

Range nodded. "Thank you, ma'am."

His voice was deep, the words spoken curtly, and his tone was like none she'd ever heard before, seeming as dark as everything else about him. Darker than the night.

At the same time it was as smooth as flowing honey, and as rough as gravel skittering across a blanket of velvet. Not cold, not warm. How many times had merely the sound of his voice instilled terror in a man's bones and given him a glimpse of eternity he wasn't ready to see?

Or instilled passion in a woman? a little voice in the back of her mind whispered. Candace stiffened, shocked at herself. She'd never had a brazen thought like that before. His gaze suddenly caught hers, and she had the horrified feeling he knew exactly what she'd been thinking.

"And this here is Brandon, Candace's brother." Garth stepped back then, allowing Range view of where Brandon sat, still near the window.

He nodded at her brother and turned away.

"If you'd care to wash up a bit, Mr. Connor," Candace said, "there's a room just off the porch for that." She indicated the washroom, whose door stood open, just beyond the dining area.

He nodded and turned toward the door she indicated.

Candace fled to the kitchen, uncertain why she felt so suspicious. Garth had explained, and that should have satisfed her. But something was gnawing at her insides. Something that said Garth and Range Connor were lying.

"Why'd you run out like that?" Brianne asked, joining her a moment later. She began to help Brianne dish the meal onto platters.

"I just wanted to get dinner on the table," Candace said, snapping the words out and instantly sorry.

Garth sat at the head of the table and Candace found, to her dismay, that Range Connor had settled himself to her right. She took her seat.

"Oh, I'm late," Karalynne said needlessly, sashaying into the room and waving a feather-tipped fan in front of her face. Everyone looked up as she made her entrance and approached the table. She stopped and stared at Range.

"Oh, someone's in my seat." Her blue eyes widened and she batted her long lashes several times.

Range started to rise.

"Oh, stay put, sugar," she purred, "I'd give up just about anything for a man who looked like you."

Jesse looked up at her. Anger blazed from his eyes, but as Range watched, he felt certain the man's anger was not derived from jealousy, but merely possession.

"This is Range Connor, Karalynne, he's working for Garth." Jesse moved over to make room for her. "Sit here." It was more an order than an offer.

Range tipped his head in acknowledgement of her. "Miss Karalynne."

Candace wondered if the outrageous, multicolored outfit Karalynne had chosen to wear was actually supposed to be a gown or a costume. Its skirt looked more like a collection of red, yellow, and blue organdy fluffs trimmed with black lace, while the bodice of her gown was bright red, the decolletage cut daringly low and adorned with black and white seed pearls. Her puffed shoulder sleeves were purple, and the velvet choker at her neck was yellow.

Karalynne smiled. "Range Connor." She practically purred his name. "I think I've heard of you, sugar." She put her hands on her waist and inhaled deeply, then pushed a wisp of red curl from her temple and sashayed toward the table.

Range rose. "I'll move."

Karalynne waved a hand at him and, ignoring Jesse, moved past him. "Oh, don't be silly, Mr. Connor. I'll just sit next to Brandon."

"Lucky me," Brandon grumbled.

Candace glanced at Garth. He would never hire a man to kill someone. She couldn't believe that. Range Connor was here because of the water rights dispute. To protect the Rolling M in case any of their neighbors decided to get nasty, that was all. Just like Garth said.

"Are you from around here, Mr. Connor?" Candace turned to look at him as she handed him a bowl of peas. If she left the conversation to Brandon, Karalynne, or Jesse, war might erupt at the table. And that she could do without.

"No, ma'am."

She frowned, sensing immediately that getting him to talk was not going to be easy. "Well, I don't detect a southern drawl or an eastern clip in your voice, so, where are you from? The midwest, maybe?"

He shrugged. "Everywhere, I guess. Don't stay in one place too long."

"But you must have a home somewhere?"

"Stop badgering the man, Candace," Garth said.

Range bristled. He didn't like answering questions, but he liked Garth's ordering his wife around even less. It was too close to the real reason he was at the Rolling M. Yet, even as he thought about ways to avoid her questions without being rude, he realized that he could use her. "Never had a reason to call anywhere home," he said, attempting for the first time in longer than he could remember to instill an edge of friendliness to his tone, if not warmth.

"So, where do your parents live, Mr. Connor?"

"They're dead."

"Oh." She handed him a bowl of baked carrots and onions. "I'm sorry." She smiled.

"Why?" Karalynne quipped, laughing. "You certainly didn't know them."

Ignoring Karalynne, Range turned and looked at Candace, pinning her with a long stare from those dark eyes that made her suddenly want to run from the table and barricade herself behind her bedchamber door. Yet this time is wasn't the coldness in those black depths that frightened her, but something else, something she couldn't even put her finger on to name. Nevertheless, she felt it, and instinctively knew it was something she didn't, and shouldn't, want to feel.

"It was a long time ago, ma'am," he said finally. "In fact, I don't even remember them."

The lie slid off his lips easily. As far as his father was concerned, it was the truth. But his mother, he would remember her for the rest of his life.

For a reason she was at a loss to explain, Candace sensed he was lying.

Range had taken off his hat when he'd sat at the table, but he hadn't removed his gun belt. She glanced at it now, as he shifted his position on the benchlike seat and it rubbed against her thigh. She suspected he almost never took it off, or if he did, that the guns were never far from his reach.

When Brandon had been able to walk he'd always worn a gun, too, but he'd worn it for protection. Range Connor wore his to intimidate, and used it to kill for money, not to protect himself.

"Have you ever been to Arizona before, Mr. Connor?" Brianne asked.

"A long time ago."

"So, who've you been hired to kill around here?" Brandon asked.

Candace's gaze snapped up in surprise as she whipped around to stare in disbelief at her brother.

Brianne gasped.

Jesse's mouth dropped open in surprise.

Outrage turned Garth's face a motley purple and he glared at Brandon, but Brandon ignored them all and continued to stare pointedly at Range.

He slowly lowered the biscuit he'd been about to take a bite out of and placed it back on his plate, then looked across the table at Brandon. "I was hired to protect Mr.

Murdock's interests during a dispute with his neighbors,"
Range said. His gaze bored into the younger man's. "Or
do you know something I don't?"

Silence fell over the room like an invisible shroud of
doom—cold, dank, and penetrating.

"I heard killing was your specialty," Brandon said, "not
protecting."

Candace held her breath, trying to decide which platter
she could reach, which one she could hit Range Connor
with, if he made a threatening move toward Brandon.

"Don't mind the boy, Connor," Garth broke in, "he
just reads too much."

Brandon turned his gaze toward Garth, not bothering
to hide the animosity he felt toward the older man. "Not
much else to do when you're saddled into a chair all day."

"Well, I gotta go into town tomorrow to pick up a few
things," Garth said, smiling. "Why don't I take the buckboard and you can come along, Brandon?"

Range looked from Brandon to Garth. One man showed
his real feelings, the other hid them so well probably
nobody even suspected what was behind the congenial
smile. When he'd been young, Range had never been real
good at hiding what he felt, but all that had changed when
he was six. After that he'd learned not to let anyone see
anything. But then, it had been a hellava long time since
he'd actually felt anything.

"Pass me that bowl of potatoes, Brianne," Jesse said,
breaking the silence that had descended over the table.

The food platters were passed around again, everyone
helped themselves and quietly went to the task of eating.

Candace reached for the biscuits and, though she didn't
want to, she couldn't stop herself from glancing at the
man sitting beside her as she extended her arm and
brushed against his.

"Excuse me, Mr. Connor."

He paid her no mind, neither acknowledging her softly spoken words or making a move to assist and pass the platter to her. Instead he kept his eyes cast downward and appeared deep in thought, or merely concentrating on the plate of food before him, eating slowly, methodically, and silently. During the remainder of the meal Candace noticed that the few times he did glance up, he looked directly across the table at Brandon.

The fear she'd been trying to ignore and hold at bay now settled over her like an icy mantle. She was no longer able to deny the possibility that a hired killer was interested in her brother. She felt her stomach muscles contract, then fought the terror back, and unconsciously straightened her spine. No, she told herself. There had to be another explanation for the man's presence. She was just reading something into the situation that wasn't there.

"Candace," Garth said, breaking into her thoughts, "would you and Brianne make up the spare room for Range? He'll be staying a few days."

"Don't bother," Range said.

Everyone turned to look at him.

"You don't want to stay in the house?" Garth asked.

"No."

He looked up and Candace noticed the icy glare that shone from his eyes as they focused on Garth. Colder than before. Harder than when he'd first arrived. Almost . . . she nearly started in surprise . . . almost like the look she saw in Brandon's eyes whenever *he* looked at Garth. But why, she wondered, would Range Connor hate Garth?

"Well, I can put you up in the bunkhouse if you prefer," Garth said, seeming a little put off, "but I can assure you, Connor, the accommodations here in the main house would be much more—"

"The bunkhouse will be fine," Range said, cutting his protest off.

Garth shrugged. "Whatever you say, Connor."

"That's what I say." His dark eyes fixed on Garth for several long seconds before his lids dropped to give everyone a moment's respite from that hard, menacing gaze. He wiped at the gravy on his plate with a chunk of biscuit and slipped it into his mouth.

From the corner of her eye, Candace watched him chew it slowly, then swallow, his Adam's apple moving and drawing her attention to his neck and the broad chest just below. His shirt was open at the collar, not enough to give her a view of anything but a silver chain around his neck, but the sight was enough to arouse her curiosity nevertheless.

Candace caught herself, shocked at her own thoughts.

After placing his lap cloth on the table, Range pushed his chair back and rose to his feet.

She glanced up at him, not wanting to, yet unable to resist. He was a cold-blooded killer, she told herself. The worst kind of man. That was the only reason she was curious about him. That, and what his real reasons were for being at the Rolling M ranch.

Range shifted his gun belt slightly, replaced the Stetson on his head, and then, as if feeling her staring up at him, he looked down.

She thought she saw a spark of warmth in his eyes as their gazes met, but it was gone before she had a chance to really catch it, and so she ended up uncertain whether it had actually been there at all. Worse, she couldn't explain why it even mattered.

"Thanks for the meal, Mrs. Murdock."

She nodded.

Range turned to Garth. "And the name's *Mr.* Connor, if you don't mind."

She heard Brianne's soft gasp and saw the faint smirk

of a smile that appeared on Brandon's face. Candace turned to look at Garth, expecting him to cut back in anger. Instead, he merely looked shocked.

She didn't understand. Garth had hired the man, was going to pay him to do a job . . . so why was Range Connor acting so curt toward him? She remembered the fleeting glimpse of hatred she thought she'd seen in the hired gunman's eyes a while ago, when he'd looked at Garth and thought no one was watching. She'd assumed Garth had hired Range Connor, but what if she was wrong? What if there was another reason Range Connor was at the Rolling M?

"Fine," Garth said, and laughed. "You get the job done, Connor, and I'll call you anything you want."

Candace started in surprise again. Garth's attitude was so out of character she didn't know what to think.

"*Mr.* Connor," Range repeated. His hands hadn't moved, both hanging loosely at his sides, each only an inch from the butts of his guns. He looked easy enough, but the warning in his voice was evident to them all.

"Fine, *Mr.* Connor," Garth replied, a slight sneer creeping into his tone in direct contrast to the smile on his face. "Like I said, you get the job done I hired you for, and I'll call you anything you want."

So she had been right. That fact left Candace more confused than ever.

"Yeah, me and my brother aren't particular, huh, Garth?" Jesse quipped.

Candace's gaze whipped to her brother-in-law.

"Mister, Miss, or in between, hell, don't make no matter to us."

Range ignored Jesse and continued to stare at Garth. He didn't say anything, but he didn't have to, at least not for Candace's benefit. His midnight eyes were filled with emotion, dark and swirling and very, very cold.

A shudder swept through her and she looked away. Garth might have hired Range Connor to do a job, but the gunman had an agenda all his own. She was as certain of that now as she was of her own name.

Chapter 4

Range swore under his breath and dragged the saddle and blanket from his horse's back.

He'd known Garth Murdock was an S.O.B., a man who would do anything, or walk over anyone, to get what he wanted. Murder didn't mean a thing to him. There was probably no telling how many bodies there were buried in the man's tracks, but hiring Range to kill a boy in a wheelchair . . .

The mere thought sent his temperature flaring and left him so mad he could face down the Devil and not think twice about it. But then, he smiled, that's exactly what he'd come here to do. Face the Devil . . . and kill him.

Range swung the saddle over a rail of the nearby stall. It was all he could do to stop himself from returning to the ranch house and putting an end to this charade. His hands ached to draw his guns and press their long barrels against Garth's forehead. Pulling the trigger as he watched would be such sweet justice. And it was exactly what Garth

deserved, to look death in the face and know there was
no way he could stop it from taking him.

He tossed some hay into the feed trough, along with
a couple of handfuls of grain, pulled a brush from his
saddlebag, and began to run it over Satan's sleek back.
The animal's black skin rippled beneath the brush, and a
soft whinny slipped from his lips.

"Feels good, huh, boy?"

A lot of people didn't bother brushing their horses down
after a ride, long or short. Hell, a lot of people treated
their worst enemies better than they treated their mounts,
but Range considered Satan his best friend. He snorted at
his own thoughts. His horse was his *only* friend and more
valuable to him than any amount of money. They'd been
together for a little over eight years, and the huge gelding
had gotten him out of several scrapes that could have
ended with a rope around his neck or a bullet in his back
if the gelding's long, lean legs had moved any slower. They
took care of each other, understood each other, and kept
each other alive.

A soft, cracking sound caught his attention. Stepping
into the shadows at the front of the stall, Range let his
gaze sweep over the interior of the huge, shadow-infested
barn. Most of the other stalls were occupied, and a huge
mound of hay had been piled in one corner. The loft
was steeped in darkness, the soft glow of the lone lantern
hanging on a pole in the center of the barn not able to
reach that high.

His right hand rested on his gun, ready to draw given
the slightest reason.

Silence . . . stillness surrounded him.

Long moments later he finally relaxed, deciding one of
the other horses had merely stepped on something.

He patted Satan's rump. "Have yourself a good meal,

fella," Range said, "and get some sleep. We'll do us a little scouting around the place tomorrow."

Satan pulled a small mound of hay into his mouth and, as he chewed, turned his head to look at Range.

He laughed. "Yeah, okay, you didn't bother me while I was eating my dinner, so I won't bother you." He stuck the brush back in his saddlebag, tossed it over his shoulder, and, after extinguishing the lantern, walked outside.

The night seemed exceptionally black, the low-hanging moon barely a silver crescent glowing softly against the darkness of a sky dotted with only a handful of stars. In the distance the ragged peaks of a mountain range cut across the horizon, its black silhouette almost, but not quite, melding in color with the stygian depth of the sky.

Darkness had always proven his friend. But the immediate area was fairly well illuminated. Pale light poured from the windows of both the main house and the bunkhouse to shine on the wide area of earth that separated them.

Range made his way toward the bunkhouse, staying close to the outbuildings and out of the light as much as possible, his black clothes blending with the night, his stealth utilizing the darkness. It was a trick he'd learned while living with the Apaches long ago, walking in the shadows, melding with them, using them to become as one with his surroundings. He paused several yards from the low-lying bunkhouse and stared at it. The sounds of laughter drifted out from one of the open windows, followed by someone cursing soundly.

This was a risk, but one he had to take. He went over the possibilities in his mind. Would there be anyone in there he recognized? The thought was a bit unsettling. But more importantly, he wondered if there would be anyone inside who recognized him . . . not as Range Connor, but as a young boy they'd known long ago?

He inhaled deeply of the cool night air and moved his

head from side to side, forcing away the kinks that had
formed during the day's ride and settled in his neck during
dinner. Shifting the saddlebag that draped over his shoulder, he rolled his shoulders several times in an effort to
rid them of the tension that still held them stiff.

He shook away the apprehension. It had been too long
to worry about running into familiar faces—no one had
ever recognized him before, and there was no reason to
think anyone would now. Especially if Garth hadn't. And
that had been the real test.

Range had changed. He'd grown up. There was nothing
left of the young boy he'd been back then . . . nothing left
of the innocence and trust either.

He leaned back against the side of the shed he'd paused
beside. This would finish it. At last. The answers were here,
and he'd find them, and then he'd see that Garth faced
what he'd done . . . and paid.

Range pulled a pouch of tobacco from his shirt pocket,
unfolded a paper, drew the pouch open, and began to
carefully shake tobacco onto the paper. But then what?
his mind asked, the question one he'd been trying to avoid
acknowledging. When this was finally over, then what
would he do?

Go back to Cold Springs? Hire his gun out to someone
else?

A long sigh slipped from his lips and disappeared quietly
onto the night. He was tired of the killing, tired of people
using him, tired of constantly looking over his shoulder.
Range rolled the cigarette and placed it between his lips.
After jerking the string on the pouch to shut it and slipping
it back into his pocket, he flicked a lucifer against the
shed's rough wooden wall and held it to the cigarette's
tip, shielding the flame with cupped hands.

He heard a door slam shut somewhere behind him.
Dropping the match, he spit out the cigarette—not willing

to let its glowing tip make him a target—and whirled
around, crouching low, his hands swinging automatically
to hover only a hair's breadth above the butts of the Colts
sheathed at his hips. For a split second everything was
forgotten; where he was, why he was there, and who else
was nearby. Without thought the intense instinct for survival that had been with him since that unforgettable night
twenty-three years ago washed over him, and he was
instantly ready to fight, to kill if necessary. Nothing moved.
His gaze darted toward the house.

She stood on the veranda, bathed in the light that shone
out through the open front door behind her. The long
strands of her dark blond hair spread across her shoulders,
and, with the lamplight touching each wave, took on the
guise of a mantle of golden silk. She was dressed for bed,
the folds of a long white robe flowing gracefully about her
legs.

He could tell, in spite of the distance that separated
them and the murky shadows within which he stood, that
she had no idea he was there. He straightened and relaxed
his defensive stance. She was a threat to his plans, he
couldn't deny that, but not the type of threat he needed
his guns for. His gaze moved over her slowly, assessing
each curve and line. She was a beautiful woman, but it
didn't make sense that she was married to a man like Garth
Murdock. He was old enough to be her father . . . but
more than that, he was a heartless murderer, and wives
always knew things like that.

But then maybe she didn't care. Maybe she'd married
him for his money. The idea didn't set well with Range,
yet he couldn't deny it made sense. Garth Murdock was a
powerful man in these parts. His ranch one of the biggest,
his holdings prosperous, his name respectable. There were
probably any number of women around who would be

thankful to call him their husband. Except they didn't know the truth about him.

Range pushed thoughts of Garth from his mind and let his eyes enjoy the sight of the man's young wife standing only a few yards away. She wasn't really beautiful in the classic sense of the word, not like several of the women he'd seen in some of the bigger towns he'd been through. Her lips were a little too full, her nose a little too short and upturned, and her cheekbones too rounded, her cheeks too hollow. Nevertheless he found her beautiful in her own unique way.

Something like feeling tried to ignite within him, but he brushed it aside as the mere stirrings of passion. He hadn't had a woman in a long time, and though his body was used to a lot of things, it wasn't used to that.

His gaze moved over Candace in slow appreciation. Her body was lithe and taut, her curves subtle, yet enticing, and though the top of her head barely reached his shoulders, he sensed that if he pulled her against him, into the circle of his arms, and pressed her body to his, her curves would meld perfectly into the long lines of his own frame.

She moved then, jerking Range from his musings. He continued to watch as she descended one step of the porch, then hesitated, as if sensing someone was watching. His gaze shot up to meet her eyes. He couldn't see them, but he did remember them. Only once before had he ever seen blue quite that dark. It had been a quiet night in Kansas. The birds had stopped chirping, the insects had stopped their humming. The earth had grown unexplainably calm, so quiet it almost hurt the ears. Then the sky had turned that color, and moments later a tornado had come ripping across the prairie. A dark, swirling blue that was as deep as the ocean, yet not as dark as the night.

Range caught himself. This was Garth Murdock's wife he was thinking about. A cold-blooded murderer's wife. He watched her descend another step of the stairs and pulled himself up, pushing himself away from the wall. It was time to get to the bunkhouse and call it a night.

Spinning on his heel, Range didn't look back as he walked to the bunkhouse. He kicked the door open, then kicked it closed behind him after entering.

Several wranglers sat playing poker at a table in the corner. They turned when Range entered. One nodded, then they all went back to their game.

Range silently surveyed the room. Things had seemed so simple only a few hours ago, when he'd been on his way to the Rolling M. So why now did he feel like complications he'd never even dreamed of were starting to intrude into his long-harbored plans?

Most of the bunks had clothes or gear on or near them, but one, against the far wall and near the corner, appeared empty. Range walked to it, dropped his saddlebag down beside it, and looked back at the wranglers at the table. "Anyone sleeping here?"

"Nope," a grizzled older man said. He looked up, shoving a hat that had seen better days years ago off his forehead, and stared long and hard at Range before answering further. "Name's J. D." He looked back at the bunk Range had taken. "That one's bad luck, though."

Range stared at him, waiting.

" 'Bout a year ago a man named Dicks slept there. Rattler got him. Then Murdock hired Brooster. He wasn't here two weeks and got hisself kicked off a bronc."

"Broke his fool neck and died on the spot," another of the men said.

The grizzled wrangler lay down his cards. "Afore that, Ben Hurley came in one night, drunk as a skunk, tripped over his own gear, and split his head wide open on that bed rail. Sorriest thing I ever saw.''

Range unholstered his gun belt and hung it, along with his hat, on the bedpost, then lay down. "Maybe I'll break the curse," he muttered.

"Yeah, and maybe not."

He flipped back the blanket on the bunk and saw a folded piece of paper sticking out from beneath the pillow. Glancing over his shoulder, he picked it up quickly and opened it.

"Meet me in the barn at midnight."

Range smiled. So, Garth wanted a private talk. One where he could speak without any of his family, or anyone else, overhearing. Range pocketed the note and lay down on the bunk. A long sigh slipped from his lips as his body began to relax. Normally he took a few weeks off between jobs, just to rest up and regroup himself. But he hadn't this time. The moment he'd read Garth's telegram he'd begun to pack, and had left Cold Springs within hours of its arrival. He felt his muscles begin to relax. Long hours in the saddle, days without rest, weeks of rugged living on the desert, the plains, in the mountains, was nothing new to his body. It had long ago become used to the rough treatment.

He closed his eyes, thinking back on just how much he'd put his body through over the years. A Sioux arrow had pierced his left shoulder, a bullet had ripped through the calf of his right leg, and some fancy dancer from New Orleans had used his rapier to leave Range with a thin line of a scar on his neck, running from just below his right ear, down across his Adam's apple, and ending just above his heart.

But at least it was better than the burn of a hangman's noose. That was something he hadn't experienced yet, and

didn't intend to. Though there more than a few lawmen
out there who'd like to change that situation.

And if Murdock knew who he really was, he'd probably
be the first in line with a rope.

It wasn't exhaustion that gnawed at his body at the
moment, however, it was another feeling, one that not
only surprised him, but angered him. Candace Murdock
was a beautiful woman, he couldn't deny that, but the last
thing in the world he wanted to feel was desire for any
woman who'd marry Garth Murdock. Nevertheless, as
memory of her filled his mind, erotic thoughts filled his
head, and desire—hungrier than any he'd ever felt
before—crept slowly into his veins.

Two hours later, unable to get even a few minutes' sleep,
Range rolled from his bunk and walked outside. It was
almost midnight anyway.

The air was cool and crisp, the silence nearly deafening.

He'd waited most of his life for the opportunity to come
back to the Rolling M, and now that he was here, he was
anxious to do what he'd come for. But he had to take it
slow. In spite of his anxiety, in spite of the fact that he could
just draw his gun and put an end to Garth's Murdock's life
whenever he chose, there were other considerations. He
needed some answers . . . answers to questions he couldn't
just come out and ask.

It would take time and patience, the latter he usually
had very little of. But this time he would make an excep-
tion, because when the time came he wanted Garth Murdock to know exactly why he was going to die, and who
was pulling the trigger.

He looked at the ranch house, memories flooding back
upon his mind. Nightmares, more than memories. His
gaze moved to the window he knew was that of the master

bedroom. Candace was in there, sleeping in bed next to Garth Murdock.

Range wondered if she knew the truth about what had happened to Garth's first wife.

Then he wondered if she cared.

Chapter 5

"I want him dead within the next two weeks."

The voice came from Range's right, and he turned, his hands automatically moving to hover over his guns, his senses alert to even the slightest movement or sound. There was no light in the barn. No lantern had been lit, no moonlight filtered in through the open doorway.

He stared in the direction the voice had come from. To the good folks of Tombstone, Garth Murdock might be a respectable businessman, maybe even some of them liked him. But Range figured there had to be someone around who knew the truth. Beneath that facade of gruff respectability he put forth, the man had no more warmth in his blood than a rattlesnake, and about just as gracious a personality. When the real one was showing, which Range figured probably wasn't all that often. But that was an opinion he was going to have to keep to himself, for a while at least. He'd been hired by Murdock to come to the Rolling M and provoke Brandon Gates into a gunfight that would, without question, end in the young man's death. And until Range found the answers to his own questions, he was going to have to make certain Garth remained satisfied that killing Brandon Gates was the only reason Range was at the Rolling M.

"I hire out my gun," Range drawled. The coldness that laced his tone was as natural to him as breathing, but instinctively intensified whenever he spoke to Murdock. "But I choose my own killing time."

"It has to be before his birthday."

Range squinted into the darkness, trying to make out the man, but all he could see, barely, was a dark silhouette, half-hidden by a stall across the barn. "I've got too much at stake here, Connor—Mr. Connor," he quickly corrected.

Range cocked his head and frowned. Garth's voice didn't sound right. Almost as if he was trying to disguise it. But for what reason? They both knew the reason Range was here. Or, Range smiled to himself, the supposed reason.

"Brandon isn't any use to anyone, you can see that yourself. He wasn't much good around here before the accident, now he's just foul-mouthed and more useless than ever. I need to be rid of him within the next week."

"Why?" It was a question Range had never asked before, never cared about. If a man needed killing, he needed killing. Range always tried to keep it a fair fight, as fair as any could be when someone who didn't make their living with a gun came up against someone who did. But the reasons for the killing weren't usually important to him. This time, however, because the man who wanted the killing done was Garth Murdock, the reason was important. Everything about this job was different. Everything about this job was important. Or at least, could be.

"Why?" Garth echoed, clearly surprised by the question. "I . . . ah . . . ." He slammed a fist against the stall gate he stood behind. "That's my business, Con—Mr. Connor. I hired you to kill him, that's all, not to worry about why. So, just do it. And do it soon.''

"Oh, it'll get done, Murdock," Range said with a sneer, not bothering to use the polite formality toward the man that he'd demanded for himself, "but as I said, I'll do it in my manner and my own time." He looked down at the wad of money Murdock had handed over upon his arrival, half his fee in advance, as always. "But if this thing is that important to you, I could hurry a bit—"

"It is."

". . . But I'll have to charge you double," Range finished.

"Double?"

Range saw Garth's dark shadow begin to pace the stall. "But you can't. . . . I mean, we made an agreement."

Range's eyes narrowed and he pushed away from the wall of the barn he'd been leaning against, the booted foot that had been propped up against the wall slamming to the ground and creating a small cloud of dust, the spur attached to his heel offering a merry jingle. "And I just changed it."

"But—"

Range shoved the packet of money into his shirt. "Double," he said again, then turned to walk away. He'd only gone a few feet when he stopped and turned back. "And another thing, Murdock," he growled. "I don't like meeting people in the middle of the night in dark barns. You want to talk to me again, do it where I can see you."

Spinning on his heel, Range blended with the darkness as he walked out of the barn. He wouldn't put it past the man to have some kind of double-cross planned. In fact, he more than expected it, he would have been surprised if it hadn't come, which was why he'd taken a precaution. Unfortunately, it wasn't a precaution that would prevent his getting killed, if Garth wanted that badly enough, but at least it was one that would, no matter what happened to him, expose Garth Murdock for the cold-blooded monster he really was.

He'd only been on the Rolling M for a matter of hours, and already Range Connor was taxing him to the limit. Fury churned inside of him, entwining itself about every cell in his body. Long ago he'd made some grave mistakes that had almost cost him everything, and all because of his temper. He'd learned since then how to better control his anger, but it wasn't always easy. And he wasn't always completely successful. His gloved fists clenched and unclenched with the power of the rage rafting through his veins.

Suddenly, a new idea flashed into his mind. He mulled it over, letting it take root in his thoughts, and found it brought him such a feeling of satisfaction that he was surprised he hadn't thought of it before. He nodded to himself. He'd pay Connor double his fee, all right. Why not? The corners of his lips turned up in an ugly smile. After the devil finally did what he'd been paid to do and gotten rid of Brandon, he would see to it that Range Connor never got the chance to spend—let alone keep—anybody's money ever again.

He nearly laughed aloud at the prospect. He was going to have things his way, and it wasn't really going to cost him a cent.

He'd stood on the porch of the bunkhouse for hours, smoking, thinking, and staring into the darkness. He had tried to sleep, and he'd paced until he felt like screaming. The sun had come up and Garth had actually come out and invited him in to breakfast, which Range had declined. Finally, after another hour of struggling not to put his fist through a wall, he knew what he needed to do to calm down. He needed to sort things out, get his bearings, and put some much needed space between himself and Garth Murdock, otherwise he just might blow the man's brains out before he was ready.

Range grabbed Satan's reins and, holding them in his hand, slipped a foot into his stirrup and swung easily up and onto his saddle, settling comfortably into its well-worn curves.

Candace moved quietly away from the horse she'd been grooming in the corral. She didn't know what was going on, but for the past half an hour she had been able to see Range Connor sitting, standing, or pacing in front of the bunkhouse, and the expression she'd seen on his face had given her even more reason to feel frightened.

The problem was, she wasn't certain exactly what, or who, she should fear.

Brandon was sure their enemy was Garth. But even though Candace had no love for the man she'd been forced to marry, she still wasn't ready to believe he was capable of cold-bloodedly trying to kill Brandon, then, failing that, hiring someone else to do it.

Yet there was also really no reason for Garth to hire a professional gunman to protect them in their water rights dispute with their neighbors. Especially since there truly was enough water for everyone, and no one wanted a fight.

Range headed west toward the Chiricahua Mountain range in the distance, a place he'd once called home. That seemed like another lifetime ago, but at least those memories were pleasant ones. Several hours later, after taking a few wandering detours, he stared at the wide valley that had once been his home. In his mind's eye he could see the people's makeshift dwellings strewn across the open acreage, deer skins stretched out on poles to dry in the sun, children playing in the fields, and the women kneeling by the shallow riverbed as they went about softening their already dried hides.

His gaze moved to an especially large and unusually shaped saguaro standing to one side of the clearing, and Range smiled, please that it was still there, alive and healthy. Two Hawks's lodge had once stood on the ground next to the massive cactus, its sprawling, needle-covered arms lending a bit of shade to the dwelling's entrance.

A hawk flew overhead, his shadow flitting across Range for just a moment. He looked up, watching the bird as it soared majestically toward a nearby mountaintop and disappeared from view.

Rising in his saddle, Range swung a leg over Satan's back and dismounted, then, leaving Satan to graze on whatever desert grass he could find, Range walked to the huge saguaro and sat down cross-legged in its shadow. Delving deep into his memory, he pulled up words from the language he hadn't spoken in years. "Hello again, old man," he said in Apache, looking up at the cactus.

Taking off his hat, he set it on the ground beside him, turned his face to the sky and, closing his eyes, inhaled deeply, letting the feel and peacefulness of the desert fill and relax him.

Long hours later he opened his eyes and noticed the sun was beginning its descent toward the horizon. If he didn't leave now, he would have to camp out for the night, and there was no need to do anything that might arouse Murdock's suspicion if he didn't have to. Anyway, he had things to do, things to find, which meant, for the time being, he needed to concentrate his efforts on the ranch, specifically at the house, which is what he'd do first thing in the morning.

When Range had received Garth's telegram, he'd thought it almost too good to be true. He'd waited so long for an excuse to return to the Rolling M without arousing suspicion that he'd nearly given up hope. A few more months, maybe a year, and his patience would have been gone, and he'd have shown up at the Rolling M anyway.

But the opportunity he'd been waiting for had finally come, and the fact that Murdock wanted someone dead was neither here nor there. Killing was what Range did for a living, and Murdock wanting another man dead, and even the fact that he'd hire someone to do his dirty work for him, didn't surprise Range one bit.

He'd learned about the brutality of death when he'd seen his mother murdered. He'd learned how to kill, both ruthlessly and mercifully, from the Apaches. And he'd learned how to make money off death from the Army. He hadn't cared much one way or another if he had to kill Brandon Gates in order to get the answers he sought, and Garth Murdock. But that was before he'd found out that Gates was a cripple.

Now that fact stuck in his craw, and no amount of thinking or rationalizing was going to get it out. He shouldn't care. What difference did it make to him what Brandon Gates was? It never had before. But this time was different, some little voice in the back of his mind kept reminding him. This time, everything was different, everything mattered. And Brandon mattered, because for some reason Range was unable to explain to himself, or understand, Brandon Gates reminded Range of himself. He'd never been physically crippled, but he'd been young, helpless, scared, and threatened by a man who he should have been able to trust.

But there was something else, and it pricked at his own

temper. He'd admitted to himself that he wanted Candace Gates Murdock in his bed, and the thought was a taint on his way of thinking. He didn't *want* to desire her, didn't want to have anything to do with her. She was Garth Murdock's wife, and that was reason enough for Range not to respect her. She was a woman who'd obviously married Murdock for his money and probably looked the other way whenever the man acted less than human. Nevertheless, it didn't change the fact that Range wanted her, and that was enough to nearly make him want to put the muzzle of his gun to his own head and pull the trigger. The last damned thing he wanted or needed was to get involved with Murdock's wife. That was one complication he didn't need.

As he approached the barn, he saw Brandon sitting in his wheelchair next to one of the corrals. Murdock was in the corral with a couple of wranglers, all of them trying to get near a spooked bronc. Range unsaddled Satan, brushed him down, walked him to a fenced pasture behind the barn, then returned and approached Brandon. If he was going to get anywhere with this thing, he had to start making it look good, so Murdock would stay off his back.

"Hey, kid," Range said, "feeling kinda useless?" He knew the comment was about as low as he could get, but that's what he wanted. The kid needed to hate him more than he feared him, and that might take some doing.

Brandon's head whipped around. Hurt filled his eyes at the cruel words, but anger pushed it aside almost instantly. "Not as useless as a man whose only talent is killing people," he shot back.

Range's brows rose slightly in surprise. He lay one arm on the corral rail and settled a booted foot on the bottom rung. He hadn't expected the kid to stand up to his challenge, and the fact that he did instilled Range with an instant sense of respect for him. But that was something he couldn't afford to pay attention to right now. What he'd come to the Rolling M to do was too important to let a little thing like respect stand in his way.

"Yeah?" he snarled. "Well," he straightened and lay a hand casually on the butt of one of his guns, as if in silent challenge, "maybe we should do something to see just how useful you are."

He saw Brandon's hand move slowly toward the blanket that draped his lap, and Range felt pretty certain there was a gun hidden there, most likely, at the moment, aimed right at his most private parts.

"Brandon." Candace exited the barn behind Range and hurried forward.

Range glanced over his shoulder and watched her approach, appreciating her beauty as he damned her greed and lack of scruples.

"I think we'd better get back to the house now. I need to help Brianne finish up with supper."

"I'm busy," Brandon snapped, his hand under the blanket now, his glaring gaze still pinned on Range.

Candace paused and glanced quickly at Range, instantly aware of what was happening. "Yes, well, that kind of busy can wait." She stepped behind Brandon's chair and grabbed its handles. "Let's go."

"I'm not helpless, Candace," Brandon snarled as she started to push the chair forward. "I'm capable of getting to the house on my own." He grabbed the chair's wheels, effectively moving away from her.

Candace paused beside Range. As she looked up at him, her eyes were ablaze with fire. "Leave my brother alone," she whispered softly, though the words were harsh and determined, "or I'll kill you."

If her nearess hadn't caused his entire body to suddenly forget about everything but dragging her up against him and burying himself in her, he would have laughed at her threat. Or at the very least, threw her a sneering retort. As it was, he could hardly breathe.

She was Murdock's wife, which meant she was everything in a woman that he despised. Yet he desired her, and the mere thought aggravated the bejesus out of him, brought him closer to self loathing than he'd ever been, and he'd been pretty close. He watched her stalk after her brother, the stiffness of her body and her gait expressing her own fury. Range swore under his breath, a string of pithy oaths slipping from his lips that would have turned any God-fearing bible-thumper white with shock and caused him to drop to his knees and pray for forgiveness just for listening.

He'd meant for Murdock to overhear his confrontation with Brandon, not Candace.

"She's off-limits, Connor."

He turned to see Jesse Murdock standing a few feet away, his halfway handsome features drawn into a surly frown under the brim of his well-worn, brown slouch hat.

"Off-limits?" Range repeated, allowing a cold smile to draw up one corner of his lips. "That you giving the warning, Jesse, or your big brother?" Range had no reason to goad Jesse other than that he didn't like him. The man lived in a world halfway between arrogance and foolishness, neither of which Range usually tolerated.

But, unlike the anger he'd seen in Jesse's eyes when Karalynne had flirted with him, there was more in Jesse's eyes this time, there was fire and jealousy. Range recognized it instantly, as well as who it was for.

Jesse Murdock was in love with his brother's wife.

"Just do what it was Garth hired you to do, Connor," Jesse snarled, "then leave here. Believe me, it'd be a whole lot healthier."

Range's brow furrowed. "Really? For who?"

Jesse kept his gaze pinned to Range's, but he also kept

his thumbs hooked over his belt and nowhere near the gun that hung from his left hip.

He was stupid, Range decided, but he wasn't a total fool. And he wasn't ready to die.

"If you need a woman," Jesse said, "take Karalynne. She ain't too particular about who shares her bed." An ugly laugh ripped from his throat.

The offer surprised Range. The man might not be in love with Karalynne, nevertheless, Jesse Murdock had impressed him as the possessive type, not a generous man. "You're offering me your woman?"

"She's everybody's woman," Jesse sneered. "I took her from a drover in town, who took her from one of her actor friends, who I heard took her from her own sister."

"Huh, the lady has diversified tastes."

"She's a whore."

Range nodded. "Good to know. I might just take you up on that offer." He smiled, but instilled the gesture with little warmth. He'd been with a lot of women in his life, some not near as pretty as Karalynne, and if it would cure his body of wanting Candace Murdock, it just might be the thing to do. But there just might be other things Jesse could tell him. Things more to the point of what he wanted to know.

"I hear your brother once had himself a wife like that. Loose," Range added, to make certain Jesse got his point. "Long time ago." Range frowned, as if trying to remember what he'd heard. "Alice or Alicia or Allison." He shook his head and shrugged. "Something like that."

Jesse's features instantly hardened, and his dark brown eyes narrowed as they stared at Range. "Where'd you hear about Allison?"

Range smiled. "Yeah, that was it, Allison."

"Where'd you hear it?" Jesse demanded again.

Range shrugged. "In town, I guess. I stopped there

before coming out to the ranch." He hadn't of course. Tombstone was the last place he wanted to go. No telling who was there that might recognize him. Not as Range Connor, but from before. Even though Garth and Jesse hadn't, that didn't mean there wasn't someone out there who would.

Jesse's expression was hard and suspicious. "People don't usually do much talking like that around here. Not about Garth anyway. Who'd you hear that from, Connor?" An ugly smirk pulled at one corner of his mouth. "Probably old Charlie, huh? Man's always drunk." He stared at Range. "Little guy, with long white hair and a limp?"

Range shook his head. "No, I don't think so, but I seem to recall being told she ran off. Her and a kid."

"Like I said, we don't talk about that around here." Jesse's tone was harder, a warning edge to his tone.

Range smiled and persisted. "Yeah, I can see why. Must have been pretty bad, her running off with Garth's kid. Ain't the kind of a thing a man usually takes lightly. I know I wouldn't, if a woman did that to me. Fact is, I'd probably go after her." He purposely turned his smile to a leer. "Course, who knows what I'd do to her once I caught up with her." He turned sober again. "But I know I'd at least get my kid back." He watched Jesse closely. "Unless he wasn't mine. Then I wouldn't give a damn what happened to him."

"Yeah," Jesse muttered, then spun and walked toward the corral. Garth was still struggling to subdue the bronc who was fighting to break free of the ropes that had been thrown around his neck.

One of the wranglers was jerked off his feet when the horse reared.

Garth smacked a fist to the animal's shoulder, threw his rope to the ground when Jesse called, then walked to the gate of the corral.

Range watched the two talk for a few minutes, having no doubt Jesse was relaying every word of their conversation to his brother. He moved away from the barn and walked toward the house. It was probably a long shot, but he'd sure as hell like to get a look at the rooms in the back of the house, though he didn't really expect to find anything. It had been too long. But he still wanted to get in there, if he could do it without being seen.

He walked into the house.

Candace was setting the table. She looked up as he entered. "Dinner won't be for another ten or fifteen minutes at least," she said coldly.

He nodded and walked toward the washroom.

"Why are you here?"

Her pointed question surprised him, and he stopped. It wasn't a question he intended to answer, for her or anyone else, at least not with the truth. But he found himself admiring her courage for asking it anyway. He turned and met her gaze straight on. It was a mistake he didn't usually make with a woman, but he'd made it now, and it was too late to change it. Lies were easier told to a woman when you didn't look her straight in the eye. He'd found that out a long time ago. With men, it didn't matter.

Most men just couldn't see past their own fear or bravado to the truth staring at them from within Range's eyes, but it never really mattered, because he had never cared if they thought he was lying or not.

She stared at him, waiting for an answer.

"Because your husband hired me," he said sharply, hoping the half-truth would be enough for her. For good measure, he made certain there was no warmth to his tone, no ease in the rigid way he held his features, or the hard, almost brazen way he looked at her.

But she didn't intimidate easily. He'd seen that the day he'd arrived, and he saw it now, both in her eyes and the defiant tilt of her chin as she stared back at him. "To do what?" she demanded.

He leaned a shoulder against the door frame, hooking his thumbs lazily into his gun belt, and crossing one foot over the other. "To protect your ranch during this water rights dispute your husband is having with his neighbors," Range said, letting the lie roll easily off his tongue. "Or don't you want your husband and ranch protected?"

Her blue gaze delved boldly into his, searching for the truth behind his words, and unconsciously drawing him toward fantasies he had no business entertaining. He felt his body begin to respond to the sight of her, and silently cursed. He didn't know what it was about Candace Murdock that aroused his libido like an iron stoking a fire, but he couldn't deny it happened whenever she was around. He'd felt it when he'd seen her standing on the porch, watching him as he'd ridden toward the ranch house upon his arrival at the Rolling M. He'd felt it when he had sat next to her at the dinner table; when he'd seen her standing on the porch last night, after she'd thought everyone else had retired for the night . . . and he felt it now, while she was staring at him with dislike and distrust clearly shining in her sky blue eyes.

He'd bedded plenty of beautiful women in his time, some ladies, some whores, and some in-between, but he'd never wanted any of them as instantly, or as strongly, as he wanted Candace Gates Murdock.

His hands fairly ached with the desire to reach out and touch her, to draw her near and claim her lips with his. His jaw ground in resistance of the sweep of heat suddenly rushing through his body. He wanted to rip off her clothes, see her naked, throw her down on the floor, and take her—hot, fast and swift.

It wasn't what he wanted to feel toward her, and it wasn't

something he was going to do anything about, but he couldn't deny that he felt it.

For just a moment he considered relenting, considered ignoring the long-ago hard-learned need for caution and taking her, but the momentary lapse of self-discipline was gone almost before it took root in his mind.

Candace met his stare and refused to look away. "Protecting people isn't what you do, Mr. Connor," she said coolly. "And it's not the real reason you're at the Rolling M." She swallowed hard, unable to believe she'd actually said the words that had been nagging at her since his arrival on the Rolling M. He frightened and intimidated her, but after overhearing his confrontation with Brandon, she wasn't going to let him see that, because she wasn't so certain anymore that her brother wasn't right about the real reason the gunman was at the Rolling M, and that thought scared her half to death. It also gave her the strength to do what she knew she had to do. Whatever happened, she would protect Brandon, even if she had to kill to do it.

"No?" Range's brows quirked upward. "Then suppose you tell me what the real reason I'm here is?"

"To kill someone."

"That could end up happening."

"I believe that's exactly what usually happens when you're around," she said. Candace didn't know where she was getting the courage to challenge him. She had never been a timid person, but she'd always picked her fights carefully. This one, however, she'd just plunged headfirst into, instinct and fear guiding her rather than planning.

The sounds of someone approaching the house echoed through the open door behind Range.

"Maybe we could continue this conversation later," he said, pushing propriety, and even caution, aside, "say about midnight? By the barn?"

He desired her. She saw it in his eyes, and, though she remained still and shocked for a moment, she quickly regained her wits and knew instantly it was most likely the only thread of vulnerability she was going to find in him. If she was smart, she could use that weakness to her advantage. Candace smiled. "Perhaps," she said softly, and went back to the task of setting the table.

Several hours later Range walked into the bunkhouse. He didn't know whether she was going to show up at the barn or not. His body wanted her to, his mind didn't. In the meantime, he'd get a couple hours' sleep. If he woke in time to meet her, he would. If he didn't, then it didn't matter.

Range pulled back the blanket from his bunk. A small figurine lay in the center of his pillow.

Chapter 6

Range stared at the small figurine. A surge of emotion swept over him that was so quick, so intense, his knees nearly buckled beneath him at the onslaught. She looked up at him and Range felt suddenly as if time had stood still, as if all the years that had passed between the last time he'd seen the statuette, and now, had never existed.

But where had it come from? More importantly, how had it gotten here? His gaze moved over the statuette's graceful curves and lines, examining each, even as he hesitated to actually reach out and touch it, as if afraid if he did it would merely disappear.

"Hey, Connor, want in on the game?" J. D. Sharp called out from his seat across the room.

Range didn't turn, but merely waved a dismissing hand at the grizzled old wrangler who'd been the only one so far who had said more than three words to him.

The delicate china figurine seemed to stare back up at him. The base was chipped on one side, and the paint on the swirling folds of her gown was faded, worn almost completely off in some places, but she was the same figurine that had sat on his mother's bureau. Range's mind reeled with memories and emotions that had been stored away and never dredged up, as much for his own sense of self-preservation as a way to keep his anger and hatred under control.

Finally, he reached out and touched the figurine. The world didn't stop. The past didn't crash down on him. Death didn't suddenly appear and beckon to him. Range picked the statuette up. It felt so light and fragile in his hand and seemed smaller than it once had, now barely longer than his palm. Emotion suddenly swept over him, bringing with it all the memories and pain of a past he'd never forgotten, but tried not to think about.

Turning abruptly, he walked out of the bunkhouse and strode toward the corrals, his dark clothes enabling him to disappear into the night. Only the sound of his spurs, jingling softly with each step he took, defined him from the nearly moonless night. Wearing them was a danger the man who'd given him his last name had warned him against, but the soft, almost musical sound was one of the few pleasures in life that Range allowed himself, and one he'd refused to give up, even after it had nearly gotten him killed.

Chapter 7

He leaned against the railing, drawing deeply on his cigarette and staring up at a vast expanse of black sky nearly devoid of stars.

Someone knew who he was.

The thought chilled Range to the bone, something he'd thought could never happen again. He'd gone through and seen more in his thirty years than most men endure or see in a lifetime. He had been orphaned, adopted, and orphaned again. He'd had two mothers, and witnessed both murdered. He had never known his real father, saw his stepfather kill his mother, watched soldiers cut down his adopted father, Two Hawks, and held old Connor in his arms while the man breathed his last as his heart finally decided to give out.

He had been both hunter and hunted, had killed and almost been killed, been lauded by some as a hero, and condemned by others as a murderer.

Except for the beginning of it all, that night twenty-four

years ago when he'd experienced more terror than any one person—let alone a six-year-old child—should ever suffer, none of the things that had happened to him since that night had caused Range even a shiver of fear.

Fury. Outrage. Defiance. Sorrow. Those feelings he knew well. But not fear. That was one emotion he'd sworn would never touch him again.

He slowly held up his hand, uncurling his fingers from around the tiny angel, and stared down at her. Golden hair spread in long waves over her shoulders, while golden wings curved gracefully from her back. She was a little more worn than the last time he'd seen her, the colors on her delicate curves a little less rich.

Uneasiness snaked up his back. Someone here at the ranch knew who he was . . . who he really was, and though it didn't frighten him, it did make him wonder what their game was, and how it would affect his own.

Smoke slipped from his lips as he glanced at the ranch house. It hadn't changed much from what he remembered. Long, low, and painted white, with a fenced veranda that ran the length of the house's raised front and wrapped around its entire width. A couple of dormer windows protruded from the sloped roof, but Range knew the house had no second story, merely an attic. His eyes narrowed as he stared up at the dormers. Could there be something up there? A clue packed away years ago and forgotten about? Something that would tell him the truth of what had happened after he'd run off?

Or maybe just some other things that had belonged to his mother.

Range rolled the figurine around in his hand, feeling its delicate curves and grooves. He closed his eyes and instantly saw his mother's dressing table, with its lemonwood-carved insets and tall triple mirrors.

He glanced down and opened his hand, studying the

angelic but worn porcelain face that seemed to smile up
at him in serene innocence. She had sat on the surface of
the dressing table, her golden wings reflected in the silver
glass, but she hadn't been alone . . . there had been two
of them. One gold, one silver. Range remembered now,
his mother telling him that his father had brought them
to her from England and she was saving them, so that
someday Range could give them to the woman he loved.

He looked back at the house. Someone knew that the
figurine had belonged to his mother, and knew if he saw
it he'd recognize it. Someone knew who he really was, and
wanted him to know that they knew.

The question was: who? And what were they prepared
to do about it? If anything.

Candace stood looking out through the parlor's window.
She hadn't been able to sleep, having done little more for
the past couple of hours than toss and turn. But it hadn't
been Garth, snoring loudly in a bedroom adjacent to her
own, that had disturbed and kept her awake. She was used
to his sounds, and most nights the wall that separated their
rooms muffled whatever noise he made enough so that it
didn't bother her ability to sleep. What had kept her from
sleeping this night were the thoughts of Range Connor
that wouldn't seem to leave her mind, no matter how much
she tried to banish them.

The gunman frightened her beyond belief, but in the
solitude of her own mind, she found it impossible to deny
that he also fascinated her.

But what had finally gotten her out of bed was neither
Garth's snoring or her traitorous thoughts of Range Connor, but hearing the creak of Brandon's wheelchair as it
rolled across the gallery.

She looked toward her brother, knowing that when his

back ached and the pain robbed him of the ability to sleep, he often sat out on the gallery, staring off into the night. When she'd first realized he spent most nights more awake than asleep, she had tried to get him to take some laudanaum to both ease the pain and help him rest, but he always stubbornly refused. At first she hadn't understood, but now she knew why. Her brother was afraid of being killed in his sleep by her husband. And with Range Connor's arrival, Brandon's suspicions had finally found their way into her mind as well.

Candace caught a movement in the darkness by the barn and looked past Brandon and in that direction. There was nothing immediately visible to her eye, but she knew someone was standing there, in the darkness, and she was certain she knew who it was. He had suggested they meet, but she hadn't really considered doing it.

A chill suddenly swept over her body. What if that wasn't it? What if Brandon was right and Range Connor was standing in the shadows right now, his gun drawn, his finger tightening on the trigger as he took aim at her brother?

Her pulses raced, but fear seized her throat, preventing her from screaming out a warning to Brandon. She turned toward the door, groping for its handle, feeling as if her arms and legs were suddenly weighted down and useless. She grappled with the door, finally got it open, but before she could rush out to Brandon's rescue, he rolled his chair over the threshold toward her.

"Couldn't sleep?" he said.

She shook her head, nearly sagging with the relief that flowed through her body.

"Me neither. I'm going to get some pie." He moved toward the kitchen. "Want some?"

"No thanks," Candace said, her voice barely above a whisper. Maybe she could talk to the gunman, find out the truth and, if Brandon was right, do something to dissuade him. She looked toward the barn. He was there. He'd asked her to meet him there.

"I . . . I'm just going to step outside for some air." She closed the door behind her, but didn't step away from it. Instead, she clung to the door handle and looked toward the barn, where she'd sensed Range Connor had been standing only moments before.

She couldn't see anything. No movement. No shadow.

"I didn't think you were going to come out."

Startled, Candace clutched at her throat and whirled toward the side of the house.

He was standing only a few yards away, beyond the veranda, half in shadow, half in the light flowing out from the parlor window.

Moving away from the door, she walked toward him. "I only came out for some air."

He nodded.

She stared down at him. There was a darkness about him that had nothing to do with the night. She sensed it, felt it reach out and touch her, and shivered, as if to shake it off. Squaring her shoulders, she summoned every ounce of courage she possessed and, pinning her gaze to his, asked the question that had been gnawing at her ever since his arrival. "Did you come here to kill my brother, Mr. Connor?"

Range smiled and looked up at her. Some people would consider her foolhardy for confronting him like that. Range considered it courage, and that was one attribute, besides her beauty, that he admired.

Moon and lamplight filtered through the thick waves of her long blond hair and turned it to tangled threads of shimmering gold that surrounded her face and cascaded down over her shoulders toward full breasts hidden from his view by only the sheer folds of her nightgown. He felt an ache of desire, ignored it, and leaned back against a hitching post. But foolhardy or courageous, she was Murdock's wife, which meant if anything was going to happen between them, it was going to be on his terms, and for his purposes. "You don't mince words, do you, Mrs. Murdock?"

His smile unnerved Candace, but she held herself rigid, refusing to give in to the squall of emotions churning within her. "No."

He nodded. "I knew another woman like that once, said what she meant."

Candace sensed something in his tone, a shadow of sentiment, and felt a rush of surprise.

"She ended up getting murdered for it."

The words, as much as if he'd reached out and slapped her face, startled her. The coldness glistening from his eyes held her gaze, and her heart skipped a bit. She hastily struggled to regain some semblance of composure, reminding herself that since she'd come out to meet him, there was no sense hiding behind caution or fear. She needed the truth. One light brow soared as she stared down at him. "Is that a threat, Mr. Connor?" she asked, straining to instill her own tone with a calmness she was far from feeling.

He shook his head. "Merely a comment, Mrs. Murdock. People react differently to things. Fact is, I prefer people tell me the truth. Makes my job a lot easier."

"And your job is important to you?"

Range shrugged. "It's a living."

Now it was Candace's turn to smile, but there was no warmth in the curve of her cheeks, no empathy in the spark of her eyes. "Living," she mused. "Interesting word, coming from a man who kills people for money."

"Would you rather I kill people for nothing?"

She stiffened. "What you do or do not do is of no consequence to me, Mr. Connor."

"Unless I'm here to kill your brother."

She swallowed hard. "Yes."

He nodded thoughtfully and, throwing his cigarette to the ground, crushed it with the heel of his boot. Jamming his thumbs back beneath his gun belt, he looked back up at her. "Why are you married to Garth Murdock?"

Surprised by him again, Candace stared at Range. "I beg your pardon?"

He didn't know why he'd asked. In the long run, whether he took her to his own bed or not, it wouldn't make any difference to him whether she loved Garth Murdock or merely his money. But Range had felt the need to ask. Maybe merely to ascertain how many people on this ranch were actually his enemies, other than Garth.

"You don't have to beg, Mrs. Murdock," Range said, smiling. His eyes roamed her body, blatantly, showing both their appreciation and their hunger.

Candace stiffened.

"I asked you why you married Garth Murdock."

"I don't think that's any of your business."

He smiled again, and shrugged. "Maybe not, but I'd like to know anyway. Was it for love?" He watched her carefully. "Do you love a man old enough to be your father? Or was it his money you were after?"

Candace glared down at him for a long moment, then turned away. "Good night, Mr. Connor."

"Good night, Mrs. Murdock." He watched her walk into the house and was surprised a few moments later when a light went on, not in the large master bedchamber, but in the smaller front bedroom down the hall that had once been his.

* * *

"Heard a few rumors when I first come here," J. D. said, holding a branding iron over the fire and slowly turning its iron handle over and over in his hand.

One of the other wranglers subdued the calf they were about to burn with the Rolling M brand.

"But, of course, people was just talking 'bout things they really didn't know up from down. Speculating, you know?" He looked across the calf at Range. "Don't reckon you do a lot of that, hey? Speculating."

Range ignored the question, as he did most. He preferred gathering information, rather than giving it. "So she just ran off? His wife and her kid?"

J. D. nodded and pressed the branding iron to the calf's hip. It bawled loudly and, as the other wrangler released it, bolted to its feet and scurried away. J. D. looked at Range, his gaze riveting and probing. "Why so much interest in Garth's first wife and kid?"

He shrugged. "I like to know everything there is to know about the men I work for. Makes my job easier."

"Yeah." J.D. grinned. "How's that?"

"Makes for fewer surprises down the road," Range said, stepping aside as a wrangler brought up another calf for branding.

J. D.'s grin disappeared into a sober frown as he nodded. "Yeah, surprises can be hell on a man."

Range stood and caught sight of Candace walking toward the barn. Brandon was maneuvering his wheelchair beside her. "Well, if Murdock's first wife looked anything like his present one," Range drawled, inflecting his tone with just the right amount of appreciation as his gaze followed her, "Murdock must have been pretty upset when she took off like that."

"Looked like an angel," J. D. said.

Range's gaze ripped away from Candace and turned sharply onto J. D. "You knew her?"

The older man looked up at him for a long moment, shrugged, and turned his gaze back to reheating the branding iron. "Saw her a couple of times." He shrugged a shoulder. "In town, before I hired on here."

Range continued to watch the older man, unable to shake the nagging suspicion that J. D. Sharp just might know a whole lot more about what went on around the Rolling M, both past and present, than he was letting on. Which meant he just might be a person Range should make an effort to get closer to, though it had been so long since he'd gotten close to anyone he wasn't certain he even knew how to go about it, or if he could do it at all.

The sounds of activity near the barn drew his attention and Range turned.

Candace, mounted on a chestnut-dappled Appaloosa, rode from the interior shadows of the barn into the morning sunlight. She reined in and looked back.

Range's gaze followed hers.

A huge black gelding, its powerful legs dancing impatiently upon the hard earth, broke into view. A white star on his forehead blazed in contrast to his already glistening, midnight-hued coat. Brandon laughed and drew back on the massive animal's reins. "Take it easy, Aramis," he said, reaching down to stroke the horse's sleek neck. "We're going."

Range watched, shocked to see the crippled young man mounted on the back of a horse, and impressed by the magnificence of the beast.

Belt straps held Brandon's legs to the skirts of his saddle, his feet secured in the stirrups.

Range looked for anything else that might be holding the young man in the saddle, but there was nothing.

He hadn't failed to notice the gun strapped to Brandon's

hip, however. Nor had he missed the fact that both Brandon and Candace had slid rifles into their saddle sheaths.

The two ignored him and rode off.

"Shame what happened to that boy," J. D. said, drawing Range's attention again.

He looked back down at the older man. "So, tell me, what did happen to him?"

J. D. shrugged and stood, looking after the departing couple who had almost disappeared into the distance. "Broke his back when his cinch gave way one day while he was out riding after strays. Leastways, that's what they say."

Again, the suspicion that J. D. knew a lot more than he was actually putting into words swept over Range. "Sounds like you don't believe it."

J. D. turned and met Range's gaze. His own was shadowed. "Ain't up to me to—"

"Hey, sugar, want to escort me into town?"

The two men turned to see Karalynne sashaying toward them, the brilliance of her yellow gown, dripping with lace and supporting a huge bustle, and the matching plumed hat, almost rivaled the glare of the sun. She stopped at the railed fence and smiled flirtatiously at Range.

"Sorry, I've got a couple of errands to do," he mumbled solemnly.

"Oh, come on. Brianne's in the house cooking up a storm, making the place all hot and stuffy and smelly, and I just have to get away for a while."

"Sorry," Range said again. "Maybe J. D. here could go with you."

"Thanks for nothin'," J. D. grumbled under his breath, and reached for the branding iron again.

Karalynne flipped her carefully coiffed curls and spun on her heel. "Thanks, sugar, but I don't usually associate with wranglers. I'll get there on my own."

Range almost laughed aloud at the thought that Kara-lynne was more than willing to associate—and who knew what else—with a hired gunman, but not with an honest, working wrangler. Though he was more than certain her rejection had more to do with J. D. being grizzled, worn, old enough to be her grandfather, and most likely hard up for his next golden eagle, than the fact that he was a wrangler. Especially since Jesse claimed to have taken her away from a drover in town.

Waiting until Karalynne left, Range walked into the barn. Since Brianne was "cooking up a storm" in the house, there was no way he was going to be able to get in there for a look around. Especially in the bedrooms or attic. He saddled Satan, but just as he rode out of the barn, Garth stepped into view and waved him toward one of the corrals.

"Where you going?"

Range looked down at him, wishing he could put his boot in the man's face. He hadn't answered to anyone in longer than he could remember, but, he reminded himself, everything was different now . . . for a while. "Riding."

"Well, don't be starting any trouble in front of my wife," he growled.

Range looked down at him, one arm draped casually over his saddle horn. Contempt edged his retort. "You hired me to do a job, Murdock, and I'll do it, but I thought I made it clear, I do it my way."

A deep red flush swept over Garth's face. "I just don't want Candace in the middle of anything," he said, his tone more subdued.

Range's cold, black stare pinned him to the spot. "I hadn't intended that she would be." Taking up Satan's reins, Range nudged his heels against the horse's flanks and headed out in the same direction Candace and Bran-don had taken, not bothering to glance back at Garth Murdock.

He picked up their trail almost instantly, but then they hadn't done anything to obscure it. The morning was still young, but the day was already blistering hot. Range pulled his hat lower onto his forehead to block the sun's glare from his eyes.

Tall saguaro cacti spotted the landscape like silent sentinels standing guard over the desert, their smaller cousins—the bunched and pancake-shaped prickly pear, the barrel cactus, agave, and fishhooks—growing in scattered clusters nearer the ground.

Range watched his surroundings closely as he moved over the landscape. Innocence could always spell danger, peacefulness could shroud menace, and beauty could turn deadly in a split second, if caution was ignored, or even forgotten for a moment. It was a lesson he had learned young, and well. Trust was something he no longer gave anyone or anything. He relied only on himself, and that was what had kept him alive for the past twenty-four years.

Though there were two exceptions: he trusted Satan, and he trusted his guns. Neither had ever let him down, and he knew neither ever would.

Half an hour later he rode onto a small plateau. Candace and Brandon were in a valley below, riding side by side at a casual pace.

Range reined in and, draping his arms one crossed atop the other over his saddlehorn, he watched them.

They rode slowly, unaware of him, and though he was too far away to read their expressions or hear their words, he heard quite distinctly when Candace laughed. It was a musical sound, reminding him of chimes upon a spring breeze. It also reminded him of his mother. A tightness gripped his chest. After twenty-four years he would have expected the anger to have subsided, diminished, or even disappeared altogether. He would have expected the hatred to have gone away long ago, too. Along with the hurt and anguish. But that hadn't happened. None of those dark, rage-tinted feelings had gone away, or waned in their intensity.

New feelings, however, had come to him since he'd returned to the Rolling M, and not one of them was welcome. He didn't want to feel compassion for a wheelchair-bound young man, or desire for the wife of the blackguard who had murdered his mother. Range didn't want to feel any of those things, and yet he did.

He watched Candace and Brandon ride toward an arroyo. Maybe they knew about the past, maybe they didn't. But whether they knew the truth about Allison Landers Murdock or not didn't really matter. He knew now he had no intention of killing Brandon Gates. He'd make it look like he was going to. He'd taunt him, antagonize him, maybe even threaten him, but that would be only for Garth's sake, to buy Range time to seek his answers, and keep Garth off guard and assuming Range was leading up to doing what he'd been hired to do.

Using Candace, however, even taking her to his bed, that was another story. If it would get him closer to Garth, closer to finding the answers he needed so that he could disperse the retribution he'd come here to mete out, then whatever he had to do to her, he would do.

After all, she was merely the wife of a cold-blooded murderer.

Candace knew they were being watched. The feeling crept slowly up the back of her neck, ruffled through her hair, and sent chills sweeping down her spine.

Her hand moved toward the butt of the rifle sheathed beside her leg, but she didn't say anything to Brandon, not wanting to unnerve him. Ever since the accident he'd been too jumpy, too ready to draw his gun and fire without asking questions, without even thinking about it. Maybe if their situations were reversed, she'd be that way, too. She hoped not, but there was no way of knowing.

Her gaze scanned the horizon, looking for the danger she felt, while praying she was wrong.

Then she noticed him, sitting on a plateau that jutted out of the ground only a short distance away, to their right. The blood in her veins stopped flowing, grew cold, and she shuddered with apprehension.

He sat astride his large horse, the sun at his back transforming him into a black silhouette against the otherwise colorful landscape. But she didn't need to see his face to recognize the man who sat silently watching them. In spite of the bright sunlight there was a darkness about him that she sensed emanated from his soul, a darkness that surrounded his heart and tainted everything he touched, even the air he breathed.

The image of him sent a sense of menace rippling through her, chilling her blood. It reminded her of the warlords of the ancient world, strong, ambitious, bloodthirsty power-mongers who rode across the land, ravaging, conquering, and destroying everything in their paths.

Fear slid through her like a rapier, swift, silent, and smooth. But she knew she couldn't give in to it, she had to act. Only that morning she had determined that she had to get close to Range Connor, to try and get him to turn from Garth and take her side, if Brandon was right that Range had come here to kill rather than protect. Yet so far she had been unable to force herself to make any advances toward him. He fascinated her, but he also frightened her, and she knew it was the fear that he instilled within her that was going to give her the strength to do what she knew she had to do.

Candace touched her reins to Tojo's neck, and the graceful gelding began to turn.

"Where are you going?" Brandon yelled.

She reined in and looked over her shoulder at him. "Stay there, I'll be right back."

"Candace."

"Stay there," she snapped. "Please." She urged Tojo into motion and galloped up the hillside toward Range.

He smiled as she approached. So far the lady had managed to surprise him several times, and she was doing it again. He hadn't expected her to confront him.

"Why are you watching us?" she demanded.

"Because you're too pretty to ignore," Range quipped.

She gave him a sneering smile. "Flattery isn't going to fool me, Mr. Connor. I know why you're here, and if you go through with any attempt to harm my brother, I swear, you won't leave this ranch alive."

He liked her spirit. She had guts. Something most women—and even quite a few men—lacked. He reached a finger to his hat and tipped the brim toward her. "I'll keep that in mind, Mrs. Murdock."

"You do that, Mr. Connor."

Chapter 8

Range raised the canteen to his lips and drank deeply. The water was warm, but at least it was wet. His parched throat felt a few seconds of relief, then began to ache for another drink. He recapped the canteen and wrapped its strap around his saddle horn. Pulling the brim of his hat lower onto his forehead, he scanned the surrounding desert, saw nothing of interest, and urged Satan into motion.

Murdock's neighbors weren't close, their spreads were miles apart, and at the rate he was going trying to get any of them to talk, he just might have a head full of white hair before he found out anything worthwhile. Assuming he found out anything at all. That they might not know anything was something he didn't want to contemplate. After watching Candace and Brandon riding the morning before, he'd spent the entire rest of the day going from one spread to another, asking questions and getting no answers.

Today wasn't proving to be much better. The only change was that he wasn't alone today. Range turned slightly, as if to reach into his saddlebag. As he did, he glanced over his shoulder toward the rim of the canyon behind him. She was doing her best to keep out of his sight, but her best just wasn't good enough, especially since she was trying to follow a man trained on the desert by the Apache. He smiled to himself. Either she was more suspicious of him than she should be, or more curious than cautious.

Half an hour later he realized she wasn't behind him anymore.

Range stopped and looked back. Since he was on his way back to the Rolling M, she should have been right behind him. He stood in the saddle and scanned the area. Nothing moved. A frown drew his brows together. He should have been able to see her, and it wouldn't have made any sense for her to go in another direction when they were headed back toward the ranch. The sun was on its way down. It would be dark in a couple of hours, and this was the most direct route back. Range flipped open his saddlebag and, after a few minutes of digging around, pulled out a spyglass he'd acquired from an army officer a few years earlier. Holding it up and standing in his saddle again, he began to scan the area.

It took three tries before he spotted her sitting on the ground beside a tall saguaro, her horse almost invisible to his sight as it stood directly behind the plant. As he watched, Candace rose and bent over beside the horse, running her hands over his left foreleg.

Range returned the glass to his saddlebag and, urging Satan to wheel around, rode back toward Candace.

She heard his approach and damned the heavens. Now he would know she'd been following him.

"What's the matter?" he said, reining in only a few feet from her.

She looked up. "Who said anything was the matter?"

"I saw you examining your horse's leg."

She sighed. The man must have the eyes of an eagle. "I think he pulled a muscle."

"What're you doing out here?"

The question she'd been dreading. She glowered at him. "I might ask you the same thing, Mr. Connor."

"You might."

"I am." She stared up at him expectantly.

"I was out riding," Range said after a pronounced silence.

"Well, I was, too."

"Didn't your daddy ever teach you that it's dangerous for a woman to be alone out in the middle of nowhere?"

She stiffened. "My daddy taught me a lot of things, Mr. Connor." She turned and drew her rifle from its saddle sheath. "One of which was how to shoot a rifle and hit what I'm aiming at."

He smiled. "Then don't point that thing my way."

"Don't give me reason," she retorted, returning his smile but keeping the rifle securely gripped in her hands.

He swung from his saddle, hit the ground, rolled, and had her rifle in his hands when he bolted back to his feet.

Candace stared, stupefied.

"Never drop your guard," Range said, and handed the rifle back to her.

Candace took the weapon and stepped back.

"Want me to take a look?" He glanced at her horse's leg.

"I know how to tell if a horse is lame or not."

A sudden tightness began to squeeze his chest as he stared at her. He didn't know what it was about Candace, but he knew he'd never seen a woman quite as pretty, quite as alluring as she looked at that moment.

Her blue eyes suddenly struck him as being the purest blue he'd ever seen, as bright as a spring sky, yet surrounded by a shadow of midnight and hinting at pleasures and secrets he would probably never know. Instinctively he knew there was a part of Candace Gates Murdock that she kept hidden from the world, a part that, like him, she might never allow anyone to see. Maybe it was a feeling that they had more in common than either had realized, maybe he was merely impressing his own feelings onto her, but he suddenly felt like he knew her better than he'd ever known any woman.

Silence hung between them, and a war raged within him. One side of him said *Use her.* Do whatever he had to do to get information out of her, and enjoy her at the same time. But the other side shouted a loud warning. She was a fire that could burn him badly. Destroy every hope he had of uncovering the truth and bringing Garth Murdock to justice.

He knew he should stay away from her, keep his guard up, his defenses intact. There could just as easily be treachery hiding behind those alluring blue eyes as pleasure.

What if Garth had sent her to follow him?

Range shook the thought aside, but he couldn't argue that it made sense. If Garth wanted to know what Range was doing every day, he couldn't follow him, or even send Jesse. They had a ranch to run, business to operate and oversee. So why not send Candace? The only problem with that scenario was that Range knew Garth Murdock, like his younger brother, was an extremely possessive man. Jealous. Suspicious. Even unreasonable. The last thing he would want was for his pretty young wife to be alone with another man. But why else would she have followed him?

It wasn't as if he was any threat to her brother while riding out here alone.

And she certainly hadn't tried to kill him.

Range bent to examine the horse's leg. He cupped his hands around it and ran them up and down its length. It was warm, an indication that the gelding's muscle had been pulled. He straightened and looked at Candace. "You're not going to be able to get home on him today."

"I know that." She pulled her saddlebags off her horse's back and threw them to the ground, then reached for her saddle's cinch. "Tell my family what happened, would you? I'll be home tomorrow."

Range frowned. "You're going to stay out here?"

With the rifle shoved under her arm, she paused in an awkward attempt to remove her saddle without setting down the rifle, and looked up at him. "Well, tell me, Mr. Connor, what would you have me do? Leave my horse out here alone to fend off coyotes or whatever?"

Not many women would brave camping out in the middle of the desert alone. He decided to play along, see what it was she was after.

"No. I'll stay with you."

She rammed both fists on her hips. "I didn't ask you to stay with me."

"No, you didn't." Range pulled the saddle from Satan's back.

A few minutes later he had a fire started. He contemplated chewing on beef jerky for dinner, or hunting down a jackrabbit or a rattler.

Candace looked at him, her head tipped slightly to one side as she studied him. "Can I ask you a question?"

"Since when do you ask?"

Candace ignored his insolence. "How long have you been a hired gun?"

He turned from stoking the fire to meet her gaze, as well as her question. "Long enough."

Range grabbed his saddlebag and pulled out a small packet of beef jerky, deciding not to take the chance that a rifle shot would bring them company. This might be his only opportunity to be alone with Garth's wife and get some answers, if she had any to give. He pulled the jerky from his bag, unwrapped it, and held some out to her. "This is the best I've got to offer for dinner," he said. A wry smile twisted the corners of his mouth upward.

Candace stared at his offering, then shook her head, and reached into her own saddlebag. "Obviously I travel a lot better prepared for problems than you do," she said, plunking a jar of canned peaches, and another of beans, down on the ground before her. She pulled out a small tin plate and, after splitting the food equally, handed Range the still half-full jars, along with a fork.

"Sorry, I only have one plate."

They ate in silence as the sun began to drop behind the mountains in the distance.

Range mulled over a dozen questions in his mind, examining each one. He wasn't sure of the best way to approach her. Small talk, or direct questions? She seemed to favor the direct route when it was her doing the asking, but she might not be so accommodating when the tables were turned.

Candace put her plate down and, wrapping her arms around her drawn-up legs, looked across the fire at him. "Why did you become a hired gunman?"

He scooped the last peach out of the jar and ate it before answering, but if he was going to get answers out of her, he figured maybe the easiest way was to give her some. "I didn't plan it. Kind of just happened."

"Where were you born?"

That questioned surprised him, and made him think. His gaze met hers. "I don't know," he answered truthfully.

Her eyes widened. "You don't know?"

He shook his head. "Why do you want to know? It's not really important where a person was born. We all come into this world helpless, and make of ourselves what we can."

"I like to know where a person started. It gives me a sense of them."

She smiled, and for the briefest of moments, Range knew he would have given her anything she asked for, answered any question she put to him. Even the ones he'd never answered for anyone else.

Candace knew she was playing a dangerous game, but she wanted to know about him. It wasn't just a need anymore, not just a way to solidify her defenses against him so that she could better protect Brandon. There was something in her now that had to know about Range Connor. About his past, what had made him what he was, what drove him on.

Maybe she'd find they weren't answers she'd want to hear, but she had to ask anyway. "Where were you raised?"

He studied her for a long moment before answering, then knew, somehow, that no matter what he said, if it was to her it had to be the truth. "I was raised by the Apache for a while after my mother died."

"Apaches?" The thought of him being surrounded by savage Indians sent a shiver snaking down her spine. No wonder he was a killer.

He nodded.

"Did they . . ." She paused, not certain how to continue. The urge to know everything about him was so strong it was almost overwhelming, yet it also frightened her. She took a deep breath and, telling herself she needed to do this for Brandon, she plunged ahead. "Did they . . . did the Indians kill your mother and . . . steal you?"

A look of pain, so intense, so deep, suddenly flashed through his eyes, and startled her.

"No," he said, moments later, so softly she barely heard him. "They saved me."

"Saved you?" Candace felt a start of surprise. "From what?"

He turned away from her to look out into the shadows that were quickly consuming the surrounding landscape. He inhaled deeply, as he remembered that day, when he'd sat huddled beside a rock, staring up defiantly at the men who surrounded him, their long black hair framing hard faces bright with paint—red, white, black, and yellow. Range sighed. "My mother was dead, I was alone and lost in the desert. The Apache were on a hunt. They found me and took me in." He looked back at her, his gaze no longer closed. "I became the son of the chief's son. They named me Range Warrior."

Range suddenly wondered if he had told her too much? Had he told her enough so that she—or Garth if she told him—would realize the truth? He damned himself and tried to read the thoughts in her eyes.

"Is that where you learned to kill? When you lived with the Apache?"

He shook his head, not wanting to dredge up any more memories of the past, and knowing he had no choice. That was part of what coming here had meant, what he'd known he had to face. "Not for money," he said softly. "They taught me how to kill, but only to survive or defend myself."

"What about your real father?"

"The only father I ever knew was named Two Hawks."

"Is he . . ."

"Dead," Range said flatly.

She saw it then, the loneliness and pain that were hidden

deep within him. It was merely a flicker of emotion that glinted in his eyes and drew at his lips for just the briefest of seconds, and then, as if it hadn't been there at all, it was gone.

Steeling himself from the tumult of his own emotions as they churned within him at the onslaught of old memories, Range watched how she absorbed what he'd said. First with shock, then with compassion, and again he sensed that there was most likely quite a lot of Candace Gates Murdock that was kept hidden from the world.

He knew, without knowing how, that there were passions within her that few people saw. Passions that lay sleeping, unaroused by any man's touch or caress.

The thought was intoxicating, and stirred something within him he knew had no business stirring. If Candace Murdock had never felt passion, if she never did, it was no concern of his, yet even as the thought took root in Range's mind, he knew it for the lie it was.

"What . . . what happened after that?" she asked, her tone tentative. The look in her eyes told him she wasn't certain she should continue. "After your Indian father died? Where did you go?"

"I didn't go anywhere," he said, his tone hard again as more old memories crashed down upon him, memories that were unpleasant, unwanted, and more than painful. "I was taken by the army to Fort Weatherford." He shrugged. "Eventually I adjusted."

"To becoming a soldier?"

"To becoming white again."

Candace gasped softly.

Range smiled, knowing he'd succeeded in shocking her. "I became a scout."

"You haven't told me how you became a hired gunman."

The amicable look on his face disappeared, and the

shadowed frown returned. "No, I haven't." The cold, hard edge had also returned to his voice.

She knew he had said more than he'd intended, and there would be no more answers. At least not now. But she had one more question. One she had to ask. "You don't like me, do you, Mr. Connor?"

It was his turn to be surprised again. His eyes bored into her. Candace Gates Murdock was fast becoming the most unpredictable woman he'd ever met. But that wasn't all she was becoming. She had gotten him to open up, to tell her things he'd never told anyone . . . and it wasn't because he'd wanted to make her feel comfortable, because he'd wanted to get her in turn to open up to him. It was because he wanted her, more than he'd ever wanted another woman.

Candace felt as if there was suddenly a fire between them, pulling them both toward its core. Yet the more she struggled against the feeling, the stronger it seemed to get. Her body was too aware of him sitting so close, yet so far away. His gaze dueled with hers, challenging her, warning her, and all the while she looked at him, hot, flowing torrents of emotion, confusing and unfamiliar, flowed through her body.

Range smiled at her question. "Like you?" He shrugged. "I don't really know you, so why wouldn't I like you?"

"You tell me."

His dark blue eyes met hers and he saw the passion, and the mistrust, that he felt mirrored his own gaze. "I have no reason to dislike you, Mrs. Murdock."

"Yet you do," she said quietly.

He pushed himself up from the ground and walked several yards into the darkness away from their camp, before he stopped, his back to her. "In my profession, Mrs. Murdock," he said over his shoulder, "you can't trust anyone. Liking a person means trusting them, and I can't afford to do that."

She stared at his back for a long time, watching how the faint rays of the moon settled on the brim of his hat, struggled to reach beneath it to his broad expanse of shoulders, and glinted off the pair of Colts slung low on his thighs. Candace rose and walked to him, not thinking about what she was doing, and not pausing until she stood beside him. Hesitating, she looked up at him, as if searching his face for something she hoped would be in his expression.

Range turned to look down at her and found himself once again enthralled by the blue depths of her eyes, the sweet curve of her lips.

"Don't kill my brother," she said softly, the plea that was in her eyes finally reaching her lips. "Please. He doesn't deserve to be gunned down."

She wanted an assurance he couldn't give. Not unless he wanted to take the chance that there was no treachery flowing in her veins. Yet surprisingly, it was an assurance he wanted to give. His presence at the Rolling M, his supposed reason for being there, was exactly what she thought it was, and now, for the first time in his life, he suddenly cared what another person thought of him, and there wasn't anything he could do about it. He couldn't take the risk of telling her the truth. No matter how much he wanted to.

Her face was only inches from his, the scent of lilac that he'd detected in her hair that first night at the dinner table when he'd sat next to her hovered in the air now, teasing him, beckoning to him.

From the first moment he'd seen her, something had happened between them. They'd both felt it, and both tried to ignore and deny it. He saw the truth of it in her eyes now. He'd seen desire and need in a woman's eyes enough times to recognize them, and he saw them in Candace's eyes as she looked up at him. The fires of desire that had been simmering between them since that first moment suddenly flared into an inferno, uncontrollable and consuming.

Need and want swept through him, like a fever claiming his body—thoroughly, swiftly, and completely. It overtook his good sense, banished all reason, and mocked the steely self-control he'd always exerted over himself, before finally vanquishing it. Stirrings of passion, deeper than anything he'd ever felt, coiled hot within him.

Some thin shred of sanity called out to him, screamed at him repeatedly to walk away, to lose himself in the caution that had been his only ally for so long. But this time he couldn't heed its call.

Her mouth was too close, too inviting, his will too weak. The need to taste her lips, feel her body pressed up against his was too strong; the desire within him to crush her to his length, if only for a moment, was too desperate to ignore. Its intensity astounded him, but he had no will left to fight it.

Nothing in Range Connor's life had taught him how to be gentle. His mouth captured hers much like a hunter captures its prey, swift and thorough, without mercy or tenderness.

The need within him was too strong, too desperate to acknowledge anything else, yet some sense of rationale remained in him, so that recognizing that need, and surrendering to it so completely, also ignited another kind of flame in Range: anger. He had come here to kill Garth Murdock, and she was Garth Murdock's wife.

He wanted to punish her for that, punish her for making him want her, but he couldn't. Her lips were too sweet beneath his, her arms around his neck too enticing. A firestorm invaded his body and reached out to inflame hers.

She kissed him back, her lips as hungry as his, her tongue as probing.

Nothing made sense anymore. Desire was consuming them both, bringing together two people who had no reason to be together, two people who disliked each other, had every reason to hate each other.

The air around them crackled with the energy of their desire, their bodies like sparks of passion, each fueling the other, teasing and stoking, until all that was left was the flame of their needs. Hungry and uncontrollable.

She was everything he'd ever wanted, and everything he'd always vowed to avoid. She was passion and coldness, light and darkness. She was his hope for a future, and a certainty that could bring him doom.

He had never made an irrational decision in his life, yet he knew he was making one now, because short of a bullet in the back, he doubted he could stop what they'd started.

His lips crushed hers with the fierceness of the need consuming him. It was a kiss of desperation, a kiss of such emotional intensity that reality was a thing of the past, and something that might never again be regained.

His tongue invaded her mouth, entwined with hers, and a new barrage of flames assaulted his body.

Candace responded with a hunger he had never before witnessed in a woman, her body seeming to both welcome and fight him at the same time. Her arms held him to her, while her hands pushed him away. Her tongue dueled with his, inviting, probing, retreating and assaulting. But never surrendering.

She moaned with the need that coursed through her, and his arms drew her up tighter against him, dragging her to him, pressing her body to his until there was no space, no air separating them.

Candace felt the hardness of his arousal push into her stomach, and, like a splash of cold water to her face, the world and all of its ugliness crashed down upon her. Horrified at what she'd just done, terrified of the possible consequences, she dragged her hands to his shoulders and, pushing, wrenched away from him.

Range's arms suddenly experienced an emptiness they had never before felt, and, as he looked down at her, into eyes shining with disdain, he felt as if someone had just cut his heart from his chest.

Candace stared at him. But it wasn't fear of him that left her tremblilng, but of herself.

Shaking her head, she backed away from him. "No," she whispered faintly, the sound barely penetrating the night air. Turning away, she moved back to where she'd dropped her saddle and huddled next to it, staring into the crackling flames of their campfire.

Hot, painful knots held her body in a tight grip, but worse was the realization of what she'd done, what she was capable of doing.

Chapter 9

Candace awoke the next morning to find herself alone. She sat up and looked around. "Well, it figures," she grumbled. He'd left her out here alone. And after he'd nearly seduced her, too. Memory of their kiss, and her response to it, turned her blood to fire and she flushed, feeling the tingling sensation of desire invade her.

Suddenly her heart began to hammer fiercely within her breast, but it had nothing to do with passion or the memory of the torrid way they'd kissed. He was headed back to the ranch to kill Brandon. She'd asked him if that was why he was here, and he hadn't answered. She'd asked him not to do it, and he hadn't responded to that either.

Fear seized her. He was going to kill Brandon, and he'd waited for her to go to sleep before leaving. Maybe he figured it would be easier to kill her brother without her around to deal with. Maybe there was some ludicrous code of killer honor that made him not want to gun Brandon down in front of his sister.

She jumped up and ran to her horse.

Tojo's leg was bandaged.

Candace stared at it, puzzled, then bent and ran her hands up and down its length.

Tojo remained still, not even flinching, but Candace knew her chances of catching up with Range Connor or getting back to the ranch before anything happened were not good. If she tried to ride Tojo hard, she'd cripple him.

Candace pulled her rifle from its sheath and grabbed her hat, then turned back to Tojo. She took the tin plate from her saddlebag and poured water from her canteen into it, placing it down on the ground before him, then slung the canteen over her arm.

"I'll be back for you as soon as I can," she said to the large gelding. "I promise."

Turning, she started to walk in the direction of the ranch.

Tojo followed.

"No, stay there," Candace said.

The horse took another step after her.

She sighed. "I don't blame you," she said, "I wouldn't want to stand out here for hours alone either." She grabbed his reins.

Range was on his way to kill her brother. She had to keep telling herself that. He was a hired gunman. A cold-blooded killer, and he was on his way to kill her brother.

He had tried to make love to her, and she'd almost let him. He had made her feel things she'd never felt before. His kiss had aroused sensations within her that had left her body trembling all night, had awakened a need within her that she now feared she would never escape. The feelings were like nothing she'd ever experienced before, and, heaven help her, even as she trudged after him deathly afraid of what she would find, her body continued to yearn for his touch, craved a renewal of the feelings he'd touched off within her, and hungered to know more.

At that moment, with the morning sun already burning the land mercilessly, Candace hated herself. She had betrayed her family and herself. She had allowed her body to dominate her senses. But worst of all, when she remembered those few moments when he'd answered her questions and she'd thought she glimpsed a shadow of the real Range Connor, of the pain and hurt that had made him what he was, she knew she'd been played for a fool.

She had almost felt sorry for him. Almost wished she could help him heal those old wounds. Almost wished she could . . . Candace clamped a cold, hard barrier down in front of her thoughts. She had almost betrayed everything she believed in because a cold-blooded, hired killer had kissed her and made her feel passion.

Her cheeks burned with humiliation, and she forced herself to walk faster.

Suddenly the sound of hoofbeats behind her penetrated Candace's thoughts. As she spun to face whoever was riding toward her, the rifle she'd held propped on her shoulder dropped to her hand and she aimed.

"Just where in the hell are you going?" Range growled, reining up in front of her. He was astride his own horse.

Candace stared at him, comprehension the farthest thing from her mind.

"I thought I'd try to scrounge up something for breakfast," he said, "but I guess you were in too much of a hurry to wait."

"I . . ." She felt like a fool.

"Never mind." He swung a leg over his saddle and dropped to the ground. "Come on."

His offer surprised her. She moved past him, her gaze averted from his, and mounted his horse. "I'll send someone back for you," she said.

Range, his hand wrapped around the saddle horn, smiled. "I don't think so," he said, and shoving her foot from his stirrup, swung up behind her.

Candace felt his body settle in behind hers, his chest pressing to her back, his thighs molding to the back of her own. She felt his breath on her cheek, his hand resting on her leg as he held the reins.

Range knew the moment he'd swung his leg over the saddle and slid down onto it that he'd made a mistake. A groan of despair nearly ripped from his throat as his body pressed against hers, but he managed to stifle it, and silently curse himself for an idiot a half-dozen times.

They rode slowly, because Satan was carrying a double load, and Tojo was favoring his injured leg.

Range knew hell could never be so agonizing. With each step Satan took, Candace's hips swayed against him, unintentionally teasing his self-control. The soft waves of her hair brushed against his stubbled cheek. The fragrance of her lilac scent swirled around him, and the aching need to touch her further, to wrap his arms around her and lose himself within her embrace, was almost more than he could bear.

To keep his raging passions under control, Range resorted to the only thing he knew that could turn his body from fiery hot to icy cold. He purposely dredged up the memories of his mother's death, letting the scene play over and over through his mind, allowing the old, painful emotions to invade his heart and tear at it as they had done so many years before.

Candace tried to hold herself away from him, but it was hard, and her back ached. She shifted position on the saddle again, trying to put some space between them. Her thighs rubbed against his, and she bit down on her bottom lip as she heard him utter a soft curse.

"Will you stop squirming around, for chrissake?" Range thundered in her ear.

Startled, Candace nearly jumped onto the horse's neck. "I . . . I was just trying to give you some room," she lied.

"I don't need room," Range snapped. What he needed was her, but he sure as hell couldn't say that, nor could he do anything about it.

They were halfway back to the ranch when he reined in and swung down to the ground.

"What's wrong?" Candace said, suddenly afraid he was going to leave her here and go in alone to kill Brandon. She twisted around, eyeing her rifle, which he'd returned to the sheath connected to her saddle before they'd started out.

"Get down," Range ordered.

She stared at him, contemplating whether or not he could stop her if she kicked the horse into motion.

Range stretched his back.

Candace grabbed the reins, then remembered that Tojo's lead rope was tied to Range's saddle. If she urged his horse into a run, Tojo would be forced to follow, and with his bad leg she knew the effort would most likely cripple him. She dropped the reins and swung down to the ground.

Range immediately grabbed the saddle horn and mounted.

She'd been right, he was leaving her.

Range held out his gloved hand. "Come on."

She looked up and frowned.

"Your turn to be in back," he said.

Relief nearly caused her knees to buckle. Candace took his hand and, slipping a foot into the stirrup he vacated, swung up and onto the back of the saddle.

"Try not to move around too much," Range growled.

Half an hour later he knew he might as well have said

that to a wall, and if he'd thought having her behind him was going to be any less enticing, any less arousing, he'd been wrong. One minute her breasts were crushed into his back, her thighs to the back of his butt, and rubbing suggestively against him with each step his horse took. The next minute Candace was wriggling toward Satan's rear.

He reined in. "Will you stop?" he bellowed, scaring her so much she nearly slid over the horse's rump to the ground.

Range caught her shirtfront just in time, hauling her back up against him. "You're going to cripple my damned horse with all your wriggling around."

"I'm sorry," she said softly.

"Fine, then just sit still and ride." Images of her hot, naked, and under him, kept dancing through his head.

They were halfway back to the ranch when Candace noticed the change in him. It was like he'd pulled a mantle of coldness over himself, suddenly separating him from the rest of the world, and completely from her.

"Where the hell have you been?"

Range turned from pulling the saddle from Satan's back to see Garth Murdock standing in the doorway to the barn, meaty fists clenched and propped on his hips.

Murdock's dark gaze bored into Candace.

She stood a few feet from Range, near the stall into which she'd just led her horse. "Tojo came up lame," she said, meeting Garth's angry glare. "Mr. Connor came across us out on Dutch Flats."

"So why didn't you come home?"

Range saw Candace's shoulders stiffen.

"I told you, Tojo came up lame."

"So," Garth sneered, "you coulda left him there."

"No, I couldn't." She brushed past him. "I need to clean up, then see about helping Brianne with supper."

Garth watched her walk toward the house, then whirled around, and turned his attention back to Range. His dark brown eyes gleamed with fire and a momentary lack of caution as they arrogantly raked Garth's length. "Anything happen out there between you two?"

Range settled his saddle onto a nearby rail, took a brush from his saddlebag, and began to rub it across Satan's back. He didn't like being questioned. He liked it even less when the one doing the questioning was Garth Murdock.

"Connor, I asked you a question," Garth snapped.

Range turned slowly, letting the older man feel the full onslaught of his cold, hard gaze. His eyes narrowed beneath drawn brows. "Excuse me?" he sneered sardonically.

Garth Murdock's bluster instantly paled as their eyes met and he heard the dark sarcasm in Range's tone. "Did anything . . ." He wiped a gnarled hand over his face. "Did my wife . . . did she let you . . . ?"

Range had been a long time waiting for an excuse to return to the Rolling M and see that justice was served, and he didn't want anything to ruin that plan. But he knew it would give him one hell of a lot of enjoyment to tell Garth Murdock that kissing his wife had been one of the most pleasurable things Range had done in longer than he could remember. Now, however, wasn't the time. It was too soon. He shrugged. "We shared a can of peaches, some beans, and a campfire," Range said evenly. "That was it."

Garth's brow screwed into a mass of furrows as he contemplated what Range had said. "That's all you shared?"

Range let the question in his own eyes be clearly seen. "Should there have been more?"

Garth backed down, as Range had expected he would.

"No. She's a good woman. Really. Just crazy defiant sometimes, you know?"

"Sometimes that can be good," Range said. He saw the suspicion return to Garth's eyes, and smiled to himself.

"I'm planning on riding over to Hatchabee's tomorrow," Garth said. "So I assume you haven't forgotten why you're here."

Range paused in running the brush over Satan's back and looked at Garth. "There are very few things that I forget, Murdock."

The two men stood looking at each other for a long time, Range's eyes sparking with, he knew, cold menace, Garth's with confusion, and just a hint of fear.

Then Garth tore his gaze from Range's and turned away. "Supper'll be ready soon."

"I'll be there," Range said, turning back to Satan. Thirty minutes later he walked into the house, hoping Garth had cooled his jealous thoughts enough to be civil, and that his own body had expelled enough of its traitorous reactions toward Garth's wife for one day.

Within minutes of sitting down at the table, Range realized that he might as well have hoped that when his time came, St. Peter was going to see fit to size him up for a pair of wings.

"Hear you and Candace had yourself a little evening under the stars," Jesse said, laughing at his own words as he looked across the table at Range.

"Mrs. Murdock's horse came up lame," Range said. "I didn't think she should stay out there in the desert alone."

"Yeah, I'll bet you didn't," Jesse said with a suggestive sneer.

Brandon glared across the table at Range, and for a while he feared the young man was going to challenge him in defense of his sister's honor.

"Mr. Connor was a gentleman," Candace said, her own

challenging gaze pinning itself on Jesse and daring him to call her a liar.

"You should have come home on his horse," Garth said, his own glowering gaze skipping past his wife to land bravely on Range. "Sent someone back for him."

Range smiled. "No one rides Satan but me, Murdock," he said easily. "Of course, if you'd like to try?" He let the question hang in the air, and felt a swell of satisfaction at seeing Garth's face pale slightly.

"I figure there's a reason you call that animal Satan," Garth said finally.

Range nodded, the cold smile on his lips still there. "Yeah, there is." He reached for a bowl of potatoes at the same moment that Candace did. Their hands touched. A path of fire ripped up Range's arm, and he drew back.

Garth and Jesse had turned their attentions to the chunks of roast on their plate, but Range caught Brandon's look and knew instantly that the young man had a much better sense of what had happened between his sister and Garth's hired gun, than either of the other men at the table.

Whether Candace had told him or Brandon had guessed, Range didn't know, but then, he told himself, it really didn't matter, because it wasn't going to happen again.

Halfway through dinner, Range had heard enough of Jesse's sly comments to last him a lifetime, but short of putting a bullet through the man's brain, which he wasn't ready to do yet, he figured there was probably no way to stop him. Pushing his chair away from the table, he rose. "Think I'll take me a ride into town," he said.

Jesse looked up and smiled. "Sounds like a good idea, Connor. Maybe I'll go with you." He pushed his chair back and stood.

"I don't rightly recall inviting you to come along," Range drawled.

Brianne and Candace, who'd been talking softly, instantly quieted.

Brandon and Garth Murdock looked up, both obviously surprised.

Karalynne watched, wide-eyed with the anticipation of excitement.

Jesse looked taken back, not having expected, or familiar with being rebuked. He puffed out his chest. "Didn't think I needed an invitation."

"To ride with me, you do," Range said. He grabbed his Stetson from the chair he'd laid it on and settled it on his head, then turned and walked out the door. The last person he wanted to keep company with tonight was Jesse Murdock, though it should have been Candace Murdock. Getting away from her before the fire in his body caused him to do something he would be damned sorry for was the exact reason he was going to ride in to town.

Range pulled Satan up in front of the Double Eagle Saloon. Music blared out through its swinging doors, as well as the raucous laughter of several dozen men and a few women. The smell of stale tobacco, leather, and cheap whiskey permeated the air.

He'd intended to head straight for the local brothel, but had decided he needed a couple of drinks first. Then again, maybe it would take the entire bottle to blot out the image of Candace's face in his mind. And he definitely needed it blotted out.

Range dismounted, strode across the boardwalk, and pushed open the swinging doors. Smoke hung like a hazy gray cloud over the saloon's interior. He stood still, surveying the room, taking stock of everyone and everything in it. No surprises, that was the rule he lived by, the rule that had kept him alive so far.

A staircase ran along the saloon's left wall. On its landing overlooking the rear of the room, stood several women, waiting, Range knew, to be taken up on what they had to offer.

None looked appealing to him.

His gaze moved to the rear of the room. A wheel of fortune spun as a dozen men laid down bets. Near the front of the stairs was a faro table. Range recognized Luke Foster dealing. The short blond's hazel eyes darted to meet Range's, he nodded, and turned his attention back to his game.

Range saw two other men he'd met in Wichita several years before, sitting at one of the poker tables.

The bar was crowded.

The piano player seemed to be in his own world, plunking the keys and staring dreamily off into space.

Range walked to the bar. "Give me a bottle."

The bartender, a huge burly man with a mustache whose ends curled up to nearly meet the outer corners of his eyes, set a bottle and shot glass down on the bar before Range. "You new in town?" he asked.

"You could say that." Range downed a glass of whiskey and poured himself another one, all the while his gaze glued to the huge mirror behind the bar as he watched everything going on behind him.

"Looking for a woman?"

A man at the faro table suddenly shot to his feet, grabbing the table and tipping it over. It pinned Luke Foster against the balustrades of the stairs, as greenbacks, double eagles, and cards went flying.

"You cheating son of a bitch!" the man yelled. He reached for his gun.

Range spun around, drew, and fired.

The man screamed as Range's bullet sliced across the outer edge of his palm and blood spurted onto his thigh.

He turned, eyes wide with the fear of seeing another bullet coming toward him. "What'd you do that for?" he shrieked, after seeing Range reholster his gun.

Range propped an arm on the bar and lazed back casually. "Luke Foster doesn't cheat," Range said softly.

The room had gone deathly still, everyone watching Range.

"And since his mother is a real nice lady, I'd say you owe them both an apology."

"He cheated me."

Luke pushed the table away from his chest and rose to his feet.

Range continued to merely stare at the man.

"Fine," he mumbled, minutes later. Turning on his heel, he darted toward the door and disappeared.

"Appreciate it," Luke said. "Consider your bottle on me."

Range nodded and turned back to his drink.

"That was some pretty fine shooting, mister."

Range looked at the man who'd stepped up to his left. Slightly built, almost wiry, with a face that reminded Range of a squirrel, a pair of spectacles resting on his nose that magnified his eyes to the size of oranges, and an Adam's apple that bobbed up and down in his scrawny neck with each word he said.

"Thanks," Range said, his hand moving cautiously to rest on the butt of his gun. The man might look innocuous, but there were plenty of men who did and turned out to be some of the most ruthless killers a man could face.

Doc Holliday and Bat Masterson were two of the most renowned, and Range just counted himself lucky that those two, at least, were his friends, not his enemies.

"I saw Doc Holliday draw on a man once, Wyatt Earp,

too, but I don't think either one of them are as fast as you."

Range turned to face the man.

He smiled. "John Donnelly. I own the general store across the street. Just stopped in for my nightly shot before going home."

Range nodded. "Good to meet you, John Donnelly."

"You're Range Connor, right?"

Range nodded again.

"Heard Garth hired you, but I doubt there's anyone around here who believes he got you down here to protect him in any water rights dispute, you know?"

"No?" Talking to strangers wasn't something he normally did, but then the situation wasn't exactly a normal one, and he needed as much information as he could get if his questions were going to get answers. "And just what do people think he hired me to do, Mr. Donnelly?"

"Kill somebody, of course."

"Anybody got any ideas on just who that might be?"

The smaller man looked at Range cautiously. "I'm not looking for trouble, Mr. Connor."

Range smiled. "I'm not looking to give you any, Mr. Donnelly."

Donnelly nodded. "Most folks figure they know exactly who it is you've been hired to kill, but we all hope we're wrong. Might even turn out to be a bad mistake for Murdock, if what we hope doesn't happen, does."

"How's that?"

The man shrugged, then looked up pointedly at Range. "You know the story behind Candace and her brother and sister? How they came to be at Murdock's?"

Range shook his head. "No. So why don't you tell it to me?"

John Donnelly poured them both a glass of whiskey, downed his, then looked back up at Range. "The Gates spread borders the Rolling M. About seven, eight years ago, Theo Gates and Garth Murdock were best friends. Good thing, too, cause the Rolling M didn't have access to the river without going across Gates End. But that never seemed a problem. Ol' Theo and Murdock shared the water and the range land, too. And Jesse, hell, he was so taken with Candace that, in spite of him being older, everyone thought the two of them would end up married someday. But her pa had other thoughts on the matter."

Donnelly paused to pour himself another drink.

Range stared at the man. "Candace and Jesse?"

"Yep. But then, someone shot ol' Theo in the back one night while he was on the way home from town. Ambushed him good. Never did catch the guy. Theo didn't die right away, though. They found him a few hours later, and he lingered. Wasn't nothing Doc could do and Theo knew it, so he called for his best friend. Asked him to marry Candace and take care of the other two, the twins, 'til the boy was twenty-one and could take over Gates End."

Donnelly shook his head. "Jesse changed then, let me tell you. Losing Candace made him mean. But in a way, you know, I kinda understand. He loved that girl."

"Range Connor!"

Range stiffened and slowly raised his eyes toward the mirror. He knew that kind of voice, the pitch and verve, had heard the challenge too many times to count, too many times not to know what it meant.

The man who stood behind him, feet spread wide, hands hovering only inches from the guns tied to both thighs, wasn't really a man at all, he was a boy, at least in Range's opinion. Purposely moving slowly, Range set his glass down on the bar, but didn't turn. "Yeah, kid, whaddya want?" he drawled, in a bored tone.

"You!" the boy snapped. "I want you, Range Connor. Now draw."

"I don't kill children."

The boy's eyes narrowed and an ugly sneer drew his lips. "I'm as old as The Kid was when he shot his first man," he said. "So what's wrong, Connor? You too much of a coward to meet your maker?"

Range turned slowly. "Boy, Billy ain't someone you want to imitate." He took a step toward the kid. "Look, son, you don't want to die, and I sure as hell don't want to have to kill you. So why don't you just go on home?"

"Getting too old, Connor?" the boy taunted. "Gun hand slowing down? Afraid I can take you?"

Everyone in the saloon grew quiet and began backing away from them. Everyone except Luke Foster. He stood off to one side of the boy and slowly pulled his black greatcoat back, hooking its folds behind his gun's butt.

"It's okay, Luke," Range said, noticing the other gunman's stance.

Luke nodded and backed away, but kept his gun obviously uncovered and his hand ready.

The boy smiled. "Found your nerve, huh, Connor?"

Range shook his head, as if in disgust. "Go ahead and draw, boy," he said coldly.

"No, you first."

"You made the challenge, kid," Range said. "It's your call."

The boy's fingers flexed.

Range kept his gaze glued to the boy's eyes. It was there he'd see the sign and know when it was time to act.

The boy reached for his gun.

Range saw the flash of light in the boy's eyes just a split second before his hand moved toward his gun. He dived for the floor and rolled just as gunfire exploded in the room. Range jumped to his feet, his fist clenched, and rammed it into the kid's jaw.

He crumpled to the floor instantly.

Loud hoots and guffaws filled the saloon.

The bartender carried the kid outside and unceremoniously dumped him in the street.

Two hours later Range had finished off his bottle, lost a couple of double eagles to Luke Foster over a few hands of poker, and was no longer in the mood to share his bed or his body with a whore.

Walking outside, he flicked the cigarette he'd been smoking into the street and stepped down from the boardwalk. "Time to head back to hell, Satan," he said, reaching for the animal's reins and chuckling softly at his own pun.

"Turn around, Connor."

Range froze and a sigh of resignation slid through his body as he recognized the voice of the boy who'd challenged him earlier. He'd hoped this wouldn't happen, but even so, he had been fairly certain it would. He'd seen it, faced it himself too many times before. Young bucks out to make a name for themselves before they were ready. He dropped Satan's reins and turned.

"No funny stuff this time," the kid said. "Draw, or I'll kill you right where you stand."

Range took several steps sideways, moving toward the center of the street and away from his horse. No sense in taking a chance on Satan catching the kid's bullet, if he had time to fire one.

Light filtering out from the windows and doorway of the saloon was the only illumination offered the street.

"You ready now, old man?" the kid sneered.

"You in that much of a hurry to die, kid?"

"I asked if you were ready, old man?"

Range shrugged. "Your call, kid."

Several men, including Luke Foster, had heard the kid's challenge and come out of the saloon. They stood crowded together now on the boardwalk, most fairly certain the kid was about to breathe his last, and knowing there wasn't anything any of them could do about it, even if they were inclined to, which none of them were.

The kid stared at Range, determination on his face, anger in his eyes.

Range prayed the kid would change his mind and walk away.

The boy's hand went for his gun.

Range drew and fired.

For several seconds nothing happened.

Range stared at the boy.

He stared back. Then, without a word, the gun slipped from his fingers, he dropped to his knees and fell face forward into the street. Dust flew up around him, then resetttled to the ground.

Range slid his Colts back into their holsters and walked back to Satan. "See to the kid's funeral for me, would you, Luke?" He reached into the pocket of his shirt, pulled out a double eagle, and tossed it to the gambler.

Luke caught the coin and nodded, then broke away from the others to walk toward the kid.

Range mounted Satan and headed for the Rolling M. In the last forty-eight hours he'd come face-to-face with the man he'd hated for almost twenty-four years, nearly seduced the devil's wife, and killed a boy that was little more than a child.

He felt suddenly very old, and very used-up. Nevertheless, he had to finish what he'd come here to do.

Chapter 10

Range paused on his way from the barn to the bunk-house. A light was on in her window, in the room that used to be his. He knew it was hers because he'd seen her coming out of it as he'd entered the house that evening for dinner.

It was like an unusual and unfamiliar touch of intimacy to his soul, knowing she was sleeping in the room that he'd once slept in, that the room she now called hers had once been his. He knew now, after what Donnelly had told him, that she was as much a victim of Garth Murdock as he was. Maybe even more. At least his mother had been put out of her misery, and Range had gotten away from the man. Candace had to spend every day with him. That would soon change, however, and she'd be free to do whatever she wanted.

Range felt a tightening in his gut, felt the fire of desire coil tight around his groin, and cursed softly, the sound hanging on the midnight air. He had never wanted a woman so badly, and it annoyed as well as puzzled him. There was no room in his life for a woman, and no need for one, other than an occasional whore to satisfy his physical needs.

And even if he did want a woman in his life, it wouldn't be Candace Gates Murdock. He could tell by just looking at her that she wasn't his type. She was the settling-down type. A woman who'd want a man around all the time, who would want him in the fields every day, and beside her in bed every night. She'd want children, security, and honesty. All things Range couldn't, or didn't want, to give.

Nevertheless, he wanted her. It had been easier when he'd thought she was no better than Murdock, when he'd believed she most likely had married the old man for his ranch and money. Then he'd planned to merely satisfy himself by taking her once he'd gotten rid of Murdock. Now he knew he couldn't do that to her, because he knew his judgment of her had been wrong, but it didn't stop him from wanting her, only from his plan of taking her. He wouldn't do that now.

There was at least that much morality left in him.

Candace stood behind the lace curtains that covered her window and watched him. She'd known when he left the ranch, and she'd known when he came back, because she'd been watching. She didn't know why. Didn't know what there was about Range Connor that made her feel the need to watch him, need to know everything she could about him. Fear was part of it, fear of why he was really at the Rolling M, what he'd really been hired to do. But she knew there was much more, deeper feelings churning within her that she was too frightened to acknowledge or analyze.

She saw him pause halfway between the barn and the bunkhouse and turn toward her, as if somehow he'd known she was standing behind the curtain, watching him. It star-

tled her, made her step back, afraid of what he was going
to do next, afraid that he would walk toward the house
and confront her. But he didn't. Instead, he merely stared
back, and soon she realized that he couldn't see her, that
he was merely staring at the house. That intrigued her.

There was more to Range Connor than any of them had
been allowed to see, she knew that, sensed that even though
Garth had hired him, supposedly to protect them in the
dispute with their neighbors, even though she feared
Range Connor was really there to kill Brandon, there was
more to the man, more to the reason he had come to the
Rolling M, more behind the darkness of his eyes. And she
wanted to know what it was.

She watched him turn away, but he didn't enter the
bunkhouse. Instead, he looked out toward the distant hills,
as if listening.

"What are your secrets, Range Connor?" Candace whispered softly. "What kind of feelings and thoughts are really
behind those cold, hard eyes of yours?"

Unconsciously she reached out, her fingers brushing
past the sheer lace to touch the cold glass of the window,
as if reaching out to touch him. What would it be like, she
thought, to slide her hands along the hard breadth of his
shoulders? To feel her breasts crushed against his chest,
her body embraced by the length of his sinewy arms and
warmed by the fiery heat of his flesh?

He turned back to look at her window, an abrupt move
that startled Candace and she gasped and stepped back,
the fear that he had somehow heard her thoughts flashing
through her mind. It was a ridiculous idea, she knew, but
one she couldn't banish from her mind.

As abruptly as he'd turned to look toward her window,
he turned back and walked to the bunkhouse.

Candace moved to her bed, the trembling in her legs
threatening to weaken them to the point of no longer

being able to offer her support. What was the matter with her? She collapsed onto the bed and closed her eyes, but the image of Range Connor refused to leave her. Nor would the fire that had erupted in her body at the thought of being held in his arms.

Range threw his gear down on the floor and flopped onto his bunk. Why Candace had married Garth Murdock wasn't his concern. What happened to her after he sent Murdock to hell wasn't his concern either. In fact, if he was honest with himself, he'd admit that having both Murdock and Range Connor out of her life would probably be for the better. She could go home then, back to her family's ranch with her brother and do whatever she wanted to do. Marry Jesse, or whomever.

The thought should have made him feel better. It did just the opposite. His gut churned sourly and his head throbbed. Range pounded a fist into his pillow, then rammed his head down on it, and ordered his mind to either help him figure out how to get the answers he needed before sending Murdock on his way to the fiery pits, or shut up, turn off, and let him get a few hours of much-needed sleep.

Dawn came flooding into the bunkhouse at the same moment the sound of horses' hooves broke the silence.

Range was instantly alert and on his feet. He moved to the window and looked out.

Two riders pulled up at the hitching rack in front of the main house.

Several other wranglers rolled from their cots, grumbling and reaching for their boots, while another started a fire in the bellied stove that sat in one corner and moved the coffeepot over its lid.

"Hey, Connor, you going out with the boys today?" J. D. Sharp said.

"No," Connor said, shaking his head but never taking his eyes off the two riders who had now climbed the steps to the house and knocked on the door.

A moment later Candace opened the door.

Range saw her smile at one of the men, then step aside, obviously having asked them inside. Moving back to the bunk, he strapped on his guns, settled his hat on his head, and walked to the stove. He took a tin cup from a rack on the wall, poured himself a cup of coffee, and walked outside. Leaning his back against the bunkhouse wall, he slowly sipped the steaming hot coffee and stared at the house, waiting for the two men to come back out.

He didn't have long to wait.

Garth Murdock appeared first, followed by both of the men who'd ridden up. They crossed the open space between the main house and the bunkhouse, and walked directly toward where Range stood.

"Mr. Connor," Garth said, carefully using the title Range had demanded, "this here is Sheriff Laney and Deputy Hawkins. They say there was a shooting in town last night and want to talk to you about it."

Range nodded, and his slow gaze moved insolently over first the sheriff, then the deputy, as he made a mental assessment of each. But he didn't straighten or push away from the wall, and he didn't offer either man his hand.

He tried to place their names, especially the sheriff's, who looked about the same age as Garth. Had the man been around these parts twenty-four years ago? Range didn't remember, even though he racked his brain in an effort to do so. If he had been in Tombstone, he'd either swallowed the story about Allison Landers Murdock running off with her kid, or he'd helped Garth cover up the truth.

That was something else Range intended to find out. He looked straight into the man's eyes, as if daring Laney to recognize him.

"Understand you were in town last night," the sheriff said. "At the saloon."

Range looked him up and down, making no secret of the blatant appraisal. He had a paunch the size of a watermelon hanging over his gun belt, and thick gray hair protruding from beneath his hat and lining his upper lip. His hazel-colored eyes were almost colorless, and his jowls heavy. The man had long ago passed his prime, but Range figured he was just too old, or maybe too full of stubbornness and bluster to admit and recognize the fact.

The deputy, on the other hand, was about Range's age and build, blond hair, blue eyes, clean-shaven, and physically fit. He also gave every impression that he knew his way around a gun. But, unlike the Earps, Bat Masterson, Doc Holliday, or any of the other gunmen Range had known who'd done their stints as lawmen, Range would bet his last double eagle that Deputy Hawkins had never allowed himself to be on the wrong side of the law. Maybe it was the set of the man's square jaw, or the pure blue of his eyes that set off that feeling in Range, he wasn't sure and it didn't matter. He knew he was right.

"And Jimmy Sawlyers called you out," the sheriff said, drawing his gaze again.

But it wasn't a question, so Range didn't bother to respond. Instead, he pulled a small white linen pouch from his vest pocket, held a small square of paper in his other hand, and, loosening the red drawstring on the pouch, poured a line of tobacco onto the paper.

Sheriff Laney obviously didn't recognize him as anyone other than Range Connor, hired gun, which was good. For him, and for the sheriff.

"That kid was always looking for trouble," Garth said. "Hotheaded idiot."

The sheriff ignored Garth and kept his gaze focused on Range. "You killed him."

Range rolled his cigarette and slipped it between his lips before looking up and letting the cold darkness of anger flood his eyes. "The kid gave me no choice." He knew challenge echoed around his words, but that's exactly what he'd intended. Too many times in the past, a sheriff had wanted to make something of nothing when a hired gunman was the person left standing after a face-off. It wasn't a situation Range liked, and it wasn't one he'd tolerate.

The sheriff nodded at Range's answer. "I know that. Already talked to Luke Foster and several other men who were there. All said that."

"It's a wonder he didn't get himself killed years ago, like his father," Garth said.

"You got rid of the kid once," Sheriff Laney went on, "but then he came back. I have to verify the facts. You understand? From you."

"Seems pretty simple to me," Garth said. "Kid went out looking to get killed, and he did."

Laney turned toward Garth. "Yeah, but the boy's brother ain't gonna be real understanding about it, if you know what I mean."

Garth shrugged. "So he'll end up dead, too. Good riddance to bad rubbish."

The sheriff nodded. "Yeah, you got a point. It would bring a little more peace and quiet to the town, having the Sawlyers gone."

Range noticed that Deputy Hawkins had moved away from them and was a few yards away now, talking with Candace. A flash of annoyance swept over Range. The man hadn't said two words to Range, yet he bothered him. More so than the sheriff. Range wanted to know what the deputy and Candace were talking about, but they were too far away for him to hear their words. And even if they hadn't been, the Sheriff's inane yakking was overriding every other sound around.

"Now, the boy did draw first, right, Connor?"

Range looked back at the sheriff, but instead of answering, he dug into his shirt pocket for a lucifer. He scraped its sulfured head against the leather of his leggings, and it burst into flame. He cupped his hands around it, held the match to the end of his cigarette, drew in a long drag of smoke, then flicked the lucifer across the yard toward the deputy. It struck the man on the side of the face.

Startled, Hawkins jumped and whirled around, his hand instantly moving to hover over his gun's butt.

Range smiled, satisfied. His aim had always been damned good. Today it was perfect. And he'd also confirmed his suspicions. Hawkins was more than just familiar with a gun. "Sorry, deputy."

Hawkins glared.

Range looked back at the sheriff. "Yeah, the kid drew first."

"So you really couldn't avoid shooting him?"

Range shrugged, pulled the cigarette from his lips, and hooked his thumbs into his gun belt. "I could have let him shoot me."

The sheriff chuckled, then fell silent when he realized no one else had laughed.

Suddenly Garth turned and strode toward Candace and the deputy.

Range watched as Garth grabbed Candace's arm and, spinning her around, practically dragged her toward the house. She tried to jerk her arm free, but she was no match, at least physically, for her husband.

Garth jerked back and nearly tore her from her feet.

Candace tripped and scrambled after him.

Long-suppressed memories of another woman trying to fight off Garth Murdock and suffering beneath his fury-inspired blows flashed through Range's mind. Rage erupted inside of him like the spewing fire of a volcano, hot and swift and deadly. His fingers ached to circle Garth Murdock's neck and squeeze for all they were worth, to steal the breath from his lungs and the light of life from his eyes. Instead, he spun on his heel and stalked toward the deputy.

"You'd better leave," Range said under his breath.

Wade Hawkins, staring after Garth, turned to look at Range. Anger shadowed every line and curve of his face, flashed from the depths of his eyes, screamed from the stiff stance of his broad shoulders.

Range wanted to ask the deputy what in the hell had just happened, to demand that the man tell him what he'd been so intently discussing with Candace. He wanted to know what was between them, why Garth had seemed to become so instantly and thoroughly jealous. But something he didn't want to acknowledge was afraid of the answers. So he repeated his warning instead. "I'm not here for you, Hawkins," Range said, a thread of warning edging his tone, "and I don't want to be. So just get on your horse and leave."

The deputy stared at Range for a long, fury-filled second before responding. "Protect that son of a bitch, Connor, and your beef definitely is with me."

"I don't expect there to be any more trouble on this Sawlyer thing," Sheriff Laney said, having moved to stand just behind Range.

He turned and looked at the man, having almost forgotten about him and the reason the two lawmen had come to the Rolling M in the first place.

"But if you come into town again, watch out for Jimmy Sawlyer's older brother, Ed. He just might get it into his fool head to avenge his brother's killing and come gunning for you, if you know what I mean."

"I know," Range said, none too happy about the prospect. He didn't want to kill another kid, but he'd never hidden from a fight either, and he wasn't about to start now.

The sheriff tipped his hat. "Well then, guess I'll be seeing ya around."

Range watched the two men walk away. "Yeah," he muttered under his breath. "No doubt."

Minutes later only a cloud of dust hanging over the long entry drive gave any evidence the two men had even been there. Range still stood leaning against the outside wall of the bunkhouse. Garth had stalked back out of the house seconds before and gone into the barn. Jesse had ridden off with several of the wranglers earlier.

Range's gaze moved back to the house. What was Candace doing? His mind conjured up too many possibilities, and some of them were enough to propel his anger into fury. He remembered his mother as he looked toward the house, remembered the last time he'd seen her. He could almost still hear her screams. See the blood. Did Candace know about her husband? Was she aware of what he was capable of?

Range took a long drag off his cigarette. They obviously slept in separate beds in separate rooms, but that didn't mean that Garth left her alone. And from what Range had seen, it obviously didn't mean that the man wasn't crazy jealous of his young wife. The look in his eyes when he'd watched her talking with the deputy had been murderous, and Range suspected that if no one else had been around, Garth just might have put a bullet in Hawkins's back.

He saw her move past the front window then.

Why the hell had he warned the deputy away? Range thought back over that moment. He'd told himself it was to save the man's life, or prevent Garth from getting into a fight that could get him killed. Not that Range really cared about Garth, he just didn't want to give anyone else the satisfaction of putting a bullet between the man's eyes. He'd waited too long to do it himself.

Both motives seemed altruistic, and both were so false it wasn't even funny. He'd warned the deputy away in order to protect Candace, plain and simple. But from whom? Garth? Or himself?

He snorted. That was the big question. Garth, he knew from experience, was capable of killing, especially while in a jealous rage. Range, on the other hand, had felt a surge of jealousy come over him when he'd seen the deputy and Candace together, that was like nothing else he'd ever felt. And nothing he wanted to feel again.

He threw the cigarette down and ground it into the earth with the heel of his boot. There was no way Candace couldn't know about Garth Murdock. She was married to the man, had been living in his house for seven years. Even if they didn't share a bed, she'd know. A wife always knows.

Pushing away from the wall, Range walked toward the barn. He needed to ride, to get away from Garth, Candace, and the sight of the house, so he could think. The neighbors had given him nothing new. They'd obviously all swallowed Garth's lame story that Allison and her son had run off with some tinker. And Range hadn't been free to look around the house yet, not that he held out much hope he'd find anything there. Even so, he had to look. Especially in the attic. His mother had brought a lot of her belongings to the Rolling M when she'd married Garth, and quite a lot of them had been stored in the attic. Range remembered that because he remembered going up there once with her and looking through an old trunk for something.

"Got yourself a plan yet?" Garth said, as he watched Range saddle Satan.

Range ignored him.

"I figure it should be over soon."

Range whirled around. "It'll be over when I'm ready to make it over. Understand?"

Garth paled and looked back at the bridles he'd been inspecting. He nodded. "Yeah, sure, fine. Just thought I'd ask, is all."

Range started to lead Satan from the barn, then paused beside Garth. "How long has Sheriff Laney been around these parts?"

Garth looked up and frowned, clearly puzzled by the question. "Laney?" He screwed up his face as if thinking. "On and off all his life, I guess. Why?"

Range shrugged. "Looks familiar."

Garth set the bridles aside as he looked at Range. "Laney's family had a place here, but lost it years ago when his pa died. He took off then, did some deputying up around Abilene, I think. Sheriffed over in Balsie for a few years. Been here for about the past two. But if he'd have run into you before, he would have said so."

Unless it was twenty-four years ago, Range thought, and he was helping to cover up a murder.

Range swung up onto his saddle.

"You going into town again?" Garth asked.

Range looked down at him, his gaze steely hard. "No." He nudged his heels to Satan's flanks, and the big horse instantly bolted from the barn. There were still a few neighbors to visit, a few questions to put to them, and maybe, if he was lucky, a few answers to get.

By evening, as he returned to the ranch, he knew exactly what he was going to do.

Chapter 11

From the directions the bartender had given him and the description of the place, Range was pretty certain the clapboard cottage he'd reined up in front of had to be the dressmaker's place.

But even if the directions had been sketchier, the description a little less exact, and the sign hanging from the fence hadn't proclaimed in faded letters "Dressmaking," Range would have known he was at the right place. He remembered it, remembered coming here often with his mother, remembered her sitting in the garden, surrounded by the roses. His mother had always given him a penny when they'd come here, and let him run down the street to the general store to buy some licorice, which he'd loved. And afterwards, he'd played with the dog who belonged to his mother's friend, a dog that was little more than a small brown ball of fur called Tansy.

Memories stung at his heart and eyes; emotion clogged his throat. He brushed it aside, drawing back the harshness of reality that had been the only thing that had allowed him to survive the last twenty-four years.

As always, his gaze took in everything before he dismounted. Surprisingly, nothing seemed to have changed. The cottage was small, painted yellow, and, if he remembered right, there were only four rooms beneath its peaked roof. White, louvered shutters adorned the two tall windows that looked out onto the street, a picket fence framed the front yard, and an arbor curved gracefully over the front gate. A variety of rosebushes and vines, all abloom in splashes of red, white, pink, orange, and yellow, grew everywhere, just as they had twenty-four years ago, under the windows, the front of the gallery, up a trellis set between two front windows, over the gate's arbor, and along the fence line.

Range dismounted, looped Satan's reins over a hitching rack near the gate, and walked up the dirt path that led to the front gallery and the door. For a brief moment he felt six years old again, and half-expected to see his mother and her friend sitting on the porch, half-expected Tansy to come bounding out of the front door to greet him, yapping happily and jumping all around him.

He chided himself for the ridiculous thought and knocked on the door.

A movement behind the lace-covered window set into the top half of the door alerted him that someone was there. A second later the door swung open and a tiny woman looked up at him. Though her hair, pulled back in a massive chignon at her nape, was more gray than brown, her face appeared nearly free of wrinkles, and her crystal blue eyes shone with life and vigor. Range would have recognized her anywhere.

She smiled up at him.

As a child he hadn't realized it, but as a man, looking at her now, he knew that at one time, long ago, her beauty would have easily taken a man's breath away. As it was now, she was still an extremely striking woman. "Francie Rouchard?" Range said, suddenly aware that beneath the black gloves he wore, his hands were trembling.

The woman nodded and smiled. "I wondered how long it would take you to get around to visiting me," she said, in a drawl that was definitely deep south.

Range stared down at her, taken aback by her words. "You expected me?" he finally managed.

She laughed, and the sound was like a jingle of merriment to his ears, a sound that instantly drew him into the past. "Well, of course I expected you." She stepped back, opening the door wider in welcome. "But I'd almost given up that you were going to come by and see me. Come on, come in here." She waved him into the house. "My first client isn't due to arrive until noon today, and Mrs. Bailey is always late anyway, so we have plenty of time to chat."

Range glanced back over his shoulder, not certain what he was looking for, but feeling suddenly apprehensive.

"There's nothing to worry about here," she said, as if aware of his wariness. "No one else knows about you. Leastways, not from me."

His head snapped back around, and his dark eyes bore into hers. "Knows about me?" he challenged.

Her eyes met his steadily. Compassion shone there. "Who you really are," she explained.

He felt as if the earth had suddenly disappeared beneath his feet, a fist had rammed into his stomach, the air stolen from his lungs. His eyes narrowed, shoulders stiffened, and his hands instinctively moved toward his guns. "You know who I am?"

She laughed softly. "Well, of course I do. I knew the moment I saw you ride into town a few days ago, but I figured when you wanted to come see me, you'd come." She grabbed his hands and, holding them out, looked him up and down. "Land o' mercy, just look at you," she said. "So tall and strong and handsome." She shook her head. "Your mama would have been so proud."

Range took off his hat when she released his hands and stepped into her house.

The parlor was small, but nicely decorated. A wooden fireplace mantel held an assortment of porcelain bric-a-brac. Over them hung an oil portrait of a man about Range's age or a few years older, dressed in a Confederate uniform. Two settees and two sitting chairs covered in green brocade were set around the room, along with an assortment of tables, etageres, and a bookcase.

Range noticed that pictures of the same soldier were set in frames here and there on the various tables.

"My husband," the woman said, noticing the direction of his gaze. "Lt. Col. Lance Delany Rouchard, III. He died during the war, at the battle of Yellow Tavern, fighting under Jeb Stuart."

Range turned back to her. "I'm sorry."

Sadness swept into her eyes and she sighed deeply. "So am I. Yellow fever took our daughter, then the war took my husband, and afterwards it took our home, too."

Silence hung over the room as Range searched for something to say, and Francie momentarily remained with her long-cherished memories.

"But," she said, suddenly brightening, the smile returning, "I was more fortunate than your mother. At least I was certain my Lance was dead."

He frowned, then shook his head. "I'm sorry, but I don't understand."

"And you shouldn't," she quipped. "Now, sit down." She motioned toward one of the chairs. "I just made a fresh batch of beignets, and I'll get us some coffee, then we'll have us a nice, long talk."

Here's a special offer for
Romance Readers!
Get 4 FREE Zebra Historical Romance Novels from the newest Historical Romance line-Splendor Romances!
A $19.96 value absolutely Free!
© ENNIS
Take a trip back in time and experience the passion, adventure and excitement of a Splendor Romance...delivered right to your doorstep!

Take advantage of this offer to enjoy Zebra's newest line of historical romance novels....Splendor Romances (formerly Lovegrams Historical Romances)- Take our introductory shipment of 4 romance novels -Absolutely Free! (a $19.96 value)

Now you'll be able to savor today's best romance novels without even leaving your home with our convenient and inexpensive home subscription service. Here's what you get for joining:

- 4 BRAND NEW bestselling Splendor Romances delivered to your doorstep every month
- 20% off every title (or almost $4.00 off) with your home subscription
- FREE home delivery
- A FREE monthly newsletter, *Zebra/Pinnacle Romance News* filled with author interviews, member benefits, book previews and more!
- No risks or obligations...you're free to cancel whenever you wish...no questions asked

To get started with your own home subscription, simply complete and return the card provided. You'll receive your FREE introductory shipment of 4 Splendor Romances and then you'll begin to receive monthly shipments of new Zebra Splendor titles. Each shipment will be yours to examine for 10 days and then if you decide to keep the books, you'll pay the preferred home subscriber's price of just $4.00 per title. That's $16 for all 4 books with FREE home delivery! And if you want us to stop sending books, just say the word...it's that simple.

4 Free BOOKS are waiting for you!
Just mail in the certificate below!

If the certificate is missing below, write to: Splendor Romances, Zebra Home Subscription Service, Inc., P.O. Box 5214, Clifton, New Jersey 07015-5214

FREE BOOK CERTIFICATE

Yes! Please send me 4 Splendor Romances (formerly Zebra Lovegram Historical Romances), ABSOLUTELY FREE! After my introductory shipment, I will be able to preview 4 new Splendor Romances each month FREE for 10 days. Then if I decide to keep them, I will pay the money-saving preferred publisher's price of just $4.00 each... a total of $16.00. That's 20% off the regular publisher's price and there's never any additional charge for shipping and handling. I may return any shipment within 10 days and owe nothing, and I may cancel my subscription at any time. The 4 FREE books will be mine to keep in any case.

Name _____

Address _____ Apt. _____

City _____ State _____ Zip _____

Telephone ( ) _____

Signature _____ SF0698
(If under 18, parent or guardian must sign.)

Terms and prices subject to change. Orders subject to acceptance by Zebra Home Subscription Service, Inc. . Zebra Home Subscription Service, Inc. reserves the right to reject or cancel any subscription.

Range didn't know what beignets were, but he knew he definitely needed to talk to her, and after what she'd said, if he couldn't have a shot of whiskey, he definitely needed some coffee. He sat.

Moments later she breezed back into the room carrying a silver tray laden with a coffeepot, china cups, plates, and a platter covered with what looked like a mountain of powdered sugar.

"Now, be careful when you bite into that," she said, handing Range a plate that held a sugar-covered pastry she'd taken from the mountain. "Otherwise you'll have white sugar all over that black shirt of yours."

Range did as he was told, then set the plate on a table next to the cup of coffee she'd given him. "Delicious," he said, sensing he needed to comment on the beignets before delving into the myriad of questions he had for her. And he had a hell of a lot more questions now than he'd had before she'd opened the door to him.

"Mrs. Rouchard—"

"Call me Francie."

He nodded. "Francie, you said you know who I am."

She smiled. "Of course I do."

His eyes narrowed slightly. "And just who do you think I am?"

"Why, little Nicky Landers, of course, though I realize that's not the name you're going by now, and," she laughed, "lord knows you're not little anymore. Range Connor is what you use nowdays, isn't it?"

He thought he'd been prepared for her answer, but the shock waves that rippled through his body told him he'd been wrong. He hadn't been prepared at all. In fact, he'd been certain she had mistaken him for someone else.

Range sat forward on his chair, the cool calm that was always his companion threatening to thoroughly desert him. "How did you know?"

She inhaled deeply. "I'm not sure. There's just something about you." Francie shook her head. "I see a lot of Allison in you, cher, around your eyes especially, but maybe that's just because I've been watching for you to come back."

"How did you know I'd come back?"

She sat forward on her chair and clasped her hands together, setting them on her knees. "Because I knew that story Garth Murdock told everyone—about your mother running off with a tinker—wasn't true."

"How?"

"Well, for one thing, several days before Garth Murdock went around claiming that awful lie for the truth, besmirching your mother's good name and reputation, your father had shown up in town."

For the second time that day, and the third since his arrival in Tombstone, Range felt as if he'd just been sucker-punched in the gut.

"Oh my, you didn't know any of this, did you?" Francie said. Concern filled her eyes at the shocked look that had come over his face.

"No," Range managed. "My mother told me my father was dead."

"That's what she believed." Francie reached out and touched his hand. "Your mother and I were best friends, cher. We had no secrets from each other."

"Tell me," he said softly. "Tell me everything you know. Please."

Francie nodded. "Your father was a seaman, captained his own ship. Your mama was eight months' pregnant when she last saw him. He had a cargo that had to get to England, but he didn't want her taking the risk of going with him, so even though she'd sailed with him a dozen times before, she stayed behind that time. Went to Boston to stay with her family. A year later Jedidiah's ship returned, but his crew swore he'd disappeared shortly after they'd docked in England, and no one had been able to find him."

"Disappeared?"

Francie nodded. "Your mama waited three years, even hired some kind of detective, but there was no word from your father, and the detective couldn't come up with a thing."

"Waited where?" Range asked.

"Maine. That's where you lived. Where Jedidiah was from. Allison went back there after you were born. Luckily your mama's family was well off. I think they owned some kind of factory that made dishes and such. Anyway, two years later, while you and her were visiting relatives in New Orleans, she met Garth Murdock. Sorriest day in the world for her, I'll say. She never really spoke ill of Garth, not in a terribly bad way, but I could tell, just from the little things she'd say. And sometimes from what she didn't say. It was a whirlwind courtship, but your mother soon became disillusioned." Francie shook her head, as if the memories were suddenly unpleasant. "My guess is Garth Murdock didn't turn out to be quite the man your mother thought she'd married."

"Yeah, I know," Range said.

"But your father," Francie smiled, "she never stopped loving him. She'd tell me about him and her eyes would just shine. She was so happy when he came back. Lord, I'd never seen her smile like she did the day she told me he was alive."

Range's guts felt coiled into a knot. "What'd she tell you, Francie?"

Her eyes looked at him tenderly. "Your father had taken a side trip to France after his boat docked in London, so he could buy some things he wanted for your mother. But his first night there he'd gotten into a fight with some duke or something, and ended up in jail. No one would listen to him, and he never even came before a judge or a court, for months. When he finally did, both his legs had been broken by a guard who didn't like "colonists," and your father was nearly crippled. They transferred him to some kind of prison hospital and he finally learned to walk again, but by the time he got out and made it back to the states, he'd been gone five years and your mother had left Maine.

"It took him almost two more years to track her to Tombstone."

"He was here? My father was in Tombstone?"

Francie nodded. "Garth was away on business the week Jedidiah arrived in town. He rode straight out to the Rolling M. Your mother was deliriously happy, but she was also an honorable woman and wouldn't leave without waiting for Garth to come home so she could explain."

"So she was going to leave Garth and go back to my father," Range said.

Francie nodded.

"But how did you know she didn't just leave with him? That the tinker Garth claimed she and I left with wasn't really my father?"

"Well, first of all, your mother would have never, ever left town without saying goodbye to me. I told you we were best friends, but we were really more like sisters. And then, of course, there's you."

"Me?" He looked at her, puzzled.

"Yes, you," Francie said. "If Allison had left with anyone, she would never have left *you* behind. Your mother loved you with all her heart, and you're here, searching for the truth, which means I was right all along: she didn't leave with anyone." Tears filled Francie's eyes and spilled over her lashes. "Which is what I'd always feared."

Range looked at her. Now he knew what had sent Garth into a jealous fury that night, and why his mother had died.

Chapter 12

An hour later, after Francie had insisted he tell her every detail of what he remembered about that night and everything that had happened to him since, and he'd complied, Range finally stood to leave.

A long sigh slipped from between his lips. "You're the only person I've ever told all that to."

"Don't worry, cher," she said, rising with him and reaching out to take one of his hands in hers, "your secret is safe with me."

He nodded, leaned down, and brushed his lips to Francie's cheek. "Thank you. It felt good to talk."

She smiled and cupped his cheek with her hand. "You just be careful. That man Murdock's a snake. Don't turn your back on him. Not even for a second."

"I'll be fine, Francie."

She sighed. "I truly hate the idea of your going back to that place."

He smiled, but Francie caught the momentary glimmer

of hatred that replaced the smoldering facade of calmness in his eyes. "He killed my mother, Francie. And maybe my father, too. I have to prove that and see that he pays. It's already been too long."

"Like I said, cher, you just be careful. That man's got more nasty tricks up his sleeve than any sidewinder could even think of. Probably learned them sitting at the heels of the devil. But if you need any help, you know all you have to do is ask. Allie was my best friend."

Range squeezed Francie's hand, then turned and walked outside. At the gate he paused as his eyes scanned the street and surrounding buildings, but found nothing amiss. He mounted Satan, but just as he was urging the big horse to turn toward the end of town, and in the direction of the ranch, he saw Candace round the corner of the general store, her arm linked with that of Deputy Wade Hawkins.

Fury, white hot and lightning quick, swept through Range, but he didn't take the time or trouble to analyze it, not even to decide who it was actually directed toward. Jerking on the reins, he sent Satan whirling in the opposite direction than he'd started.

The woman was going to get Hawkins, and maybe even herself, killed.

The big stallion wasn't pleased with the abrupt change. He whinnied loudly and threw his head up, sending black tendrils of mane splitting the air.

Pressing his heels into the animal's flanks, Range commanded, and got, instant speed. Within seconds he was beside Candace and the deputy. Pulling back on the reins, he forced Satan to skid along the dirt street in an effort to stop. A cloud of dust billowed up around them.

Range swung to the ground and stalked around Satan, one thought, one intent in his mind. He stepped onto the boardwalk and stopped before Candace and Wade, who, startled, had already paused to stare at him.

"What the hell are you doing here?" Range growled, his tone soft, but filled with menace and challenge.

She stared up at him, obviously shocked by both his sudden appearance and question. Then, as quickly as surprise had overtaken her, anger pushed it aside and took hold. Candace threw back her shoulders, raised her chin defiantly, and propped clenched fists on her hips. "Excuse me," she retorted coldly, blue eyes burning into his, "but since when do I have to answer to you, Mr. Connor?"

"Since you don't seem to have the good sense God gave a horse," he snarled.

"Listen, Connor, that's no way to—"

Range turned his fiery gaze on the deputy. "Hawkins, I don't take you for a stupid man, so I'm only going to say this once: stay out of it." He turned back to Candace. "I'll see you home now."

Candace seethed at the man's audacity. "I'm not ready to go home yet."

"You're going anyway."

She stamped the point of her folded parasol on the boardwalk. "No, I am not going home, and even if I was, I came into town alone and I can very well manage to get home that way, Mr. Connor. I certainly don't need the likes of you to escort me."

He glared at her, shoving his face toward her so that their noses were barely an inch apart. "Get in your damned buggy, Mrs. Murdock, or I swear, I'll pick you up right here, throw you over my shoulder, and dump you into it."

She gasped. "You wouldn't dare!"

"I'll count to five."

Her eyes threw darts of hatred. "I doubt you can even count that high."

"One."

"And you have no right to tell me what to do."

"Two."

"Connor, this isn't any of your business," the deputy said.

Range threw him a murderous glare. "Three."

"I'll have my husband fire you for this, Mr. Connor," Candace snapped.

"Four."

She stared at him and suddenly knew he wasn't bluffing. He would force her to go with him, and she had no doubt he'd do it in the exact fashion he'd threatened. Turning on her heel, an expletive unfit to greet a lady's ears, let alone slip from her tongue, lashed out from between Candace's lips, and she stalked toward her buggy, tied at the hitching rack before the milliner's a few doors down and across the street from where they stood. "I swear, of all the arrogant, self-righteous, nosey—"

Range turned back to Wade Hawkins. "I don't want to have to tell you again, Deputy Hawkins," he said softly, an acrid aura of menace lacing each word, "stay away from her."

Spinning on his heel, Range grabbed Satan's reins and stalked after Candace. Didn't the woman know how to use the brains she was born with? he fumed. Or maybe she wasn't born with any. Maybe she was a pretty little package with nothing inside.

Candace threw her parasol on the floor of the buggy, lifted her skirts, and grabbed onto the seat's rail.

A series of curses spewed softly from Range's mouth. He didn't give a damn what her feelings were for Wade Hawkins. She could be in love with the man, be his mistress for all Range cared. Hell, she could be a two-timing little harlot married to Hawkins as well as Murdock, for all it mattered to him. Who she did or didn't dally with wasn't the point, and just because she had the extremely annoying ability to make Range want to rip off her clothes and drag her into his bed, didn't mean he actually cared about her.

His physical needs and desires had nothing to do with anything else. He just didn't want to see another woman die because of Garth Murdock's jealous temper, that was all. Even if her silly little brainless actions were provoking it.

Candace placed a foot on a wooden spoke of one of the wagon's wheels and pushed off the ground. Her other foot instantly caught in the lace trim of her petticoats. At the same time that she heard the sound of ripping fabric, she felt her balance falter. She clung to the metal rail and tried to lower her foot.

The movement pulled on her petticoat and threatened to send her tumbling backwards. She tried to raise her foot higher and found her petticoats being pulled in another, equally awkward direction.

Candace suddenly knew how a skewered turkey felt. She couldn't move. Up or down, she was doomed to disaster.

Range paused on the boardwalk beside her buggy.

She glared up at him.

He leaned against the pillar supporting the milliner's overhanging roof, crossed his arms, and looked down at Candace. He fought to keep a smile from making itself known to his lips. "Need a hand?"

His voice sent a shiver of anger rippling over her skin. It was his fault she was in this predicament in the first place. And now he was laughing at her.

"No," she snapped, "I thought I'd just hang here for a while and watch the rest of the afternoon drag by. Maybe I'll chat with a few friends here and there. Whenever they pass by, that is."

"Okay." Range reached into his pocket for his tobacco pouch, pulled out a paper and, holding it curled between thumb and middle finger, prepared to pour tobacco into it.

"Are you going to make a cigarette?" Candace asked, in sheer disbelief.

He didn't bother to look up, or stop. "Yep."

She fumed. The man was a beast. An insensitive, inconsiderate, totally rude beast.

He pulled the string on the tobacco pouch tight with his teeth and tucked it back into his pocket.

"A gentleman would help me."

He ran his tongue along one edge of the paper and rolled his cigarette. "Said you didn't want help, remember?" He slipped the cigarette into his mouth.

"A gentleman would help anyway."

He looked at her then. "Guess I'm not a gentleman then, am I, Mrs. Murdock?"

If she killed a hired gunman, would they put her in jail? Or give her a medal? She fumed. "No, Mr. Connor, I guess you're not." Her fingers were practically screaming in pain and her leg, still stuck in her ruffled petticoats, was beginning to cramp.

"So, what are you doing in town?" He leaned forward and looked into the buggy. "I don't see any supplies, bolts of cloth, or what not."

"I was visiting friends," Candace snapped, "not that it's any of your business."

"Like Wade Hawkins?"

She glared up at him. "Yes, Mr. Connor, Wade Hawkins is a friend."

"Stay away from him."

She blinked, taken back by the harsh-sounding words. "I beg your pardon?"

He smiled then, and lit his cigarette. "I told you before, you don't have to beg."

She knew full well that what he was referring to had nothing to do with his "pardon." Candace also knew that she wasn't going to get his help if she didn't ask for it.

She nearly sighed in frustration. "All right," she said, as if in total resignation, "will you help me?"

"Help you do what?" he taunted, enjoying their little tête-à-tête, and not even quite sure why.

"Get off of here, what do you think?" she practically shrieked.

Range's black brows rose slightly. "Say please."

Candace's temper flared out of control. "Get me off of this damned buggy!"

"Tsk, tsk. That's not very ladylike language," Range taunted. Out of the corner of his eye he saw Wade Hawkins hurrying toward them. He looked up and, the cigarette dangling from his mouth, glared at the man.

Wade stopped dead in his tracks.

Candace considered letting her foot drop. Her skirt would rip and she'd fall flat on her back in the middle of the street. She looked at Range. "Please," she fairly snarled.

He smiled. "What?"

"Please," she snapped.

He frowned. "My mother had a saying when I was a kid. When you want something, put a little sugar on your please and thank yous."

"Mother?" Candace quipped, her tone dripping with sarcasm. "I never figured you for having one."

"Doesn't everyone?" Range said. God, but he was enjoying this.

"Don't snakes just lay their eggs and slither away?"

He almost burst out laughing. Instead, he keep his features hard and solemn. "Oh," he said, trying to sound harsh, "so you think I'm a snake."

She threw him a smile that made a total mockery of the gesture, "Well, I hate to insult the snake world like that, but yes."

He nodded. "I've been called worse."

"I'm sure."

He flicked his cigarette into the street and pushed himself away from the pillar. "Well, I guess I'll be heading
back to the ranch."

Candace stared at him in disbelief. "You're just going
to leave me here?"

He looked back at her questioningly.

"Okay," she sighed, coating her tone with as much
"sweetness" as she was able to without gagging, "please
help me get up . . . or down, from here."

He tipped his head and walked around the buggy toward
her. "My pleasure, Mrs. Murdock."

The sudden pressure of his hands on her waist sent a
shock wave of feeling coursing through her. It was almost
as if she could feel the warmth of his flesh through the
fabric of her gown.

He lifted her away from the buggy as effortlessly as if
she'd weighed nothing.

When her free foot touched the ground she grabbed
hold of the wagon wheel, expecting Range to release her.

He didn't. Instead, his hands remained on her waist,
strong, hot, secure. He pulled her to him, her back pressed
against his chest.

She felt his warm breath on her neck, felt his heartbeat
as it thrummed against her shoulder blade. The world
tilted just slightly, and Candace suddenly felt a bit winded,
a bit flustered, and way, way too hot. She also felt slightly
weak, as if, if he let go of her, she'd tumble to the ground.
It was a ridiculous notion, but one that held her in its grip
all the same.

"Untangle your foot," he said softly. "I won't let you
fall."

With his hands still on her waist, supporting her, sending
her senses reeling and scurrying for cover, she raised her
skirts and, bending forward, pulled the lace from the knot

it had formed around the heel of her shoe. Satisfied she was free, she dropped her foot and straightened. "Okay," she said breathlessly. "Thank you."

He didn't release her.

She grabbed the wagon seat's metal rail again, slid her boot onto the spoke again and . . . he lifted her up. For a brief second she'd felt almost as if she were floating. Then the padded wagon seat was beneath her and his hands were gone. Annoyingly, she felt suddenly deserted. As if something she wanted had been given to her, then abruptly taken away again.

Candace pushed the ridiculous thought from her mind. She neither had wanted him to touch her, nor was disappointed that he no longer was. What she did want, however, was for him to go away and leave her and her family alone.

"I'll ride with you," Range said.

Candace whirled in her seat, his words breaking through her thoughts. "Ride with me?" she squeaked. She slapped a hand over her mouth, embarrassed by the lack of her voice and the surprising shriek of her answer.

He looked at her carefully for several seconds, but said nothing. Instead he tied his horse to the rear of the wagon, walked back, and, stepping onto a wheel spoke, grabbed the railing and hoisted himself into the seat beside her in one gracefully fluid motion.

His leather-clad leg brushed against her skirts.

In spite of the material, she felt the touch as if suddenly branded by fire.

Candace jerked away from him.

Range smiled.

She noticed and gritted her teeth. The man was absolutely the most infuriating person she'd ever had the misfortune to come into contact with.

Range picked up the reins. "Ready?" he asked, glancing at her.

Candace threw him a scathing look. "Humph. Do I have a choice?"

"No." He snapped the reins and the carriage horse instantly moved forward.

Candace glanced over her shoulder.

Wade Hawkins was standing in the middle of the street. She looked back at Range. "Why did you do that?" she asked.

He stared straight ahead, but she noticed the clench of his jaw.

"Would you rather I talk to my husband?" she challenged, though running to Garth for anything was the last thing in the world she'd do. She was sure that Range Connor, however, didn't know that.

"Running to your husband would probably be the most dangerous move you could make," Range said.

The outskirts of town fell behind them.

Candace continued to stare at him. "Really? And why is that?"

He was probably being stupid. The woman knew more than she was letting on, he felt certain, but he'd tell her enough so that she could stay out of trouble anyway, just in case. Put a little sense into that pretty little head of hers. Then, if she still insisted on flirting with disaster, it was no concern of his. "Your husband is a jealous man."

Candace nodded. "I'm very much aware of that, Mr. Connor. But my husband wasn't in town, so there was no reason for you to barge into my conversation and—"

"He's got friends, hasn't he?"

"Well, yes, but—"

"I doubt there's anything you could do he wouldn't know about. Including coming into town to flirt with Deputy Hawkins."

Candace gasped in outrage. "I was not flirting with Deputy Hawkins!"

"Could have fooled me."

"Then obviously that isn't too hard to do."

His dark look instantly told her she was wrong. She suddenly realized that fate had sent her a perfect opportunity, and she'd been wasting it bickering with him. Candace turned away and stared at the passing scenery. If she was going to succeed, she had to do it just right. He couldn't suspect a thing. She waited another ten minutes, until they were a good distance from town and nowhere near the ranch yet.

Sad. She had to think of something sad. Closing her eyes, she brought forth her memories of the night her father had died, and she had been forced to marry Garth Murdock.

Emotion snagged in her throat, and hot, scalding tears instantly stung the back of her eyes.

At Candace's abrupt and continued silence, Range glanced at her, but she had turned in her seat so that her back was to him and he couldn't see her face. He had the feeling something was wrong, more so than if she was just angry with him, but he wasn't sure why he thought that, or what it was that could be wrong. She didn't have a gun or any other weapon that he could see, and there was no one else around. Most likely for miles. Nevertheless, the nagging feeling persisted.

Suddenly Candace sobbed, and her shoulders shook.

"Mrs. Murdock?"

She sobbed again and dabbed a hankie at her eyes.

Damn. He hadn't intended to make her cry. "Mrs. Murdock?" He touched her shoulder.

She jerked away.

A thousand and one pithy oaths danced through Range's head. Now he'd done it. Damned fool. He'd most likely ruined everything, unless he could console her somehow. Make her not hate him so much she'd tell Garth to fire his sorry hide. If that happened he'd never find out the truth, and Garth Murdock would never face his justice.

Range pulled back on the reins as he urged the horse to move to the side of the road. They stopped beside a tall outcropping of saguaro that helped partially block the sun's blistering rays.

She was hunched lower in her seat, and every few seconds her shoulders shook as she sobbed.

Range wound the reins around the brake lever and turned toward Candace. "Mrs. Murdock, listen, I didn't mean to hurt your feelings." Damn, he'd never been too good with words. Especially around women. "I mean, if I said something that offended you . . . Hell, I mean, I was just having some fun with you back there and . . ."

And what? he thought. I'm an idiot? Well, obviously that went without saying. He hadn't meant to hurt her, that much was true. She'd married Garth Murdock because she'd had no choice. How could he go on blaming her for that? His own mother had married the man.

Candace was most likely as much a victim of the man as he was. Maybe even more so. At least, with the death of his mother, he'd gotten away. Because of her brother and sister, Candace had been forced to stay.

Candace dabbed at her eyes, and a soft moan slipped from his lips.

"Aw, hell, Candace, I . . ." He hadn't meant to call her that.

She whirled around at the sound of her name on his lips, and threw herself into his arms.

Chapter 13

Startled, Range's arms slipped automatically around Candace's waist.

"Oh, Range," she breathed softly, her lips only a hair's breadth from his own.

Teardrops glistened on her cheeks, and he suddenly ached to kiss them away and taste their moisture on his lips.

"I knew I could trust you," she whispered.

He looked down at her, felt her breasts crushed against his chest, her body pressed up against his, and found it suddenly difficult to breathe. A thought, surprising and unbidden, flashed into his consciousness: he could take her, he could have what he wanted, and use it as part of his revenge. He could seduce Garth Murdock's wife. She was obviously willing, so why should he refuse her?

The vengeance he sought against Garth Murdock would be just that much sweeter.

Guilt slammed into him as quickly and thoroughly as

his lascivious thoughts of seduction. It was a feeling, an emotion, he wasn't used to. Guilt usually played no part in his life or actions. He tried to shake it away, but it refused to be banished.

Maybe it was because of all the memories of his mother that, with his return to Tombstone, had crowded back into his mind. Maybe they'd brought with them a shred of his mother's decency and compassion. He didn't know. He only knew that he hadn't come back to the Rolling M to hurt anyone else. Only Garth Murdock. And though taking his wife would be sweet vengeance against the man who had murdered Range's mother, hurting Candace along the way wasn't in his plans. And for the first time in a long time, hurting someone just wasn't in him.

He started to push her away.

"Oh, Range," she whispered again, this time as if pleading with him. Her arms slid up to encircle his neck, to hold him to her. She was playing with fire, but it was the only game available, and she really had no other choice. It didn't matter what happened to her. She had no choice but to do whatever was necessary to find out the truth, because if he really was here to kill Brandon, she had to know. At least then she'd have a chance to stop him.

Range had always prided himself on his willpower, on the cold, emotionless, steely self-discipline that had gotten him through more bad times, more dangerous incidents over the years than he cared to remember. Yet both willpower and self-discipline suddenly deserted him as he stared into Candace's eyes.

He had wanted her from the very moment he'd seen her standing on the gallery, watching him ride toward the Murdock house.

He had wanted her even more when he'd walked into that same house and she'd greeted him, all manners and

politeness masking the fire he'd glimpsed in her eyes, that
he sensed simmered in her blood.

He'd wanted her every moment since.

And he wanted her now.

For twenty-four years he had taken whatever he wanted,
and given back nothing. And that was exactly that he would
do now. He was playing the fool, and he didn't care. There
would be enough time for self-recrimination later, if there
were any to be made. But they could wait until after he'd
taken what he wanted.

His lips crashed down on hers, demanding she give him
what he craved, while he did not spare a thought for her
needs or desires. He tightened his arms around her, crushing her body to his until there was no hint of light or air
separating them. His hands splayed upon her back, feeling
the fragileness of her bones, the raggedness of her breath,
the rapid beat of her heart. One hand moved upward, its
fingers delving into the long tendrils of her hair, disappearing within the golden curls and silken waves. He held
her to him as he ravished her mouth, taking what he
wanted and demanding more.

Other women had aroused his passions. Other women
had incited his desires. Other women had stirred his needs.
No woman had taken away his control . . . until now.

He'd kissed her, he had thought, because he wanted to.
Now, as his tongue wrapped around hers, as his breath
melded with hers and the hot coil that had invaded his
groin tightened as if about to squeeze the life from his
body, he knew he'd been wrong. Want was only a small
part of what he felt toward Candace Murdock. Need was
more.

He needed her, like the air he breathed, the water he
drank.

It wasn't something he had thought about, merely something he suddenly knew.

His passion impelled her own to respond, demanded her acquiescence. As much as Candace tried to hold herself back from him, from feeling anything, her senses leapt to life at his touch. A delicious shudder heated her body as his tongue forced her lips apart. Her heartbeat hammered in her ears. The heat of his body enveloped her, and a pulsing knot formed in the pit of her stomach.

It wasn't supposed to be this way.

Her tongue danced with his.

Blood surged from her fingertips to her toes as a strange aching overwhelmed her body.

A message of passion silently moved from his hungry lips to hers.

The savage caress of his lips on hers set her body aflame with the need for more. Her arms tightened around his neck. Her body pressed against his.

His lips were hard and searching as they moved over hers, leaving each area they touched burning as if touched by a stroke of fire. It was an intimacy she had never known, and feelings she had only dreamt about, but never experienced, sped through her body.

She succumbed to the forceful domination, while at the same time matching it with demands she had never known were in her.

His kiss was urgent and demanding, exploratory and savage, and she reveled in it, arcing her body toward him, pressing against him, silently pleading with him to continue, even though she knew she should want him to stop.

She returned his kiss with a reckless abandon that caused the blood in her veins to race, her brain to pound, and turned her body weak with want.

Shivers of delight followed his hand as it moved from her back to her breast.

Her thoughts spun.

His hand gently outlined the circle of her breast, then closed over it.

His seduction was masterful, and Candace knew without giving it even the slightest of thought that her surrender was inevitable.

The sound of hoofbeats suddenly broke through the haze of their passion, shattering the infinite silence of the desert that had surrounded them and bringing reality back to them with a resounding crash.

Range jerked away from Candace, one arm moving across her, as if to shield her, the other moving swiftly to the gun sheathed to his thigh.

A rider rode around a curve in the road and directly toward them.

Range recognized him as one of the wranglers from the Rolling M.

The man tipped his hat. "G'afternoon, Mrs. Murdock. Connor."

Range didn't relax until the man was well past them. Then he picked up the reins and, without a glance toward Candace, slapped them against the horse's rump. The animal and buggy immediately moved forward.

Candace stared out at the scenery passing by; the tall saguaro, the short, barrel-shaped fishhook, the prickly pear with its red fruit. Her gaze roamed over the endless landscape of burnt orange desert floor, the outcroppings of arroyos and plateaus, the mountains in the distance. Yet she didn't really see any of it.

What had she done? Good lord in heaven, what had she done? The simple question nearly sent her into a fit of hysterical laughter. She had tried to seduce a hired killer. Swallowing hard, she raised a hand and touched fingertips to her lips, now slightly swollen and most likely bruised, she knew, from his kiss, from the passion they'd shared.

A passion that had touched her as well as him. But it wasn't supposed to have been that way.

She shivered. What had happened? How could she have felt like that toward him? She wanted to turn and look at him, to find the answers to her feelings in his eyes, on his face, but she was afraid. What if instead of finding answers, she merely felt passion again?

Tears filled her eyes. At the same time, something joyous filled her heart. She wanted to reach out to him, to feel those feelings he'd aroused in her again. Yet she was afraid. Not of him, but of feeling that way toward him. He wasn't the kind of man who would want a woman to love him, who would settle down to share her life.

She had merely wanted to find out the truth from him, and if need be, sway him to her side. And she'd made a mess of things. She blinked rapidly to stem the tears that threatened to overflow her lids. She'd always dreamed about falling in love. In the last few months she had thought more and more about the time when Brandon would turn twenty-one and inherit control of Gates End. She'd planned to end her marriage to Garth then and go home. She would have left him long ago, but there had been nowhere to go, no way to survive, and she'd always had to think of Brandon and Brianne. They'd depended on her, and, much to her chagrin, she'd depended on Garth.

Range ignored Candace and stared straight ahead. *Fool.* The word kept repeating in his mind, over and over. What the hell had he been thinking?

Lust, that's what, he answered himself. He hadn't cared for anyone in years. It was too dangerous. A good way to get killed. And he wasn't going to start caring now. What was it to him if Garth's wife was a loose woman? What was it to him if she was willing to share a bed with a man other than her husband? Even if her marriage had been arranged, Garth Murdock was still her husband.

And Range still wanted her.

"Are you here to kill my brother?"

Her question pulled him from his reverie faster than a bullet through the gut could have. Range looked at her. "You've asked me that before, Mrs. Murdock."

"And you didn't answer me, Mr. Connor."

He turned back to the road. "Your husband hired me to protect the—"

"Oh, never mind," she snapped, cutting him off. "If you're not going to tell me the truth, just never mind telling me any lies."

"How do you know they're lies?" he challenged.

She held his gaze for a long moment, her blue eyes piercing his, as if trying to catch a glimpse of his soul, to see, to reassure herself, that he had one.

An insolent smile pulled at his lips as he watched her, and knew what she was doing. If she'd have merely asked, he could have told her; his soul was dead. It had died twenty-four years ago when the horror of death had replaced cradling arms, soft kisses, and whispered words of love.

A cold shiver slipped through Candace's body, and she turned away from him. Emptiness. That's all she'd seen in his eyes. Cold, dark, stark emptiness.

His passion had been scathing. His kisses had stirred something in her the likes of which she'd never felt before. And for a brief second, as he'd held her in his arms, she had glimpsed something in his eyes. Maybe it had been life. Or hope. Or a dream.

But now there was only emptiness.

She wrapped her arms around herself, hugging tightly. How could there be such coldness, such vast-seeming emptiness in a man who'd only a few moments ago emanated such hot, arousing passion, who had stirred her emotions to the point of reckless abandon?

The question frightened her, but the answer was something she knew just might frighten her even more.

Range stood in the darkness and stared at the house. He'd ignored Candace for the remainder of their trip back to the ranch, and he'd ignored her when he had gone to the house and eaten dinner with Murdock and his family.

He would have eaten in the bunkhouse with the wranglers, but he didn't want to give Murdock any reason for suspicion or ire.

But ignoring Candace and not thinking about her were two different things. The first he could do. The second was proving impossible, and that was something that annoyed him. Not thinking about things he found unpleasant had always come easy to him. It was almost as if he had the ability to shut off certain parts of his brain. Especially the part that stored memories. But for some reason, not thinking about Candace was proving impossible.

He raised his cigarette to his lips and inhaled deeply, pulling its smoke into his lungs, feeling its heat swirl through his body. Coolness followed as he let the whiteness slip back out through his lips. It drifted upward and disappeared into the darkness.

Range dropped the cigarette to the ground. Its burning tip glowed in the darkness, then his booted foot moved over it and he extinguished the small smoldering butt. He hooked his thumbs over his gun belt and, leaning against the wall of the bunkhouse, looked at Candace's bedroom window. A light glowed on the other side of the drawn curtains. They were too thick to see through, but it didn't matter. He remembered every inch of that room, and it wasn't that hard imagining Candace in it, her long hair brushed out over her shoulders for the night, her body naked except for the covering of a nightgown.

He smiled. Maybe a sheer batiste gown, its voluminous white folds flowing about her legs gracefully as she moved, its low, dipping neckline, which would just skim the top of her breasts, embroidered by twisting vines and tiny blue flowers the exact color of her eyes.

He'd always had a very good imagination.

He felt his body grow hard and hot. Her window was open a crack. He could wait until her light was extinguished, let a few moments pass until she was nearly asleep, and then he'd slip quietly into her room. His hand over her mouth would muffle her scream of surprise, then, once her eyes became accustomed to the darkness and she recognized his face, he could remove his hand and replace it with his lips.

He could make love to Garth Murdock's wife, while Murdock slept unawares just down the hall.

The thought, the image, almost brought a moan to Range's lips.

He could do that, but he wouldn't. Not because of Murdock, but because he knew he couldn't do that to Candace. She might be married to the man Range had hated almost forever, but she wasn't the money-grubbing gold digger he'd first thought her to be. Nor was she a cold, heartless schemer.

Candace extinguished the lamp next to her bed, and the room plunged into darkness. Knowing she shouldn't, yet unable to resist the urge, she moved to the window and carefully slipped a finger around the edge of the curtain and pushed it aside, just slightly. Enough for her to see out, but not enough for anyone to see her.

She spotted him almost instantly, leaning against the

front wall of the bunkhouse, his black clothes lending him a near invisibility within the night's darkness. Except for the silver conchos attached to the sides of his leather leggings. For a hired gun, she knew that was a dangerous show of vanity. Or perhaps it was daring.

Thinking on it, she knew it was the latter. Range Connor was not vain. She knew that instinctively. He was dangerous, and he was fearless, and he was daring. Not because he was brave, but because he didn't care.

A shiver ran through her then. She had looked into his eyes, she had felt his embrace, tasted his kiss, and though she knew now that an intense passion burned deep within Range Connor, she also knew there was an emptiness in him. Something, somewhere, sometime, had stolen part of his soul and left him wanting.

Perhaps, she mused, that was why he'd taken up hiring out his gun, because he was a man who didn't care whether he lived or died.

Tears suddenly filled her eyes as the chilling thought filled her mind; and the memory of his lips on hers, and how he'd made her feel, filled her heart.

How could she have felt that for a hired killer?

She saw him push away from the building and walk toward the barn.

Was he leaving the Rolling M? Would she wake up tomorrow and find him gone forever? It was what she should hope for. It would mean Brandon was safe.

She let the curtain fall forward to cover the window. She should hope that he was leaving, yet she didn't.

Morning seemed like it would never come. It was like that a lot when things were on his mind. Sleep seemed merely a waste of valuable time, even energy. Range had gone over everything again, the past and the present, looking for anything he'd missed, any clue that he might possess but was unaware of. His frustration was mounting, and he knew that if he didn't find something soon, some proof of what Garth had done, some way to bring it all out and expose him for what he really was, his anger would explode.

Range looked toward the barn where he'd seen Garth headed only moments before. He could walk in there now, confront the man, and kill him. It would be easy. One, two, three, bang, and the whole thing would be over. Murdock would be dead. Allison Landers's death would be avenged. But no one would know, Range reminded himself. Murdock would be remembered as a good man, a respected man, a man whose first wife had run off with a peddler. The truth would be buried forever, and Range knew he couldn't let that happen.

Which meant he couldn't kill him yet. He had to do this the way he'd always planned. Talk to people, find out what they knew, search the house, the ranch's outbuildings, even the land itself if necessary. He had to do it right, which meant he had to be patient. But he was good at being patient. Two Hawks had taught him how, even when his insides were churning for action, even when his fingers were itching to delve into motion, he could pull on a mantle of patience so that no one would know his true thoughts or desires. He would appear calm. Nonchalant. Untroubled. Patient. It was one of the traits that had made him one of the best at doing what he did.

Range paced.

He cleaned his guns.

He brushed Satan.

He oiled his saddle and gear and sat for an hour in a dark corner of the barn, cradling the small statuette he'd found on his pillow the night of his arrival, staring at its sweet, smiling face. Someone knew who he was. Someone knew why he was here. It was the only logical explanation of why the tiny angel had been placed on his pillow. But who? Who knew the truth about him? And why didn't they just come out and talk to him?

Range mulled over the thought, considering everyone he'd met on the ranch so far. Obviously it hadn't been Garth or Jesse. They may have had the easiest access to the statuette, but if they'd known who he really was, Range had no doubt in his mind that he'd be dead already. Most likely with no warning. Merely a bullet in the back.

That only left Candace, her brother and sister, Karalynne, and the other wranglers. None seemed likely prospects. Yet there was no one else.

Shoving the statuette back into his saddlebag where he'd decided to keep it, Range saddled Satan. He usually thought better when he was on the move.

Chapter 14

By late afternoon he was more frustrated than ever. Over the last couple of days he'd ridden to every ranch and farmhouse that surrounded Murdock's property. He'd just gone to the last few, asked the same question of their owners as he'd asked the others, and unfailingly received the same answer: Garth's first wife had taken her son and run off with a peddler. Everyone seemed to genuinely believe that, and everyone seemed to respect, if not like, Garth Murdock.

As far as the water rights dispute went, however, that was another story. Several ranchers who professed to respect Garth, made no secret of the fact that they also disliked him, and they weren't all that happy about his way of doing business. Especially when it came to water rights and grazing land.

It was usually at that point of the conversation that Range excused himself and rode away. He didn't care about Garth's business persona or ethics, or whether or not the other ranchers liked the way he conducted his business dealings with them.

By the time the sun was starting to sink behind the mountains in the distance, Range was hungry, frustrated, and in no mood for polite conversation and manners. Which meant that the last thing he wanted to do was sit at the table with Garth Murdock on one side of him and Candace on the other. He turned Satan toward town.

An hour later he reined up in front of the Oriental Saloon. The sounds of piano music flowed through the open doors. It was Saturday night and the place was crowded, wranglers, drovers, gamblers and miners all vying for a chair, a space at the bar, or a few minutes with one of the girls who worked there. Laughter, shouts, and just a general hum of noise filled the place. Along with a heavy cloud of smoke.

Range walked in, pausing just inside the swinging doors to survey the room before actually moving into it. It was a habit formed over the years, one that had kept him alive, and one he wasn't about to break.

Six men were seated around a corner table engrossed in a poker game. Luke Foster was one of them. There were about eight more clustered around the wheel of fortune, and another five at the roulette table. Four were playing faro. Five stood at the bar, drinking and watching. Four girls moved about the room, plying drinks, flirting, laughing, or dancing. In the back corner the piano player plunked at his keys.

Range walked to the bar. "Whiskey," he said, "without the rat."

The bartender looked at him sourly.

It was no secret that some bars doubled the amount of their whiskey by adding a little water. Then, to get back the kick they'd robbed it of by watering it down, they dropped a couple of rats into the barrel and let it ferment for a few weeks before bottling it.

A bottle and shot glass were plunked down on the bar before him.

"An eagle for the good stuff," the bartender said.

Range smiled and dug one out of his shirt pocket. He poured himself a shot and turned his back to the bar to survey the room again. One of the men at the poker table had removed his hat, and Range now recognized Jesse Murdock.

Half an hour later Jesse was still playing, and still losing. The stack of greenbacks on the table in front of him was nearly gone, as were his coins.

Luke, on the other hand, from what Range could see, was doing quite well. Range was pretty certain that a good portion of the money sitting in front of his friend had probably started out being Jesse's.

One of the men pushed back his chair and stood. A moment later he left the saloon.

Range grabbed his bottle and glass and walked over to the table. "Mind if I join the game?" he said, looking in turn at each man.

"Hell, I could stand a little competition here," Luke said, laughing. "Never did like my pickin's to be too easy."

Range set his bottle down and settled into a chair across from Jesse.

Two of the other men, both of whom looked like farmers, folded their cards and excused themselves from the table.

"Well, well, well," Jesse drawled, "if it ain't my brother's hired gun."

Range nodded. "Good evening, Jesse."

The last wrangler at the table, looking bleary-eyed and over the top by at least one drink—not to mention just about broke if the lone greenback still on the table before him was any indication—grabbed his money and stood. "I'm through," he announced, and staggered away.

"Looks like my pickin's went from easy to sparse," Luke said, and chuckled. "So, Range, what are you doing down this way? Last I heard, you were up in Abilene."

Range shrugged. "You know me, Luke, never stay in one place too long."

"Wears out his welcome," Jesse said, his words slurred. He downed another shot of whiskey and immediately grabbed a bottle and refilled his glass.

"Sometimes there isn't one to begin with," Range said. His dark gaze pinned itself on Jesse. "But that's not something that ever bothered me."

Luke shuffled and dealt the cards.

"What about you, Jesse," Range said pointedly, "you ever tread where you're not welcome?"

Jesse glared at him, then reached out and drew the cards that lay face down on the table toward him before picking them up. "I don't rightly recall ever not being welcome somewhere," he snarled finally.

Range smiled, his brows rising slightly. "Really?"

Jesse downed another shot of whiskey, slammed the glass onto the table, and glared at Range. "Yeah, Connor, really," he snarled.

Range shoved a greenback into the center of the table. Jesse and Luke did the same.

"How many men you killed, Connor?" Jesse asked a minute later.

Luke looked up warily.

Range shrugged. "Don't know, really."

"Ten?" Jesse prompted, the word so slurred it was almost incoherent. "Twelve?"

"As many as needed killing at the time, I guess," Range said.

Over the next twenty minutes Jesse lost the last of his

money and finished off half a bottle. He slouched back in his chair and eyed Range. "You know what's good for you, gun man, you'd better stay away from Candy."

"Never eat the stuff," Range said. He knew what and who Jesse was talking about, but he'd never drawn on a drunk, and he wasn't about to start now.

"Candace," Jesse snapped loudly. He abruptly pushed away from the table and staggered to his feet. "Stay away from Candace!" His hand hovered dangerously close to his gun and, though he swayed precariously, he stood with feet spread, as if ready to draw.

Luke sat half-turned in his seat, facing Jesse.

Range knew from experience that Luke's gun had been drawn the moment Jesse pushed away from the table. Right now it lay in Luke's lap, its barrel pointing at Jesse's gut, Luke's finger curled around the trigger.

Range tilted his chair back until it sat on its back legs. The heel of his right boot was hooked over the table ledge. He looked relaxed. Calm. Unready. And that was the furthest thing from the truth.

His guns were holstered, and although his left arm lay draped across his chair arm, his hand dangling free, his other hand was already on his gun, his finger on the trigger. He didn't need to draw in order to shoot. Nor did he need to move to hit his target dead on. If he wanted to.

"She's taken, Connor," Jesse said, staggering slightly. "You can't have her."

"Never said I wanted her, Jess," Range countered.

Jesse's eyes narrowed. "I seen the way you look at her."

Range sighed. "Fine, I won't look at her anymore, if it makes you that unhappy."

Jesse's jaw clenched. "What's this? The great Range Connor backing down?"

Range shrugged. "I don't have any reason to kill you, Jesse."

"You mean you're not getting paid to do it," he growled back.

Range nodded. "Yeah, you could say that. Way I see it, just because you got a thing for your brother's wife," he shook his head, "isn't any of my business, and no reason for me to waste a bullet."

"You just stay away from her, Connor, unless you want her to disappear like Garth's other wife. You just stay damned far away from Candy."

Range had to steel himself to keep from bolting out of his chair. Every cell in him ached to lunge into Jesse's face, wrap his fingers around the man's throat, and order him to tell him whatever it was he knew. He looked at Jesse coldly. "I thought his other wife ran off with a peddler," Range said, forcing his voice to sound calm.

"Yeah, sure, whatever." Jesse turned and staggered across the room toward the bar. "Give me another bottle," he yelled at the bartender.

Range looked after him. Jesse knew something, and Range intended to find out what it was. Even if he had to pull Jesse's brain cells out one at a time in order to see what was hidden in them, if anything. His gaze surveyed the room again. The crowd had thinned out. He turned his attention back to the gambler sitting across from him. "Luke, I've got a favor to ask," Range said.

Luke nodded and slid his gun back into its holster. "On a job?"

Range shook his head. "No, I've got that covered. It's something personal."

"What?"

"I need you to ask around town after a woman named Allison Landers . . ." He paused. "No, her name would have been Murdock when she lived here. But it was a while ago. See who you can find who remembers her, would you?"

"Didn't hear you were hooked up with anyone," Luke said. "She run out on you?"

"No. This was a long time ago. Over twenty years. I just need to know what people say about her. If anyone remembers what happened to her."

Luke shrugged again. "Sure. I'll start tomorrow when I have breakfast over at Nellie's place."

"Good." Range stood. "Now I guess I'd better get our friend over there home before he swallows enough rotgut to kill himself."

"Wouldn't count as much of a sin if you let him," Luke said, smiling slyly.

"Maybe, but since I'm working for his brother at the moment, I doubt that's a good idea."

Walking to the bar, Range slapped Jesse on the back.

Jesse choked on a gulp of whiskey he'd just started to swallow.

Range smiled to himself. Damn, but sometimes it felt good to be ornery.

"Black tarnation, Connor," Jesse sputtered as he staggered toward the door, half on his own, half propelled by Range's hand wrapped around his upper arm. "You can choke a man doing things like that."

"Really?" Range said, feigning surprise. "Guess I'll just have to be more careful in the future."

They shoved through the swinging doors.

Range dragged Jesse several feet down the boardwalk until they were past the saloon's large window and stood in the shadows, then turned the man around to face him. "What in the hell did you mean in there?"

Jesse sagged against the overhanging roof's support pillar and looked at Range through red eyes. "Huh?" The man was quickly losing himself to the alcohol he'd been consuming all evening.

Range had kept a tight rein on his temper ever since

Jesse had mouthed off about Garth's other wife disappearing, but he was quickly losing his grip on it, and frankly he had no desire to correct that situation. Range grabbed Jesse by his shirt collar, pulling him toward him, and nearly hauled him off his feet as he shoved his face into the other man's. "What the hell did you mean about Garth's other wife 'disappearing'?"

Jesse pushed his hands against Range's shoulders in an effort to escape. "Nothing," he whined. "I didn't mean nothing."

Range shook him. "Dammit, tell me, Jesse."

Jesse tried to twist away. "No, I didn't mean nothing." He slapped at Range's arm. "Lemme go."

Range shook him again, harder this time. "Jesse, I swear I'll—"

"I'm gonna be sick," Jesse screamed.

His face suddenly lost all color, then abruptly took on a greenish cast as his stomach rumbled.

Range instantly released him.

Jesse whirled around and stumbled down the steps of the boardwalk and into the darkness.

A few seconds later the sounds of his retching were all too distinguishable from the sounds drifting out from inside the saloon.

Range cursed under his breath. Whatever it was Jesse knew, he still wasn't drunk enough to open up with it. Which meant that the odds of making him talk were about zilch, since if he got any drunker he'd either pass out in a drunken stupor or keel over dead.

Several minutes went by, but Jesse didn't reappear. Range finally tired of waiting and descended the steps of the boardwalk and entered the alley into which Jesse had disappeared. He was on the ground, his back against the building, his chin resting on his chest. The ruffled sounds of snores emanated rhythmically from his throat.

Range swore again, then bent and, slipping an arm under Jesse's and around his back, hoisted the man to his feet and dragged him toward his horse. He threw him over the saddle, belly down, then mounted Satan and grabbed the reins of Jesse's horse. It was going to be a long and very slow ride back to the ranch.

"Hey, Range."

He reined up and turned in his saddle to look back at Luke, standing on the boardwalk in front of the saloon.

Another man stood beside him.

"Got someone here says he remembers that lady you were asking after."

Range looked the young man up and down. He was extremely tall, skinny as a rail, with a head of hair that was straight, dark, and slicked back, a nose that looked more like an eagle's beak, and a chin that was nearly nonexistent.

Leaving Jesse draped over his horse in the middle of the street, Range turned Satan back and urged him toward the saloon. At its steps he reined in again.

"This is Rodney Hubert," Luke said. "He runs the local telegraph office here in town, and he's got a pretty good memory."

Range nodded. "You remember Allison Murdock?" he asked, eyeing the man.

Rodney nodded his head enthusiastically while his long, knuckle-knotted fingers fidgeted with the brim of the bowler hat he held in both hands. He tried to smile. "Yes, sir, I surely do. She was married to Garth Murdock. Right pretty lady, she was, too. And real nice."

"You're pretty young to remember her," Range said, realizing the man couldn't be all that much older than himself. "How'd you know her?"

Rodney smiled shyly, the curve of his mouth accentuating the long, beakish slant of his nose. "My pa died when I was seven. We needed money, so I used to work at the general store after school, stocking shelves, helping clean the place, and sometimes delivering orders. My ma wouldn't let me quit school to work more.''

"And you saw my—you saw Allison Murdock in the general store.''

Rodney nodded. "Oh, yeah. She used to come into town a lot.''

"So, why do you remember Allison Murdock, Mr. Hubert? There must have been a lot of women who came into the general store when you were a kid.''

"Oh, yeah, sure there was, but none of the other women used to buy me a stick of penny candy.''

"And Allison Murdock did?''

"Every time she came in. She'd buy one for her own little boy, and one for me. She was a right nice lady, and I was real sad when she . . . went away.''

Range's eyes narrowed at Rodney's hesitation. "Went away? Where?''

Rodney shrugged. "I don't know. Everyone said she . . .'' He hesitated again.

"Yeah. It's okay,'' Range said. "Tell me what everyone said.''

"They said she ran off with a peddler, but I didn't believe them.''

"Why not?''

He shrugged. "She was a nice lady. I just didn't believe she'd do that.''

"Anything else?'' Range asked, feeling a little disappointed. He'd hoped for more than the man's impressions. He'd hoped for answers, and proof.

"Well, there was that other man who came looking for her. Right after she disappeared. But then he went away, too.''

Range's attention was piqued again. "Other man? Who was he?''

Rodney shook his head. "I don't know. If I ever knew his name, I don't remember it. I just remember he was real upset when he found out she was gone. Then a few days later, he was gone, too."

His father. The man had to have been his father! But where had he gone?

The sinking sensation in the pit of his stomach alerted Range to the thoughts in his mind even before he was aware of them. If his father had ridden out to the Rolling M to find out why Range and Allison hadn't come back into town so they could all leave together, he had probably confronted Garth Murdock about it.

Knowing what Garth had done to his mother, Range had no doubt that if his father had indeed ridden to the Murdock ranch in search of his wife and son, he was also probably dead.

He stared at the tall, gangly man, yet his mind's eye was elsewhere, back in the past, where he'd never really ever wanted to go again.

"Range?"

He shook off his memories and looked at Luke.

"You heard enough?" Luke asked, then raised a long cheroot to his lips.

Range nodded. "Yeah, thanks." He wheeled Satan around, then stopped, and looked back over his shoulder. "Keep asking, Luke, would you?" He turned his gaze on Rodney Hubert. "You remember anything else, Mr. Hubert, anything at all, tell Luke, would you?"

Rodney nodded. "Sure thing, Mister." Rodney slammed the bowler hat he'd been fidgeting with onto his head and, in just a few strides of his long legs, had hurried down the boardwalk and away from them.

Range grabbed the reins of Jesse's horse, then spurred Satan. The huge stallion burst forth into a lope and Jesse's horse was forced to keep pace.

Jesse bounced mercilessly on his saddle. Consciousness slammed back through him almost instantly.

"Stop!" he screamed, the word more a groan of agony than anything else. "Stop, damn you, or I'll—" An attack of dry heaves hit his stomach and threw his body into a spasm. Jesse felt his body slipping from the saddle. He grabbed a stirrup skirt with one hand, and tried to reach up and grasp the saddle horn with the other. He missed.

Range urged Satan into more speed.

Jesse grappled for the saddle horn and pushed his foot into a stirrup. He tried to sit up.

The world swerved, tilted, and threatened to turn upside down.

He clutched the saddle horn as if it were the only thing between him and certain death. "Stop, you s. o. b.," he screamed again.

Range ignored him.

Jesse grabbed for his gun, pulled it from his holster, fumbled, and nearly dropped it. He managed to get his finger around the trigger. Pain throbbed through his head. Another assault attacked his gut. "Stop!" he shrieked again, and pointed the gun toward Range.

They kept riding.

Jesse pulled the trigger.

Chapter 15

The bullet whizzed over Range's head. Too far away to do any damage, too close for comfort.

Fury flashed through him like lightning through a tree. Jerking on Satan's reins, he jumped to the ground even before the big horse managed to stop. "You stupid, low-life, worthless son of a—"

"I told you to stop," Jesse screamed, pushing off his horse and throwing out his hands to ward Range off. One leg buckled beneath him and he fell to the ground, his gun tumbling from his grasp.

Range grabbed Jesse's shirtfront and hauled him back up to his feet, then drew back a fist. The man deserved to have his brains pulverized, and Range was just in the mood to do it.

Jesse's eyes rolled heavenward, and he sank to the ground again before Range had a chance to throw his punch. With a snort of disgust, he released his hold on the man's shirt. Jesse dropped in a heap, and Range turned away to walk into the darkness.

This wasn't the way to get what he wanted. Jesse most likely had the answers Range sought, or at least some of them, but there was no way he was going to give them up, short of being half-beat to death. But he wasn't certain whether it was loyalty to his brother or fear of his brother, that was keeping Jesse silent. Then again, maybe Jesse didn't even know the truth.

Range looked back at the sorry lump of human being lying beside his horse. A sigh of resignation slipped from his lips. No matter what the reason was for Jesse's silence, Range knew he was going to have to find another way to get the answers he sought.

Walking back to where Jesse lay on the ground, Range hoisted him up on his horse. He picked up the other man's gun from the ground where it had dropped and walked back to where Satan stood, shoving the weapon into his own saddlebag.

Mounting, he grabbed the reins to Jesse's horse and urged Satan into a walk.

Candace stood at her window. It was late and the rest of the household, including Garth, had been asleep for hours, but she hadn't been able to relax. She'd lain in bed and stared up at the dark ceiling. She had tried counting sheep, having a warm glass of milk, and pacing the floor until her legs had grown weary. Nothing had worked. But this time it wasn't Brandon she'd been thinking about. It wasn't the accidents of the past, or the fears for him the present seemed to hold. And it hadn't been the thought of his upcoming birthday, or even the prospect or hope of finally leaving the Rolling M and Garth, that had kept her awake.

A week ago those would have been the thoughts filling her mind and keeping her from sleep. But tonight was different. Tonight her thoughts were all of Range Connor.

He hadn't come to the house for dinner, and there had been no explanation. Garth had nearly snarled everyone's head off because no one seemed to know where Range was.

Brianne had nearly withered at Garth's announcement that the man he wanted her to marry—some banker from Yuma—was due to arrive at the ranch any day, and she should be preparing her trousseau.

Brandon had been surly because he claimed to have found some error in the ledgers concerning Gates End, an error that involved a goodly amount of money, and all in Garth's favor. And Garth's assault on Brianne had just added another black cloud to Brandon's mood.

And then there was Karalynne, who had done nothing put pout and simper and whine because Jesse had gone into town and left her behind.

The time spent gathered around the dinner table had been torture, and she'd never been so glad to finish with it and get to her room as she had been tonight.

Candace knew she should hope that Range had left for good. But for some reason she couldn't. Instead, all she could think about was how she'd felt when he'd held her in his arms and kissed her, and that if he had gone, she might never feel that way again. It was a horrible thought; it was selfish, and it was wrong. She was a married woman. She shouldn't be thinking like that about another man. Rather, she should remember that it was still possible her brother was in danger from Range, that he was a hired gunman, that he was everything her father had always warned her away from.

But no matter how many reasons she gave herself not to think about him, no matter how many reasons she came up with to wish that he'd go away, she couldn't help hoping, with each second that passed, that he would appear.

And then, as if in answer to the prayer she hadn't even been aware she'd offered, the faint sound of hoofbeats echoed on the still night air. A few seconds later Range rode past the house with another rider in tow.

They stopped at the hitching rack before the bunkhouse. Candace watched Range dismount, then walk around his horse to the other rider.

She frowned. The other rider was slumped forward on his horse, almost lying on the animal's neck. Her breath caught in her throat for just one brief second as she suddenly recognized Jesse and feared the worse. But then after Range dragged him from his mount, Jesse staggered to his feet, and she breathed a sigh of relief. She watched as Range helped him to the house, then, turning and walking back to where he'd left his horse, he left Jesse on the porch to get inside on his own.

Grabbing Satan's reins as well as those of Jesse's horse, Range started toward the barn. Halfway there he stopped and looked back over his shoulder toward the house.

Candace instantly dropped her curtain and stepped away from the window.

"What's going on?"

She spun around at the sound of the gruff voice, the challenging words.

Garth stood in her doorway, his solid form nearly filling its width.

She realized then that she hadn't locked her door, as she usually did, and he'd had no hesitation in opening it without knocking. But how long had he been there, watching her? She met his gaze, but as usual saw nothing but anger there. "Jesse's home," she said softly.

"You waiting up for him?"

She wasn't certain whether he was referring to his

brother or to Range Connor. But it didn't matter. Garth didn't love her, most times he didn't even care to have anything to do with her, which was more than fine with Candace, but he considered her his possession, which left his jealousy with no bounds.

Four years ago he'd fired a wrangler just for smiling at her.

Last year he'd nearly beat one of his ranch hands to death because he'd overheard the man make a disparaging comment regarding a young wife and an older husband.

Her only friend, other than her brother and sister, was J. D., the ranch's handyman, and Candace knew that the only reason Garth didn't care if she talked to J. D. or spent time with him was because Garth didn't feel threatened by the older man. J. D. Sharp was about the same age as Garth, but he limped due to, he'd said once, a fall while breaking a horse. His hair was white, his hands gnarled, and in Garth's opinion, since J. D. didn't have money, he wasn't worth anything, let alone a woman's serious attentions.

"I just couldn't sleep," she said finally. "So I sat up reading. I heard horses a minute ago and got up to see who it was." Her gaze challenged Garth to call her a liar. Years ago she never would have stood up to him, let alone show any kind of daring, but that had been before she'd come to realize what kind of man Garth really was, and how much of a sham her marriage would be.

"Maybe you need a kid around here to keep you busy," Garth snarled.

It was a worn-out threat, one he'd never acted on, and one she'd long ago stopped fearing. She walked to her bedside table and reached for the lamp. "I'm going to go to sleep now, Garth," she said, her fingers on the little switch that, with a turn, would lower the lamp's wick and extinguish its flame.

His gaze bored into hers, angry. But then she'd never seen it any other way. Without another word he abruptly turned and strode down the hall. She heard the door to his bedroom slam shut, and breathed out a sigh of relief. Candace turned out the lamp, but instead of slipping into her bed, she moved back to the window.

Pale light glowed from within the barn, then, as she watched, it suddenly went out.

He was halfway to the bunkhouse before she saw him, a spectre cloaked in black moving through the inky blackness of the night, the only thing truly distinguishing him from the darkness were the faint reflections of moonlight that played upon the conchos on his leggings.

Then she heard the faint jingle of the spurs on his heels as he walked across the porch of the bunkhouse and disappeared inside.

She dropped the curtain and slipped beneath the covers of her bed, but for the first time in her life, it suddenly felt empty . . . and she felt lonely, lying there by herself in the darkness. Pushing the covers aside, Candace rose and, moving to the window again, drew its curtains aside. Returning to her bed, she lay on her side and stared across the way at the dark bunkhouse.

Brianne stood in the doorway of Candace's room. "Well, I'm ready, how about you?"

Candace glanced at her. Brianne had taken great care with her appearance. Her gown was white poplin with yellow gingham trim. A sash around her waist turned into a yellow beribboned bustle at her back, and the gown's matching jacket had puffed shoulder sleeves and a pert preacher's collar. A small straw hat sat upon her crown, its brim surrounded by a profusion of white and yellow ribbons.

She twirled her closed parasol in front of her sister impatiently. "Candace," she fairly whined, when Candace didn't answer.

"All right, all right." She grabbed her own parasol from the bed where it lay, along with her reticule, and started for the door.

"Your hat," Brianne reminded her.

Candace nearly groaned. She would have much rather just put on a pair of riding breeches and shirt, but they were going into town, which made riding breeches and a shirt totally inappropriate, at least in everyone else's opinion but hers.

She threw the parasol and reticule down and walked back to her dressing table, grabbing a blue hat from a wall rack and plopping it down on her head amid the curls she'd pulled up and pinned to her crown, then pulled its sheer blue lace down over the top half of her face.

Her gown was of white poplin with blue gingham trim, very smart and very tailored. She turned back to Brianne. "Now am I ready?" she asked, her tone dripping with sarcasm.

Brianne beamed. "Yes. And Brandon is already in the carriage."

Candace suddenly looked wary.

"Don't worry," Brianne said, interpreting Candace's look, "J. D. helped him."

Candace was just descending the front steps of the ranch house when she looked up and found Range Connor watching her. He was standing in front of the bunkhouse, leaning against its front wall, one leg crossed lazily over the other, his thumbs hooked inside his gun belt.

A deliciously warm shiver raced over her flesh, leaving it covered with goose bumps.

"You getting in, or what?" Garth sneered, breaking the spell that had momentarily fallen over Candace.

She pulled her gaze from the gunman's and allowed her husband to help her into the carriage.

"Don't be gone all day." Garth instantly turned away and walked toward the barn.

Brandon picked up the reins.

Jesse suddenly appeared from around the side of the house and, walking in front of the carriage horse, stopped beside Candace. He looked up at her. "Sure you don't want me to come into town with you, Candy? Kind of escort you around and such?"

She looked down at her brother-in-law. "No, thank you, Jesse. I'm sure we can all do just fine on our own."

"I was thinking about just you and me," he said. The suggestion in both his words and eyes was loud and clear.

Candace tried to keep herself from shuddering with revulsion. "I know you were, Jesse, but I doubt Garth would approve."

Something akin to fury shone in Jesse's eyes, but it was there and gone so fast Candace wasn't even sure she'd really seen it.

She glanced at Brandon. "Let's go," she said.

Range noticed the riders when they were still a good distance away, but there was no doubt they were headed toward the Rolling M's ranch house. "Got visitors," Range said.

J. D., who was sitting nearby oiling down several pieces of tack, looked up and squinted into the distance. "Yep," he said, and went back to his chore.

Range reached for his guns, pulling each partway out of their holsters, then letting them slowly fall back into place. A second later he pulled each out, held it up, spun its ammunition cyclinder, and reholstered it.

"Expecting trouble?" J. D. said. He spit a wad of tobacco juice onto the ground.

"Always pays to be prepared," Range said. "Expecting or not."

The older man eyed him pointedly. "Yeah, I guess," he said, and rubbed his oil-soaked rag along the leather strips of a well-worn bridle. "You musta had a hard life, huh?"

Range turned to look at the old man, eyes slightly narrowed in suspicion. "Why do you say that?"

J. D. shrugged. "Just seems that way to me, is all."

Range remembered the statuette. Someone knew who he was. "No harder than most, I reckon," he said easily. "What about you?"

J. D. looked up then. "Had a family once."

"What happened to them?"

J. D. shook his head. "Can't say for sure."

Three men reined up a few feet away.

"Where's Garth Murdock?" one of them said.

Range turned his attention to the man who'd spoken. He looked to be about forty, stockily built, hair and eyes the same bland shade of brown. The two riders who flanked him were no more distinguishable. Maybe even less so. "Who wants to know?" Range countered.

"Neighbors," J. D. said, before any of the three men could answer.

"That's right. I'm Kyle Longert, and this here is Sam Watersby and Eli Crown. We own some of the property around here, and we want to know what Murdock intends to do about our access to the water."

Range stared at the three men. He didn't recognize any of them, but then that didn't mean anything. When he'd ridden to the ranches surrounding the Rolling M, some of the men had been out and he'd talked to their wives. In a couple of cases he'd had to be satisfied with foremen, or handymen like J. D.

"I don't plan on doing anything about the water," Garth said, suddenly appearing from the barn. He walked toward the group of men who were still mounted.

"We been hearing things," Kyle Longert said.

"Yeah, so have I," Garth countered.

"Like you're planning on fencing off your property and cutting off our pass through to the river."

"Yeah, well I heard that several of you have been talking to a lawyer in town to try and find a way to force me to give you legal right-of-way across my property," Garth countered.

"We gotta watch out for ourselves," Eli ground out.

"By stabbing me in the back?" Garth snapped back.

"Ain't us started doing the stabbing, Murdock. You did when you had legal papers drawn up for us to sign."

Range tensed as he saw one of Sam Watersby's hands move to rest on the butt of his gun.

"Look," Garth said, moving closer, "I don't have any intention of cutting you off from the water."

"You hired a killer," Eli said.

"I hired a man to protect my rights after I was informed you were all consulting with that no-good lawyer in town to force the issue. Man's so damned crooked a rattler'd break his back trying to trail him."

Kyle laughed. "He said the same thing about you."

Sam Watersby's eyes darted from Kyle to Garth and back to Kyle. "You come here to make jokes, or get something settled?" he growled, his hand still on his gun.

"I don't have any intention of cutting anyone off from the river," Garth said again. "You sign the right-of-way leases, that's all I want."

"What about that young brother of your wife's?" Sam said. "Don't he inherit the land in a couple of weeks? What's his intentions?"

"Same as mine," Garth said. "All I want to do is control

the river so that we can all profit. That might mean dam-
ming it up sometimes, but no one would be cut off.''

They talked for another ten minutes, then, seeming satisfied—at least for the moment—the three ranchers said
their goodbyes and rode away.

Range looked at Garth. ''If you didn't intend to stop
their right-of-way, why'd you hire me?'' It was a question
he knew he shouldn't ask. If Garth didn't feel threatened
by his neighbors, he had no further use for Range, and
that would mean leaving without getting the answers he'd
waited so long to get.

Garth looked at him. ''You were hired to protect the
Rolling M.'' Turning, Garth walked back toward the barn.

J. D. shook his head. ''Too bad,'' he mumbled. ''I was
kind of looking forward to attending that man's funeral
this afternoon.''

Range turned his attention to J. D. ''I take it you don't
like Garth Murdock.''

J. D. smiled. ''You take it right.''

''Any particular reason?''

''Yep.'' J. D. picked up several pieces of tack and started
walking toward the barn, effectively putting an end to their
conversation.

Someone knew who he was. He stared after the older
man. Range had come to Tombstone fairly confident that
no one would recognize him, or know who he was. That
assumption had been shot to hell when Francie Rouchard
had recognized him instantly. He knew someone at the
Rolling M ranch was also privy to his secret, and he wondered now if that person was J. D. Sharp.

But if J. D. Sharp had been on the Rolling M twenty-
four years ago and knew what happened, knew who Range
really was, wouldn't he have said something by now? And
wouldn't Range have at least a vague recollection of the
man?

Range spent the next hour sitting silently and staring at the ranch house. He had to get in there. Yet even as he told himself this, as he tried to concentrate on the reason he'd come to the Rolling M, on what he needed to do, what he needed to accomplish to finally plug up the dark hole that had existed for so long where his heart was supposed to be, his thoughts kept veering elsewhere ... to Candace. What she'd made him feel when he had held her in his arms, taken her lips with his, wouldn't go away, and that made him nervous.

It was as if from the moment he'd seen her, a part of his mind had been unable to stop thinking about her, a part of his body had been unable to stop wanting her. It was a feeling he'd never experienced before, and it frightened him. He had no control over it, and control was what his life was all about. It was what got him through each day, what had enabled him to survive.

She threatened that, and yet the last thing he wanted to do was walk away from her. And he felt fairly certain that even if he did, the feeling wouldn't go away. At least not until he took her to his bed. Then, after he'd satisfied the intense need his body felt to possess her, after he'd given in to the lust that gnawed at his insides whenever he saw her or even just thought about her, then he would be able to forget about her, he was sure.

Range rolled and lit a cigarette, his gaze moving from her window to the front door of the house. Candace and her sister and brother had gone to town. Garth was busy doing something or other in the barn. This was the opportunity he'd been waiting for. Now was the time. He rose.

Before he'd taken two steps toward the house, Jesse suddenly rode up, dismounted, and walked into the house. Range cursed soundly under his breath and walked to the barn. Frustration churned inside of him like a restless snake, coiling, uncoiling, and whipping about viciously.

Minutes later he was riding Satan across the desert, the wind created by their speed whipping past Range's face.

In the distance, at the edge of a raised plateau, J. D. sat on his horse and watched.

Chapter 16

It was midnight. Range stared down at the pocket watch he normally carried in the front pocket of his trousers. Ben Connor had given it to him just before he'd died.

Range snapped the watch shut as memories of Ben filled his mind. After the Army had taken him from the Indians, he'd done everything he could to make the soldiers hate him as he hated them. They thought they'd rescued him, but to Range all they'd done was rob him of his family, the same way Garth Murdock had done several years before.

Then Ben, part-time scout for the army, part-time prospector, and a man who'd lived by his gun longer than most, had befriended him. Ben had taught him how to speak English again, how to ride a horse with a saddle on it, use utensils to eat with, wear clothes, and use a gun. But most importantly, Ben had taught him how to survive in the white man's world.

Two Hawks had given him the name Range Warrior.

Ben gave him his own last name: Connor.

And when Ben had finally died, having ridden over one hill too many, he gave Range his other most prized possession, his gold watch.

Range slipped it back into his pocket. It was time to do what he'd come here for. He walked across the open area between the bunkhouse and the ranch house. Nothing moved. Nothing stirred. The night was quiet. Even the birds were silent. And the air was heavy and still. Candace had left her bedroom window partially open. Range ignored that easy access, not because he was afraid of waking her, (Two Hawks had taught him well how to move silently through anyone or anything) but because he didn't trust himself to be so near her and not reach out to touch her. He quietly mounted the front steps and crossed the gallery to the front door.

It was locked.

He smiled and pulled a small needlelike pin from a pocket sewn onto the inside of his gun belt. Within less than the time it takes a man to blink, Range had the door open. He walked inside and carefully closed the door behind him, so silently even someone standing next to him wouldn't have been aware of it. His eyes were already accustomed to the darkness, and since he'd been in the house several times already, he knew where the furniture was situated, at least in the parlor, dining area, and kitchen, so he had no reason to hesitate in his movements through those rooms.

But he felt fairly certain those rooms weren't the ones he needed to search. Moving through the parlor he grabbed a candle from one of the tables and entered a small room situated at the rear of the house. Garth's study. Closing the door behind him, he took a lucifer from his pocket and, striking it with a flick of his thumbnail, held the small flame to the candle's wick. Pale light surrounded him, but left the outer reaches of the room in darkness and shadow.

It was enough for his purposes, however. He looked around.

A large desk sat to one side of the room. Two leather chairs sat facing it, a cabinet was positioned between two windows and another beside the desk, while shelves crammed with everything from books, ledgers, and bric-a-brac covered two walls. A mirror hanging over the fire-place mantel caught his movement into the room. He whirled, his free hand whipped to his gun, but even before he drew it, Range realized it was his own image reflecting back at him that had spooked him, and he laughed silently at himself.

He decided to start with the desk. Twenty minutes later he finished searching it, and had found nothing. For several seconds he sat in Garth's desk chair and didn't move, listening to the house, confirming that its residents were still all asleep.

Satisfied, he moved to the shelves, checking each book and looking into each piece of bric-a-brac. Again he found nothing, and again after his search he paused and listened before moving on to one of the cabinets.

An hour later he was more frustrated than ever, anger pulling his nerves taut and pushing him closer toward the verge of explosion. He rose to his feet. His fingers clenched and unclenched beside his guns, as if aching to draw them. He could walk down the hall right now, into the man's room, put his gun to Garth's head, and pull the trigger. It would all be over then. The hate inside of him would go away finally, and his mother would be avenged.

Except he wouldn't have the answers he needed, a little voice at the back of his mind whispered. And no one would know the truth about Garth Murdock but him.

Resisting the urge to slam his fists down on the desk, Range walked to the window and looked out.

Something moved beside the bunkhouse.

The hair stood up on the back of his neck, and every cell and muscle in his body became alert and ready to heed his slightest command. Range quickly stepped to one side of the window, but his eyes never left the point where he'd seen movement. A moment later he saw a man move away from the side wall of the bunkhouse and hurry toward the barn.

Range whipped the curtain aside and, bending, stared at the retreating figure. Unfortunately, what little moonlight shone down on the earth tonight was too feeble, and the darkness too intense, for him to recognize the man. But he had made out the fact that the man seemed to limp.

Like J. D., Range thought. But why would J. D. be watching him?

Range cursed softly. Someone knew who he was, and obviously that same someone was watching his every move. But was it J. D.? And if so, why? He could leave the house and go to the barn to confront the man. Which he knew could also get him killed. Whoever was out, whether J. D. or someone else, they had an advantage over Range. They knew who Range was, but Range had no idea who his unknown watcher was. Only a suspicion with no foundation.

He turned and was about to leave the room when his gaze flashed past the clock sitting on the mantel of the fireplace. Range paused, a frown pulling at his brow as he stared at the elaborate old timepiece. Familiarity tugged at him. He walked to the fireplace. In the center of a raised black metal platform sat a block of red marble. On each side of that was a horse cast of bronze, each rearing, their forelegs raised and supporting a golden timepiece, its pendulum swinging rhythmically back and forth in front of the red marble block.

Range watched the pendulum, suddenly becoming aware of the soft *tick, tock, tick, tock* sound that had filled the room the entire time he'd been there, but he hadn't noticed.

Now he knew he hadn't noticed because somewhere, buried deep in his subconscious, he'd known it would be there, had expected it to be there.

Candace stood in the hallway, staring at the door to Garth's study, all too aware of the pale light that shone beneath its door and who was in there. She'd seen him cross the grounds toward the house, had been aware when he'd entered, and, standing in the dark with her door open only a crack, she'd watched him silently slip into Garth's study.

The thought of waking Garth and alerting him that Range was in the house, and in his study, never entered her mind. She did, however, consider confronting Range, until she realized that by doing that, Garth might hear their voices and wake.

So she stood at her door and watched and listened. She knew he was searching for something. But what? What could there be in Garth's study that would be of interest to Range Connor? As far as she knew the two men had never met before. And Garth didn't keep money in his study. Of course, no one outside of the family would know that.

Candace bit down on her bottom lip. Was that what he was looking for? Money? But somehow she didn't think it was that simple.

Range grabbed the candle from Garth's desk, returned to the fireplace, and held the light up before the clock. The gold surrounding the clock face and the delicately shaped pendulum glistened against the flame's light.

Range felt a sudden tightening in his chest. Memories pressed down on him, fighting for release and recognition. He closed his eyes, momentarily giving in to them and letting them flow freely. He suddenly saw himself setting the clock with his mother, opening the small crystal glass and touching the delicate black hands.

She took a soft cloth to the glass, rubbing gently, then moved to polish the lines of the momentarily still pendulum. "This is our treasure, Nicholaus." Her voice was like the delicate music of a windchime stirred by a soft summer breeze.

He smiled up at her.

"A treasure your father brought to me all the way from France before you were born. And someday it will be yours, and you can have it in your home."

Range opened his eyes and looked at the clock. His mother's clock. And then he remembered the hidden compartment. He stopped the pendulum's silent swing and, carefully pushing it to one side, swung the red marble block outward from the right side, then bent to look under it. Pressing the tip of a finger to the metal plate there, he pushed that aside, too.

He had expected the compartment to be empty, as it had always been. Instead, he saw the whiteness of a folded piece of paper.

Shock held him immobile for several long seconds, then he pulled the paper out. His hand trembled as he unfolded it and stared at the words written there. It had been so long, and he had been so young the last time he'd seen it, but he recognized his mother's handwriting instantly. The florid swirls and lines were unmistakable. And if he'd needed any other proof, he merely needed to look at her name, signed with a flourish across the bottom of the page.

His gaze moved back to the top of the letter, and he read.

Dear Garth,

Range's pulse started to throb.

I don't really know how to start this letter. I never intended to hurt you, never thought this could happen, but now that it has, I know what I must do. I must follow my heart, and pray that you can forgive me. When we met I told you I was a widow, that my husband had been lost at sea, but that wasn't entirely the truth. My husband was a seaman. He had an important cargo to deliver and sailed for France while I was carrying Nicholaus. I never heard from him again. When his ship returned to the States, his business partner, who had sailed with him, explained that after they'd reached England and Jed had gone ashore, none of them had heard from him again. They searched, but there was no sign of him. I waited several years, but then I had to face the fact that Jed was most likely dead. I reasoned that he was dead because I always knew he wasn't the kind of man to desert his wife and child.

Range stared at the words, rereading them several times before going on. He remembered now, how his mother would sometimes sit on his bed at night, waiting for him to fall asleep, and talk about his father. She used to tell him they had the same jet black hair, the same quirk of their upper lips when they laughed, how she knew just by looking at him that he was going to grow up tall and strong like Jedidiah Landers, and how he already had his father's stubborn nature.

He'd always laughed at that, and she'd always reached out and playfully ruffled his hair and told him she loved him so very, very much.

A lump of emotion formed in Range's throat, and he continued to read.

And I was right that he wouldn't desert us, because he has finally come back, and now I know the truth about what happened to him. Jedidiah had arranged to buy something special for our child, and had gone to France to pick it up. Unfortunately, he never told anyone where he was going, since he had plenty of time to conduct his business and make it back to the ship before it was time to set sail for home. But, while in a small tavern just outside of Paris, he found himself in a fight with Ralston Drake, the Duke of Glouchester. Within no time Jed was in jail, and no one knew about it. He didn't even see a lawyer or a judge for a year, and wasn't released from that horrible place for several more. By the time he returned to our home, I was gone. He began to search for me and Nicholaus right away, but it has taken him two years to track us down.

I hope you can forgive me, Garth, but I must follow my heart and go back to Jed.

God bless you, Allison

Range read the letter again, refolded it, and slipped it into the pocket of his shirt. Numbly he closed the clock, looked around the room to make certain he'd left no telltale sign that he'd been there and searched it, then blew out the candle.

Candace stiffened and quickly closed her door until only a hair's breadth of a crack remained open, just enough to allow her a view of the hallway.

Range walked to the door of the study where he paused, listening. Silence met his ears.

He opened the door and stepped out.

Candace watched him stand in the hall. He looked toward her door and she stopped breathing, suddenly afraid he could hear her, afraid he could see her watching him. Then he moved silently but hurriedly from the hallway toward the parlor. The soft click of the front door closing followed a few seconds later.

She turned and ran to her window.

At the hitching rack before the bunkhouse, Range paused, gripping it with both hands and holding on tight, his head hanging down to his chest. His heart was thumping crazily within his chest, his pulses were racing madly, and fury was churning in his gut like a runaway prairie fire.

The ache to charge into Garth Murdock's bedroom and kill him had been almost too strong to resist as Range had stood in the hallway of the ranch house, his mother's letter in his pocket, burning through the fabric of his shirt and into his chest. But he'd done it, because he hadn't come this far, waited this long, to let the man get off that easily.

He moved across the porch of the bunkhouse and, with his back to the wall, sank to his haunches and pulled the letter out again. But he didn't need to reread it to know what it said. It was as if every word, every flourish and swirl, had been indelibly imprinted on his brain.

Nevertheless, he opened it, read it again, then sank to the ground and sat staring out at the night. Emotions he'd never known he had, never known he was capable of feeling, overwhelmed him. Grief for his mother, a yearning to know the father he'd never met, the loneliness of having his life ripped apart too many times.

He'd lived with merely the instinct for survival and the need for revenge for so long, it had been all he'd believed himself capable of feeling. Now he knew he'd been wrong, yet those familiar feelings were still strong in him.

Both confusion and compassion swelled in Candace as she stood at her window watching him. She had no idea why she was feeling the way she did, but that wasn't something she was concerned with at the moment. Rather, she wanted to know what Range had been doing in Garth's

study, and what he had taken from it that had so obviously
upset him. It seemed like an eternity that he sat on the
ground in front of the bunkhouse, staring at the piece of
paper he held in his hand.

She frowned. Something in her yearned to go to him
as he sat there, seeming so dejected.

Suddenly, Range shoved the paper back into his pocket
and rose. But instead of going into the bunkhouse, he
headed into the desert. He had to be alone, had to digest
these new feelings, had to think. His mother's letter didn't
change his plans, merely reinforced them, instilled within
him even more firmly the conviction that what he'd come
back to the Rolling M to do, had to be done. Justice had
to be served. The truth had to come out. It had already
been hidden for too long.

Not taking the time to think about what she was about
to do, what she would say if someone saw or intercepted
her, Candace grabbed her robe from the bed where it lay
and hurriedly slipped into it. At her door, she turned back.
She didn't dare try to make it through the house to the
front door. She might wake someone, or they might already
be up. She climbed out of her bedroom window.

On the gallery she paused, looking in the direction
where Range had disappeared. She was being foolish.
Whatever was happening was most likely none of her business. Walking out into the night . . . she suddenly paused
and looked down at her feet. Walking out into the night
. . . barefoot, was an insane notion. Following a hired gunman into the darkness was crazy. She was asking for trouble.
Even if she didn't find him, she might find something else,
like a rattler.

Ignoring every good, solid reason that her mind was
conjuring up for her in an attempt to dissuade her from
following Range, she stepped from the porch and hurried

across the yard in the same direction he'd taken. She didn't know why, but she had to know what he was up to.

The moon was only a sliver in the sky, the light it threw down onto the earth feeble and pale. It barely touched the top of the tall saguaros, which during the bright daylight hours reminded her of green giants standing about the desert, pointing this way and that. But the night transformed them, the blackness of shadows and the pale moonlight turning them to tall, dark behemoths that enabled danger and menace to hide behind their solid forms, waiting to strike whoever passed by.

Candace shivered and tried to banish the almost sinister thoughts from her mind. She caught sight of a sparkle of silver in the distance and paused. A moment later she caught sight of it again, just off to her left. Hoping it was one of the conchos on his leggings reflecting the moonlight, she veered in that direction.

She stepped on a rock and, as it dug into the soft flesh of her sole, she flinched and nearly stumbled. Cursing beneath her breath, she walked on, but the flash of silver she'd seen was gone. Darkness surrounded her. She looked around frantically, suddenly unsure of which direction to take. Looking back over her shoulder she saw the dark shadows of the barn, the bunkhouse, and the ranch house behind her, now a goodly distance away. She hadn't been aware she'd walked that far.

She turned back, her gaze trying to pierce the darkness again, trying to see him. Indecision gripped her. There was no point going on if she didn't know where he was. Yet she was reluctant to turn back. But even if she found him, what was she going to do? What could she say? She couldn't admit she'd seen him in Garth's study.

Candace took several steps forward, praying she wasn't standing on the edge of a plateau that would suddenly give way beneath her to nothing but thin air.

*   *   *

He knew someone was behind him. It wasn't so much that they'd made a sound, but that he sensed them, almost as if they'd disturbed the stillness of the desert, slightly tilted the slant of the earth beneath his feet. Standing still he barely breathed as he waited and listened.

Years ago Two Hawks had taught him everything he needed to know to survive in the desert, including how to sense if someone else was out there with you.

Whoever it was stood only a short distance away.

Range waited.

The person moved and he knew it instantly, even though no sound met his ears. He merely sensed the movement of the night air, the change in its stillness. He breathed in slowly, deeply, and smelled jasmine. Range frowned. Jasmine didn't grow on the desert. He breathed in again and smelled the same strong, heady fragrance.

Suddenly a rock moved, a hiss of breath followed, and the air churned furiously.

Range's hands moved faster than lightning. They whipped his guns from their holsters as he whirled to face whoever was trying to advance on him.

Candace was so startled the shriek that ripped from her chest became clogged in her throat. A mere squeak emanated from her lips as she jumped back, clutching at a heart that was now threatening to thump itself right out of her chest. "Oh, my stars," she said, bending forward and gasping for breath, "oh, my stars."

"You nearly got yourself killed," Range retorted, snarling to keep her, and maybe even himself, from realizing how badly she'd shaken him.

"I'm sorry. I just . . . I mean, I didn't expect . . . I mean, I did, but I didn't—"

"What the hell are you doing out here?" Range snapped,

cutting off her incoherent ramblings. He looked her up and down, then instantly wished he hadn't. Though the light shining down on them from the moon was weak, it was strong enough to pierce the thin threads of both her robe and nightgown. It sliced through them like the brightness of a lightning bolt, caressing her curves as it passed, and obligingly leaving nothing to his imagination.

"I could ask you the same thing," Candace said, finally managing to catch her breath and take insult at his snarly tone at the same time.

"I'm taking a walk." He reholstered his guns, looking away from her as he silently struggled to regain his composure. God, he could have killed her.

"I saw you in Garth's study," Candace said.

He instantly jerked back around to stare at her.

"And I want to know why you're really at the Rolling M, Mr. Connor."

He stared at her, the darkness of his blue eyes melding with hers, self-restraint quickly ebbing from his grasp.

Then suddenly it was gone altogether.

Chapter 17

She felt his mouth, hard and hot on hers, and though she knew she should resist, should push him away, it was the last thing in the world she wanted to do.

His lips moved over hers hungrily, need and loneliness shadowing the urgency of his ravaging kiss.

His arms were crushing her body into his, robbing her of breath. His lips were bruising upon hers, but she didn't care. A trembling weakness spread through her body.

No one else had ever kissed her the way Range Connor did. She had thought that maybe the feelings he'd aroused in her before had been merely those of excitement. A sense of thrill heightened by the shadows of a forbidden act. Now she knew that wasn't true.

Candace knew that at any moment she was going to lose complete control. If she didn't stop him now, she would give in to the swirling ache of desire that had attacked her body the moment his lips had claimed hers.

His tongue plunged into her mouth, and what little

sanity she had left, vanished. This was what she'd wanted for so long, this feeling that his touch invoked within her. This was what she had been waiting for all of her life, this tall, dark, dangerous man who made her feel things she'd only dreamed about, whose mere touch or look made her oblivious to everything else in the world.

His hands drew her nearer, so that she was molded to his long length.

Her own arms encircled his neck, holding him closer, wanting never to release him.

Her movement against his body, her arms around his neck, her tongue meeting his, dancing with passion, ignited an explosion within him that exposed everything Range Connor was, had been, or could be. Cravings so strong he knew they had to be satisifed or he would die, assaulted him in waves, one after another, mercilessly pummeling him with feelings that had been denied, ignored, and hidden away for too long.

Her kiss and acquiescence were nearly his undoing. It inflamed him beyond the heat of fire, aroused him beyond the realm of reality, and unforgivingly woke all the passions and desires that he had held in check for so long.

Her lips brazenly allowed him to ravage her mouth as Candace gave herself up to the passion that, for the first time in her life, was consuming her. Fire sped through her veins as hot, hungry emotions clawed through her body.

Lost in the desires that had overwhelmed her, she was nonetheless more aware of him than she had ever been. The scent of sagebrush and leather clung to him, while beneath that was the aroma of the man himself, a melding of flesh and soap and passion that was heady and satisfying and exhilarating.

As his lips moved from hers and trailed down her neck, Candace felt the sleek muscles of his powerful body close around her. She felt his breath gently skim across her skin, the heat of his hands on her back searing her flesh.

Suddenly he pulled back, knowing instinctively that he needed to give them both a moment before it was too late, but he did not release her. His thumb and forefinger touched her chin and turned her face up to his. He looked deep into her eyes, knowing he had to warn her, even though everything in him screamed for him not to do it. "Stop me now," he whispered raggedly, struggling against his own passion to get the words out, "or I won't be able to stop."

She felt the warmth of desire prickle her skin as fear and longing warred within her.

"I don't want to stop you," she whispered at last, knowing it was more truth than she'd ever spoken in her life. She tightened her arms around his neck and pulled him toward her. There was no turning back; there had been no turning back since the moment she'd seen Range Connor.

What little sanity and restraint Range still possessed instantly disappeared as his lips met hers again and he felt the hunger of her kiss. Yet as quickly as he wanted to take her, as desperately as his body craved the satisfaction of melding with hers, of branding her with his touch, he kissed her slowly. He traced the soft fullness of her lips with his tongue, explored the recesses of her mouth, and kissed the pulsing hollow at the base of her throat.

Candace moaned in his arms, and the fire in Range's blood intensified.

His lips moved over her neck, her shoulders, then recaptured hers, demanding more this time.

Candace returned his kiss with an abandon that was reckless as she drank in the sweetness he offered.

"I've wanted you since the moment I saw you." His voice was ragged, husky with emotion, deep with passion.

She arched her body toward him, needing his touch.

Range's hands swept under her nightgown, sliding up over her thighs, past the curve of her waist. He hesitated as his fingers brushed over her bare breasts, and she felt his sharp intake of breath and the quivering in his fingers.

He pushed the nightgown and robe from her shoulders, lifting it over her head.

Candace raised her arms and the gown billowed upward, then, as he released it, settled to the ground at her feet. Never before had she stood naked before anyone. The heat of a blush swept over her, and she moved her arms to cover herself from his view.

"No, don't," he said softly. "Don't hide yourself from me."

She dropped her hands then, all embarrassment suddenly, unexplainably gone.

"You're too beautiful," Range whispered, his eyes devouring her. He felt something tighten and coil hot and hungry within his gut. She was more beautiful than he'd even imagined, her golden hair falling around her shoulders like a halo, her eyes taking on the depth of the night as they looked up at him, her breasts moving up and down, teasing him, beckoning him to reach out and touch them.

His need for her was stronger than anything he'd ever felt in his life, and because of that, for the first time in longer than he could remember, he felt off guard, and he didn't care.

Candace met his gaze and, as if the darkness she saw there was calling out to her soul, she knew what it was that she had been feeling for Range Connor almost from the moment he'd ridden onto the Rolling M. Slipping her hands beneath his vest, she brushed it from his shoulders, knowing she had finally found the one man she would love forever.

Undressing him was an erotic adventure that teased at

their passions and taunted the hunger growing inside both
of them.

As her hands moved over his chest, pushing away the
front of his shirt, Range felt the breath in his throat stall.
Her fingers touched the silver crucifix that hung from a
chain around his neck, and he suddenly stiffened and
grabbed her hand. His eyes caught hers. "No," he said
harshly, then released her without another word, as if trusting that she knew what he meant and would not betray
him.

It was something to think about, to ask him about, later,
Candace thought. Not now. Her fingers slid down the
ropey length of his arms, pushing his shirtsleeves.

He started to reach for her.

"No," she said breathlessly, smiling, and moved away.

As he dragged another lungful of air into his body in
an effort to calm himself, she stepped back to stand before
him and undid his gun belt, setting it carefully on the
ground. Then she released his trousers, pushing them,
along with his johns, downward.

Because of the years he'd spent with the Apache, living
the way they had lived, thinking the way they'd thought,
the vulnerability nakedness could bring to a man meant
nothing to Range. But he nearly groaned at the touch of
her hands on his legs, at the need to drag her into his
arms and wrap himself around her. He steeled himself
against the urge and remained still, knowing that was what
she wanted.

Candace stared at him, a slight smile pulling at her lips.
He was the most beautiful thing she'd ever seen. His body
a long length of muscle, now hard with anticipation. His
shoulders were broad, the sinewy muscles of his arms well
honed. A light matting of black hairs covered his chest,
coming together in a V just over his stomach and plunging

downward until they spread and thickened at the juncture of his thighs.

There was no denying his arousal, yet even as her eyes were drawn to that evidence of flesh, she drew a sharp intake of breath at the sight of it jutting fiercely from that tangle of black hair.

"I think this has gone on long enough," Range snarled, unable to resist touching her any longer.

Moving faster than she thought possible, he reached out and dragged her into his arms, crushing her naked body up against his length. His mouth trapped hers, effectively cutting off any protest she might have uttered.

Neither of them were aware of the man who had watched them both pass his window on their way into the night.

J. D. hadn't been certain what had woke him. Curious, and always cautious, he had gotten out of bed, pulling on a pair of trousers and walking out to the porch of the bunkhouse. A smile pulled at his craggy features as he watched Candace follow Range, not quite sure whether or not he should really believe what his old eyes were telling him he was seeing.

Completely oblivious to J. D's awareness that they were together, Range slowly released Candace, letting her slender body slide slowly down the hard, hot length of his. Unconsciously the demanding pressure of his lips on hers slackened, and his kiss turned strangely gentle. His lips began to explore her mouth once again, his tongue pushed its way into the inner sweetness beyond her lips, and his hands began their own hungry exploration of her body.

As his mouth moved to trail a series of fire-hot kisses down the side of her neck, Candace drew a long, shud-

dering breath. She hungered for the feel of his body
pressed to hers. Everything about this man was forbidden
to her. Everything about him was dark and dangerous
and even deadly, but it didn't matter. Deep in the private
recesses of her heart, where feelings she'd never shared
with anyone else dwelt, she knew he was the one. She
wanted him, only him, and at the moment nothing else
mattered but that he was here, holding her in his arms
and loving her.

Without knowing how or when it happened, she found
herself lying on the ground, his body resting half over
hers.

His hands began a feather-light exploration of her body,
setting off flames of need wherever they touched. His fingers moved to gently cup one breast, his thumb rhythmically stroking back and forth across her nipple, teasing her,
then deserting her to move slowly, tauntingly, tormentingly
downward, past her waist, over her hip, caressing the soft,
silken plane of her skin as it went.

Candace felt her senses reeling under the assault of his
touch. Reality as she'd known it was abandoned, and she
gave herself up eagerly to this new world his kisses and
caresses were carrying her into. There was only one
thought left in her mind now, only one desire left in her
body: to be wholly possessed by Range Connor, to know
what it was like to be a woman loved.

No one else had ever touched her the way he was touching her, kissed her the way he was kissing her. Each caress
of his hands to her flesh was an intoxicating sensation
that pushed her further into the world of passion she had
dreamed about, but never thought to traverse. Even so,
when his hand moved across her stomach and slipped
between the softness of her inner thighs, Candace wasn't
prepared for the jolt of raw desire that swept through her.
She twisted under him, her body arched uncontrollably,

and she cried out his name, almost as if pleading with him . . . yet she was unsure for what.

His mouth moved to cover hers again as his hand moved between her thighs, his fingers, like fire against her flesh, increasing the gnawing ache of anticipation that had invaded her blood.

Passion held his senses prisoner, blotted out all strain of reason, warded off reality and rationale; even so, Range knew one thing: he needed to make her want him as she had never wanted another man. He needed her to desire him as much as he desired her.

Being with her, making love to her, was an exquisite agony he didn't know if he could bear much longer, and it was a sweet torment he knew he would carry with him forever. His mouth roamed her body, tasting and nuzzling, traversing her neck, breasts, stomach, and even the length of her legs. And all the while his hand continued to gently move between her thighs, drawing her passion ever higher and hotter.

It was all he could do to control his own body, to hold back, but he wanted, needed, to prolong this time with her, to enjoy loving her for as long as he could. She was the most beautiful woman he'd ever seen, her eyes as blue as the sky, her hair touched by the pale moonlight, like white gold, and her body so perfect beneath his.

Until this very moment he hadn't realized the depth of loneliness into which his soul had plunged, hadn't realized how intense the darkness in which he existed had become. Now he knew, and for just a little while, she offered him sunlight. His body trembled with the force of emotions her touch unleashed within him. Suddenly knowing he could wait no longer, Range moved to cover her body with his.

A soft scream slipped from Candace's lips, then, as she felt her body fill with him, felt him slowly begin to move inside of her, she wrapped her arms around him again and began to move with him. She felt the soft, silky black hairs on his chest brush against her breasts, teasing her nipples; felt his long, lean legs straddling hers, the power in them framing her. She looked up and into his eyes, the blue almost black now, and suddenly became lost in their depths, seeing all the pain and loneliness he had endured, but more than that, she saw the love he craved, and the love he had to give.

A muffled moan escaped her lips then as a storm of pleasure washed over her. She drew his head down to hers, seeking his mouth, wanting to taste him, wanting him to continue his sensual assault on her body, needing him never to stop.

As he moved on her, Candace instinctively moved with him, raising her hips to meet his, each movement more urgent.

She knew, when the pleasure became so intense, so mind-numbing, that she could do nothing but give herself up to it, that she cried aloud, that she sobbed his name over and over and over, but she couldn't help it, anymore than she could help the way he made her feel. The way she knew she would feel, toward him, for the rest of her life.

They lay together for what seemed hours, but was really merely minutes, each lost within their own thoughts. Their bodies were satisfied, the passions satiated, at least for the moment, but the unspoken questions between them remained. Yet each was leery of voicing them, and so they remained silent and struggling against the doubts and suspicions that had immediately crept back into their minds as passion had ebbed away.

Candace stared up at the star-strewn sky. She had never felt so complete, never felt so alive, and she had never felt so afraid and alone. How could she go on now, knowing

how she felt about him, and still suspecting that he had
come to the Rolling M to kill Brandon for Garth so that
he could continue to control Gates End?

Range Connor had made love to her, had made her feel
love, and yet he was still nothing more than a dark stranger
to her. A man whose reputation was as black as the night.

But his soul isn't, her heart argued. And she knew that
was true. She had seen that much for herself. And yet, did
it make any difference? He was a man who lived by his
gun, who hired it out to the highest bidder and killed
whoever they wanted killed. And she was in love with him.

A tear slipped from the corner of her eye, and Candace
turned quietly away from him, suddenly wanting to curl
her body up into itself, fall asleep, and never wake up
again.

Range lay with one arm under his head, the other still
wrapped around Candace's shoulder. Disbelief and wonder had nearly overwhelmed him to the point that, if he
hadn't desired her so much, if he hadn't wanted her so
desperately, when he'd entered her he would have gone
completely torpid right there on the spot from the shock
of suddenly realizing that she was a virgin.

It was something he'd never considered, something that
amazed him. She was Garth Murdock's wife. She had been
married to the man for seven years, and yet she was a
virgin. He didn't understand, but at the same time, he
didn't care to understand. He was merely glad.

He closed his eyes and listened to the battle going on
inside of him. Hope, joy, despair, and doubt roiled within
him. When this thing he'd come to do was over with, would
she understand? Would she still want him?

Or would she hate him? After all, he really was nothing
more than a man who killed other men for money. He'd
always been selective about what jobs he would accept,
always making certain that the men he was hired to kill

were men who deserved killing. But that didn't lessen the fact that he was a hired gunman. Killing scum didn't make him any less of a killer, it only allowed him to justify it in his own mind, and stay just this side of the law, most times.

He would have nothing to offer her but himself, and that, he realized, wasn't much. He had never charged excessively for his services, so he didn't have a lot of money stashed away. Enough to keep him going, that's all he'd ever needed.

Now there was Candace, and his past suddenly seemed a lot more sordid to him than it ever had before.

But it wasn't something he could change. And he wasn't even certain he could change the future. After he'd accomplished what he had set out to by coming to the Rolling M, he could hang up his guns for good, but was that really possible? Wouldn't there always be someone out there looking for him, someone out there who wanted to draw on Range Connor, beat the unbeatable in order to make his own name?

He sighed deeply. It wouldn't be fair to put her through that. With that decision made, Range closed his eyes. But instead of falling asleep, he felt the depth of the loneliness that had always dwelt with him, intensify. He knew then that after he left her, with each day that passed, the feeling would grow worse, until the day came when he couldn't stand it anymore and he was forced to end it.

Range felt her stir, but didn't move as she rolled away from him. He wanted to reach out and pull her back, hold her against him forever and a day, but he remained still. From beneath lowered lashes he watched her gather her gown and robe, slipping quietly into both, and hurry away from him, back toward the house.

Once he'd thought making love to Garth Murdock's wife would be nothing but sweet revenge. Range nearly laughed aloud. "Sweet revenge," he said into the night, his tone holding a note of rancor. What he'd accomplished had been anything but revenge, and the joke was on him, because he would be the one to suffer for it. He would be the one who would remember this night for the rest of his life. He would ache to hold her in his arms again, yearn to taste her kisses just once more, feel her body pressed up to his, and instead he would know nothing but the loneliness of longing.

He had been a fool to give in to his emotions, a fool to let that floodgate open and overwhelm him, and yet, as he thought back on it, of how she had tasted and smelled, of how she had felt beneath him, of how he had felt when inside of her, Range knew if he had it to do all over again, he would.

Chapter 18

The smell of coffee woke him. Range, already fully dressed, reached under his pillow and pulled out his gun as he rose from his bunk. Sitting on the edge of the bunk, he ran a hand through his hair and found it still damp.

After Candace had left him, he'd walked to a small, nearby creek and given himself a good dousing. It was a wonder how chilling, cold water could rid a man's mind and body of every thought and feeling but of how to get warm again.

He shook the memory of her from his mind. Today he had to get back to business, to do what he'd come here to do. There were still a few more people to talk to. Range rose and slid his gun into the holster he'd hung on one post of the bunk, then lifted it down and prepared to put it on.

That's when he spotted the folded piece of paper that had been secured by his holster's tie-down. The message was brief, and he didn't recognize the blunt handwriting.

Don't forget what you've been hired to do.

Range stared at the note and his temper instantly flared. He didn't like to be pushed. Range squashed the note into a small, wadded ball within his clenched fist and threw it to the floor. Obviously Garth was getting impatient, which meant Range was running out of time.

Buckling on the holster and grabbing his hat, Range stalked out of the bunkhouse and strode toward the ranch house.

The sounds of voices raised in anger reached him before he was even halfway there.

It didn't deter him. He took the six entry steps two at a time, strode across the gallery, and entered.

Most of the family was already seated at the breakfast table.

Candace looked up at him as he entered, and suddenly the fury that had been roiling about in him disappeared. Something intensely sensuous passed between them as his eyes held hers, and Range had to fight the overwhelming need to drag her into his arms.

"Hey, come join the party," Brandon said, glancing at Range and grinning devilishly.

Range tore his gaze from Candace and moved toward the table.

Garth, paying no heed to him, slammed a fist on the table and glared at Candace. "I will not tolerate this, Candace. You both knew about my plans. Leland Rochester will be here any day now. You should have stopped her!"

Range struggled against the flaring urge to grab Garth by his collar, haul the man to his feet, and warn him to never, ever talk to Candace like that again. Instead, he sat down.

"She left in the middle of the night," Brandon said, drawing his brother-in-law's attention. "How was Candace supposed to know?"

Garth swung toward him, his face nearly purple from his rage. "And you probably helped her."

"Yeah," Brandon sneered, "I gave her a ride out on my chair. Want me to give you one?"

Range scooped a ladle of eggs onto his plate.

"Want me to go after Brianne?" Jesse asked. He lazed against the back of his chair, a match protruding from one corner of his mouth, and grinned at his brother. "Candy could even come along to convince her to come home nicely."

"Candace is not going anywhere," Garth growled. His eyes bore into Jesse's. "And neither are you!" He turned to Range. "Connor, I need you to go after Brianne."

Range looked up slowly, his features hard. He noticed the smile on Brandon's face, the resentment on Jesse's, the look of apprehension on Karalynne's, but he didn't look at Candace. He turned to Garth. "Are you speaking to me, Murdock?"

Garth opened his mouth to snap, then closed it again. "Yes, Mr. Connor, I am."

Range remained silent.

"It seems my wife's little sister has run off to elope with Deputy Hawkins."

"And that's a problem?" Range asked.

"Since I have arranged for her to marry a man who should be arriving here any day from Yuma," he glared at Candace, "a respectable young man employed with one of the area's best banks, yes, it is a problem."

Range nodded slowly. "Guess she didn't like your plans, huh?"

Brandon chuckled. "To say the least."

"Brianne is old enough to make up her own mind who she wants to marry," Candace said.

"No," Garth growled, slamming a fist onto the table.

Range felt a slow heat move over his body and his muscles

began to grow hard. Clenching his jaw tight, he purposely conjured up a picture of his mother on that last night, her dress torn, hair tumbling from its usually neat bun, blood streaming down her face from a gash on her temple. Instantly the desire that had started to burn within him disappeared.

"I need you to go after her, Mr. Connor," Garth said. "And bring her back."

Range had no intention of chasing after Brianne Gates and Deputy Hawkins. If it was what Garth wanted, then it obviously wasn't what Range wanted. But he'd feign going along, and that would buy him time. He nodded. "I'll leave right after I finish eating." He looked at Garth. "Got any idea where they were heading?"

Garth stood. "My guess is Tucson." He walked to the door, paused, and looked back. "Jesse, we got stock to round up."

"Yeah, right," Jesse groaned. "We always do." He pushed his chair away from the table and stood, but hung back after Garth walked out.

Range looked up, feeling the man hovering over him.

Jesse's dark eyes moved between Range and Candace. "You coming?" he sneered.

"When I'm done."

Jesse's eyes narrowed and bounced back to Candace, but his words were directed at Range. "Wouldn't be proper of me to leave you in here with the ladies, unchaperoned."

"I'm here," Brandon snapped.

"Yeah." Jesse smiled. "Useless as you are."

Range caught the man's gaze, and Jesse's smile instantly disappeared. "Your brother's waiting."

"Let him wait."

Range bolted to his feet, the move so abrupt his chair toppled over backward, crashing to the floor, and Candace

gasped, startled. "I don't think that's a good idea, Jesse."
Range's eyes spit fire at the older man. "Do you?"

Jesse's gaze dropped to Range's hips, the guns that rode
there, and the hands that hovered only a hair's breadth
from the weapons' butts. Turning, he left without a word.

"Sorry," Range said, looking at Candace, Brandon, and
Karalynne.

"Don't apologize to me," Karalynne said, smiling. "We
could use a little excitement like that around here more
often."

Range righted the chair, downed the last of his coffee,
and also turned to go.

Candace hurriedly rose and stepped in front of him.
"Don't do this," she said softly.

Range stared down at her.

"Don't go after Brianne," she pleaded again. "Please.
Let her go."

His gaze moved over every inch of her face, drank in its
beauty, imprinted the image on his mind, as if for all time,
then he purposely shut off awareness of her and wrapped
himself within the cold mantle of apathy that was his normal guise. Turning, he brushed past her without a word.

"Bastard," she said after him.

Range held himself stiff as he walked out the door. It
was better that she hated him again. At least that way, she
could put what had happened between them last night
behind her. Call it a mistake. Damn him, and blame him
for taking advantage of her. Because that's exactly what
he'd done. He had planned to seduce, and he had, even
though he'd known nothing could come of it.

Within minutes he had Satan saddled and was riding
away from the Rolling M.

Two hours later he had picked up Brianne and Wade's
trail. Another hour of riding hard and he spotted their
buggy. Range approached them.

"I won't go back," Brianne screamed, the minute she recognized him and Wade stopped the buggy.

Wade drew his gun, pointing it at Range. "You're not stopping us, Connor."

Range draped his hands over his saddle horn. "Hadn't intended to, Hawkins."

Wade's eyes narrowed. "Then what do you want?"

Range looked at Brianne. "Go do what you have to do," he said, "get married, whatever. But after that, come back. Don't worry about Garth, he won't be able to interfere, but your sister will need you."

Brianne looked at him, puzzled. "What do you mean?"

He shook his head. "Don't worry about it. Just come back." Turning Satan, Range started to go, then paused again. "I'll cover your trail. That should buy you a couple of days if Murdock decides not to believe I couldn't find you and sends someone else." Not waiting for a reply, Range nudged the huge stallion into a gallop.

By late afternoon Range was more frustrated and angry than ever. If he'd thought he would get any different answers from the people he questioned that day, he was wrong. Again, everyone said the same thing, and again, he rode back toward the Rolling M with just as many unanswered questions nagging at him as he'd had when he'd started out.

Someone had to know something. They had to know the truth, and he couldn't give up until he found them. The letter he'd found in the clock in Garth's study was revealing, but it didn't prove the man to be a murderer. If anything, it merely confirmed his story that Allison Landers Murdock had run off and left him, though not for a peddler, but for her first husband. And Range knew that wasn't true.

Coming over a rise he suddenly spotted movement in a deep arroyo off to his right. Range reined up instantly and, as Satan stopped, Range swung from the saddle and hunkered down on the ground.

A man on horseback made a much easier target than a man hugging the ground.

He pulled the Stetson lower onto his forehead, blocking out the glare of the sun, and stared down into the arroyo, squinting deeply and straining to see beyond the bright sunlight and distant shadows.

An old man, his body stooped, long gray hair flowing out from beneath a ragged hat, walked along the river that flowed through Gates End. He carried a rifle in one hand, while the other held the rope of the pack mule that trotted along behind him. A pick axe, shovel, and sifting pan protruded from the pack on the animal's back.

Range smiled. A prospector. He was about to grab Satan's reins and remount to head back to the Rolling M, when he had another thought. Turning back, Range urged Satan down the side of the plateau and toward the river.

Elijah Crebbs heard the sound of hoofbeats and, moving as fast as his gnarled old fingers could move, he shoved a bullet into the rifle's firing chamber and swung around to meet whoever was approaching. "Ain't got nothin' for you to bother stealing, bucko," he yelled at Range. "So you best jes' be on your way."

Range reined in and held up his hands. "Hold it, old-timer. Name's Range Connor, and all I'm looking for here is some water and a little friendly information."

Elijah looked at Range warily. "Get your water, the river ain't mine. But I ain't got no information. Friendly or otherwise."

Range smiled and dismounted, grabbing his canteen as he did. He walked to the river and hunkered down beside it, unscrewing the cap of his canteen and submerging it beneath the steadily moving water. He looked over at the old prospector. The man had to be at least sixty. His fea-

tures were as craggy as the desert floor, and burned just
as brown, while his clothes were so faded and covered with
dust and grime their original color was almost indistin-
guishable. "How do you know you don't have any information for me until you hear what it is I want to know?"

"Jes' know," the old man said, shrugging. "Don't know
nuthin' about nuthin'."

"How long you been prospecting around these parts?"

"Awhile," the old man said, still eyeing Range cautiously.
"I just cross peoples' land to get from one place to another,
don't camp on the private stuff."

"That's not my concern," Range said. "What I want to
know is, were you around here twenty-four years ago?"

"Nope. Up north then. The Dakotas." The old man
smiled, revealing that his front teeth on the top were gone.
"We had some good times up there. Yes, sir. Deadwood,
now that was a real city."

"Yeah, I've heard," Range said, trying not to show the
disappointment he'd felt at the old man's answer. "You
know anyone around who was here twenty-four years ago?"

"Nope." Elijah's eyes suddenly widened. "Why, lookee
there." Turning to the mule, he grabbed his sifting pan
and squatted down at the water's edge, plunging the pan
beneath the surface and into the river's bottom.

As Elijah bent forward, Range caught a glimpse of silver
peeking out from beneath the faded red neckerchief the
old man had tied loosely around his neck.

"See you already struck it once, huh?" Range said, closing up his canteen and sitting back on his heels.

Elijah looked at him and frowned.

Range nodded toward the old man's neck. "Pretty nice
piece of jewelry you've got there."

Elijah smiled. "Ah, hell, this old thing?" He pulled the
the chain out from within his shirt and, holding it out,

looked down at it. "Yeah, it is pretty, ain't it? My lucky piece," he said, grinning.

Range stared at the silver crucifix whose four arms depicted vines and leaves sprouting out from the engraving of a rose in the center.

The world seemed to suddenly stop. Range struggled for breath as his pulses pounded so loudly they seemed to drum out all other sound. He stared at the cross, half-expecting it and the old man to disappear. He blinked, shook his head, and stared at the cross again. Range felt like grabbing the cross, grabbing the old man, shaking him until he told him what he wanted to know. Instead, he steeled his body to remain still. "Where—" His voice was little more than a choked whisper. He swallowed hard and squeezed his eyes shut, trying to stop the roaring sound rushing through his mind.

Past and present crashed down on his senses. Images, memories, nightmares crowded into his mind, all vying for control, all demanding acknowledgement, all battling for his attention.

With a trembling hand, Range tore open the front of his own shirt and grabbed at the chain that hung there, holding it out so the old man could see it.

"Well, I'll be hog-tied and horsewhipped," Elijah said. "They look the same, don't they, young fella?"

Range still felt breathing was a chore. He dragged in a long, slow gulp of air and ordered his body to calm down. He couldn't remember the last time he'd nearly lost control of himself like this, unless he counted just a few hours ago, when he was with Candace. This was different, however. He stared at the old man's crucifix. "Is there . . ." His voice broke. He cleared his throat and tried again. "Is there anything on the back of it?"

Range was nearly holding his breath as the old man shrugged and turned the cross over. He squinted down, looking at it. "Can't rightly tell, but then my eyesight ain't what it used to be, you know?" He pushed the crucifix toward Range. "Here, you have a look-see."

But Range didn't need to take it, he could already see exactly what was engraved on the back. He remembered when his mother had given him his cross. It had been on his fifth birthday. His mother had taken him into his bedroom and, sitting on the bed with him, had pulled it from her reticule.

Dangling from her fingers as she held it up, it had caught the sun streaming in through his window and reflected it in a rainbow of dazzling color.

"Your father and I had this made for you," she'd said softly. "Before he went away. We had one made for me, one for him, and one for you. All just alike. But he wasn't here to have your initials and birth date engraved on the back of yours, so I did it for him. We were going to start a family tradition and give one to each of our children."

She'd slipped it around his neck. "You're old enough to wear it now, Nicky, and take care of it. But never take it off, sweetheart," she'd said. "Not ever."

And he hadn't.

Elijah, no stupid man, knew that whoever the man before him was, the cross he wore around his neck had something to do with the one Elijah wore. They were identical. Sweeping off his hat, he pulled the chain over his head and handed it to Range. "Here, look close," he urged. "It's got carvings on it, something on the back, too, letters and such, but I can't read, so I ain't got no idea what it says."

Range let the chain and crucifix fall into his open palm. Though they were light, they felt as heavy as all his memories and nightmares. For a brief second he closed his fingers around the cross, holding it tightly, not realizing until that very moment, as he unconsciously prayed that he was wrong, that he'd always hoped that somehow his mother had survived.

It was a fruitless hope, he knew. A ridiculous one. But now he knew it had always been at the back of his mind anyway.

He opened his hand and stared at the cross with its spreading leaves and vines and delicately engraved rose. He reached out with his other hand and turned the cross over, knowing what he was going to see.

Nevertheless, the shock hit him with the force of a bullet between the eyes. He stared down at the engraving.

AEL, 2-17-37.

"Allison Elyse Landers," Range whispered. "Born, February 17, 1837."

"Yeah?" Elijah said. "Who was that?"

Range lifted his own crucifix up beside the other. "My mother," he said softly.

The old man's face fell into a mask of compassion. "Oh, my," he said, and shook his head. "Oh my, that really is too bad."

Range looked up, instantly certain there was more behind the old man's words than mere compassion. "What is?" he demanded.

The old man looked suddenly leery.

Range wanted to reach out and grab him and shake the answer from him. He steeled himself against the urge. "Where'd you get this?"

Elijah frowned. "You sure you want to follow this path, young fella? Go where I been?"

"Take me to where you found this."

Elijah nodded. "Okay, but I don't think you're gonna like what you see. I sure as hell didn't."

Range mounted Satan.

Elijah walked in front of his mule, Sara, who he intro-

duced to Range at the same time he told him his own
name, just before setting out.

"How far, old man?" Range asked after only a couple
of minutes.

"Not far," Elijah said. "Found it last time I was through
here, maybe six months ago. But I don't expect nothing's
changed. I'da heard about it if it had. Mines closing, opening, caving in, lone bird's finding a strike, gettin' killed or
jumped, things like that. I hear about 'em all. Ain't no
secrets out here."

"Yeah? How do you hear?" Range asked. "You being
out here all alone."

Elijah grinned. "I got my ways," he said. "Plenty of ways.
And," he patted the mule's neck, "I ain't alone. I got Sara,
and she's all the company I need."

Range knew how the old man felt. He had Satan, but it
seemed lately, especially in the last few days, when the
memory of a pair of sky blue eyes wouldn't seem to leave his
mind, Satan's loyal company just wasn't enough anymore.

From a nearby hill, Jesse lay on his stomach, a spyglass
pressed to his right eye. Nothing had been going the way
he'd planned. He watched Range and the old prospector
as they walked toward a canyon in the distance.

He didn't know who the old man was and he didn't
care; he only knew that they couldn't keep going in the
direction they were going.

Suddenly there was movement off to his left. Jesse swung
around and trained his spyglass on the small cloud of dust
rising from the horizon.

"Damn," he spit, feeling the urge to squash something
beneath his fist. He watched Brandon ride toward Range
and the old man.

* * *

"Hey, Connor."

Range stiffened and turned to look at the approaching rider. He recognized Brandon Gates immediately and, though Range remained alert, even somewhat leery, he relaxed the hand he'd raised to settle on his gun.

"That's a pretty fancy saddle you got there, young fella," Elijah said, looking over Brandon's tack as the younger man reined in beside him.

"Yeah, well, it wouldn't seem so fancy to you if you had to use it," Brandon said. "More like a nuisance." He looked at Range. "What's going on? Did you find Brianne?"

"Do you see her?"

Brandon smiled. "That's not an answer."

"Well," Range shrugged, "it's the only one you're going to get."

"Garth said if you don't bring her back, he'll hire someone else to do it."

"That's his prerogative."

"But it'll be too late by then, right?"

Range saw the mischievious gleam in Brandon's eyes. He raised his mouth in a shrug. "Could be."

Brandon looked down at him. "Who would of thought it? Range Connor actually has a heart."

"Or maybe I just didn't find them," Range growled, harsher than he needed to. "So, if you'll excuse us, kid, I'm a little busy right now."

"Really? Well, maybe I'll just ride along," Brandon said. "I could use some fresh air. Especially after that row at the house this morning."

"You're not invited," Range snapped.

Brandon grinned, then made a point of looking around. "Well, you're headed east. I'm riding east. But if you don't want my company, I guess I could just tag along behind you.''

Range threw him a hard glare, then bristled at the defiant smile on Brandon's face.

Twenty minutes later the three had traversed the canyon and paused near its rear wall. Scrubbrush covered a good portion of the canyon floor, and its walls were nothing more than sheer red cliffs.

''So, now what?'' Range asked, looking from the canyon to Elijah. ''It's a dead end.''

''Most canyons are,'' Brandon quipped, bringing another of Range's harsh glares down upon himself.

''Like I asked before,'' Elijah said, looking at Range, ''you sure you want to do this?''

Range's patience nearly snapped, but he caught it in time. ''Yes,'' he said, forcing himself to sound and appear calm.

''Okay.'' Elijah left Sara munching on some wild grass and made his way past several mounds of scrub brush, until he was standing facing the canyon's east wall and a large mound of bramble. He reached out and, grabbing a dried limb, pulled it easily from the wall and threw it aside, then reached for another. ''Could use a little help here,'' he said over his shoulder.

Chapter 19

The opening of a cave soon became apparent.

"Years ago, before all this land was bought up by ranchers, this used to be the Haverton Mine," Elijah said. "I worked here for a while, maybe a year or so, back when I had more kick in my bones."

Range dismounted and began to help the old man move the remainder of the dried brush.

"Hold on," Elijah said, when Range started into the mine. "Let me get my lantern. Too many ways a man can break his neck in there."

"Guess I'll wait here," Brandon quipped.

Elijah sidled back to where Range stood waiting. Holding the lantern up, he struck a lucifer and held the flame to the lamp's candle. "Okay, young fella, guess if you're bent on doing this, we might as well get to it."

Shadows danced off the wall as Elijah's lantern swung in front of him. Dust clogged the air, kicked up from their boots, while here and there something sparkled in the wall in reflection of the lantern's glow.

"Thought there might still be something in here worth mining," Elijah said over his shoulder. "That's why I came back in here last year. But there wasn't."

"You found the crucifix in here?"

"Yep." Elijah paused and pointed down at the ground. "Right here."

Range stared at the bare ground. There was nothing else there. Dirt and a few rocks. That was it. He looked back at the old man, wondering if his memory wasn't as good as he thought it was. "You're sure this was the spot, Elijah?"

"Yep." Elijah chewed on the wad of tobacco he'd tucked into his mouth before entering the cave, and nodded. "Damned near broke my fool leg on that old shovel over there." He pointed to a shovel lying on the ground, so covered with dust it was almost invisible. "Didn't see the danged thing and tripped over it. Thought I was a goner for sure, falling through the air and landing face down in the dirt. That's how I found the cross. About pressed my nose into it when I hit the ground."

Disappointment swelled within Range. This couldn't be the end of it. It couldn't. Her crucifix was here, and she would never have taken it off. That had to mean she was here. "This is all?" Range said. "This is all you didn't think I should see?"

The old man looked at him wearily. "I'm old, boy, not crazy. No, there's something else." He pointed into the mine. "Back there."

"Give me the lantern," Range said, and not waiting for Elijah to move, reached out and took it from the old man's hand. "And stay here. This place looks like it's about to fall in on itself any minute."

"Most likely is," Elijah said.

Range brushed past Elijah and moved deeper into the mine. The tunnel veered to the left. Range felt the ground slanting downward beneath his feet. He held the lantern higher, the pale light barely piercing the darkness more than two feet in front of him. If this thing came to an abrupt dead end, the odds were he'd walk into the wall before he saw it.

The tunnel curved. Range held his hand to the wall, skimming it with his fingertips as he moved. Something ahead caught his eye. He stopped, held the lantern higher, and took another step forward. The breath nearly clogged in his throat when he realized what he was looking at.

"Oh, God." He had known what he'd find, but it still came as a shock. Range ran forward, setting the lantern on the ground as he dropped to one knee.

She was sitting up, her back resting against a wall of rock. The remains of the quilt she'd been wrapped in was now nothing more than a few rotten shreds of faded cloth, as was the dress she still wore. Range stared at what was left of the skirt, and memories flooded his mind. Blue gingham. The pattern and color were barely discernible. Nevertheless, he recognized it. She'd been wearing a blue gingham dress that last night, when she'd stumbled, bleeding and disheveled, into his room and told him to run.

Blue gingham. He reached out and touched the fabric, only to see it crumble to dust beneath his fingers.

"He'll pay, Mama," Range whispered. "I swear to you, he'll pay for what he did." Tears stung his eyes as he remembered the woman who had been so quiet and gentle, who had held him in her arms and rocked him to sleep after he'd had a bad dream, who had sung him lullabies and knelt by his bed each night to join him in his prayers.

Rage filled his heart. She hadn't deserved this.

He wiped at his eyes with the back of one hand and reached for the lantern, then paused as something else caught his eye. He looked down at the skeletal remains of what had once been his mother's hands, resting in her lap. On the fourth finger of her right hand was the intricately designed gold and amethyst ring she'd always worn.

"It belonged to your father's mother, and someday, Nicky, you will give it to your wife."

He slipped the ring from his mother's hand and tucked it into the pocket of his trousers. "I doubt I'll ever have a wife, Mama," he said softly, "I don't live that kind of life, but there is someone I'd like to give this ring to anyway." Wiping away a traitorous tear that slipped from his eye and fell to his cheek, Range started to rise, then stopped as his gaze fell on something that had obviously slipped from her hand as he'd touched it. He stared down at the button, and might have disregarded it, if he hadn't recognized it instantly.

Memories swirled through his mind, feeding the rage that was already seething through his blood.

He remembered the jacket it had once adorned. A lightweight jacket his mother had made for Garth the summer before that night. She'd used the buttons from his army jacket. Range stared down at the button in his hand. Gold buttons, their faces engraved with the image of an eagle. Range's hands trembled. He might not have remembered such a trivial thing, except that one night, shortly after his mother had given Garth the jacket, Garth had caught Jesse wearing it and his temper had flared.

Range pocketed the button and rose to his feet. Everything in him wanted to ride hell-bent for leather back to the ranch and find Garth Murdock. The man didn't deserve one more minute on this earth. Instead, he walked purposely back to the spot in the tunnel where Elijah stood waiting. "Let me borrow your poncho, old man," he said softly.

"You find her?"

"Yes."

Elijah nodded sadly and pulled the old Mexican cape over his head and, shaking it out, handed it to Range. "You need any help?" he asked.

"No," Range said softly. He turned away. "I'll be right back."

Spreading Elijah's poncho on the ground beside the skeletal remains of his mother's body, Range carefully pulled the tattered quilt and his mother's bones onto the once colorful material, rolled it up around her, and collected it in his arms. Standing, he took a deep breath to steady the emotions raging through his body, and carried her toward the entrance of the mine. A sense of satisfaction filled Range. Now, at last, the world would know the truth about his mother, about what had happened that night on the Rolling M, and Garth Murdock would finally pay for what he'd done.

Just as Range and Elijah stepped into the sunlight at the mouth of the mine, several shots rang out.

A bullet hit the wall of rock beside Range and ricocheted wildly. Clutching his grisly treasure to his chest, Range dove for a cluster of large rocks. In one swift move he set Allison Landers Murdock's remains on the ground, drew his guns, rolled partially back into the sight of whoever was shooting at him, and fired his own weapons.

A second later he was back behind the rocks. That's when he noticed that the old prospector was lying facedown in the dirt, and Brandon Gates was slumped over in his saddle.

"Son of a—Brandon," Range whispered.

The younger man didn't move.

"Brandon."

Range glanced over the rock in the direction their assailant's shots had come from. He didn't see anyone, and no bullet came whizzing toward him, but he knew that didn't mean that whoever was out there wasn't just waiting for him to make himself a better target. "Son of a bitch," he hissed. Getting to his feet, but remaining hunched over and firing toward where the shots had come from, Range ran toward Brandon, whose horse was just now starting to prance about nervously and look as if preparing to bolt.

Snatching up the animal's reins, Range put the horse between himself and the shooter. He grappled with the belt strap that was holding Brandon in the saddle. It was the damndest thing he'd ever seen, and there was no time to figure out how to undo it. He pushed the horse toward the cover of the rocks.

The animal threw his head and sidestepped.

"Whoa boy," Range said, trying to calm him. "Take it easy." He pushed again.

The horse snorted, sidestepped again, then finally cooperated.

Once behind the rocks, Range stood still, breathing deeply and listening.

But the only sound he heard was that of silence.

Two Hawks had taught him better than to trust silence, however. It was one way to insure leaving this world a little sooner than one expected. Moving stealthily, Range placed a good-sized rock on the reins of Brandon's horse to keep the animal from bolting away and began making his way down the canyon, weaving in and out between the tall outcroppings of rock and mounds of scrub brush. The shots had come from a small cluster of rock just a short distance away. If he could make his way around whoever it was—and he had very little doubt that it wasn't Garth Murdock—he just might be able to get the drop on the man.

He was almost there when he heard the sound of retreating hoofbeats. Cursing soundly, Range ran into the open. Horse and rider were several hundred yards away. Too far for him to recognize whoever it was who'd been firing at them. But he recognized the horse. It was a large, muscled, and very distinctively marked paint, a horse he'd seen Garth riding just the other day. Range raised his guns and, taking aim, pulled the trigger. But even as he did, he knew his assailant was out of range of his Colts.

Turning, he hurried back to the mouth of the mine. A quick check verified that Elijah Crebbs wouldn't be looking for the big one anymore, unless it was hidden in a cloud somewhere. But Brandon had been luckier. The bullet that had gotten him had merely grazed his temple. He was unconscious, but he'd survive, and when he woke he'd probably have a headache that would more than likely make him wish he was dead.

He needed to get Brandon back to the ranch right away, but he had something else he had to do first. Walking to the mouth of the mine, he dragged Elijah's body inside. Moments later he carried the remains of his mother's body into the mine and laid her down next to Elijah. Then he covered both with the rain poncho he'd taken from his saddlebag and secured it over them with several rocks . . . to keep the coyotes at bay. He would return later for his mother and to bury the old man, but for now he had to see to Brandon.

Range mounted Satan and, taking hold of his reins as well as those of Brandon's horse and the old prospector's mule, he headed back toward the ranch house.

Candace saw the two riders approaching the house, and though they were still a goodly distance away and the shadows of night were quickly overtaking the landscape when she first noticed them, it didn't take long for her to discern who they were. She felt her mouth go dry at realizing that one of them was slumped over in his saddle. Her heart slammed against her breast. Jumping from the porch, she ran to the gate just as they neared it.

"You monster!" she screamed at Range. Tears exploded in her eyes, blurring her vision. A sob ripped from her throat as she grabbed at her brother. "You killed him." Her hands were shaking so badly she couldn't even grasp Brandon's shirt. "How could you?" she sobbed. "How could you?"

He dismounted before the house, but as he walked around Satan and moved to pull Brandon down and into his arms to carry him inside, Candace lunged at him.

Her arms flailed wildly as her fists pummeled him. "How could you?" she screamed. "You're a monster. A monster." Her sobs filled the air.

Range raised an arm to shield himself from her hands. Out of the corner of his eye, he saw Garth and Jesse suddenly appear near the barn. J. D. was hurrying toward them from one of the corrals. Range grabbed Candace's arms, gripping them tightly at her wrists as she writhed and twisted in an effort to get away or hit him.

"Stop it, Candace," he growled softly. "Brandon's not dead."

She stopped instantly and stared up at him, blue eyes meeting blue, and within a heartbeat Candace knew how wrong she'd been to even accuse him of murdering Brandon. Guilt assailed her. Range Connor might be known as a hired gun, a man who killed others for money, but still, she should have known better. He had held her in his arms, his lips had caressed and cajoled hers with such sweet tenderness that for hours afterward, just remembering had sent shivers coursing through her body and desire flaming anew within her loins. Range had made love to her, taken her to a world she had never visited before, a world that was theirs, and theirs alone, a world she wanted to live in forever with him.

Much as she wished it hadn't happened, he had stolen her heart, and because of that she knew he could not be the cold-blooded murderer so many people said he was.

She knew now that even if Brandon *had* been dead, Range would not have been the one who killed him.

He released his hold on her arms so abruptly she nearly stumbled. "Someone shot at us and Brandon was hit, but the bullet only grazed his head. You need to clean the wound, get him into bed," Range said, "and have some ice ready when he wakes. He'll have one hell of a headache."

His eyes were deadly cold as they looked down at her, his stance hard. The man before her was not the same man who had made love to her beneath a star-strewn sky the night before. This was not the man she had lain beside and lost her heart to. This was a man she didn't know.

Hearing footsteps behind her, Candace looked over her shoulder.

Garth and Jesse were approaching.

She looked back at Range, and for a brief, almost infinitisimal second, the coldness in his eyes was gone as he looked back at her. And then it returned.

Turning away from her, he jerked the saddle belt off of her brother and pulled him down into his arms.

"What happened?" Garth said, coming up behind Candace.

"He dead?" Jesse asked, sounding not at all displeased at the prospect.

Range didn't answer. Instead, he turned and carried Brandon up the steps and into the house.

Candace watched him walk away, then glanced at Garth and Jesse, who were staring at Range's back. Suddenly she felt an inexplicable sense of intense fear. The malice shining in Garth's and Jesse's eyes was unmistakable.

Garth turned to her. "What happened?"

She shook her head. "I . . . I don't know. He said some-one shot at them and a bullet grazed Brandon's head."

"So he's alive?" Garth said.

Candace nodded and hurried into the house. In the kitchen she grabbed some rags she'd saved to use for bandages, took some hot water that she'd been boiling to make soup, and, pouring it into a bowl, went into Brandon's room and sat on the bed beside him. She wet one of the rags and dabbed it to the bloody wound on her brother's temple. "Did you find Brianne and Wade?" she asked quietly.

Range had just started to turn toward the door. He paused and looked back at her.

Garth walked into the room before he could answer. The older man glanced down at Brandon, then looked at Range. "How'd this happen?"

"Someone bushwhacked us," Range said.

Garth's eyes narrowed. "Who?"

Range shook his head. "I didn't get a look at them."

"Why?"

He smiled. "Good question. I was going to ask you if *you* knew."

"Me?" Garth snapped. "Why would I know anything about you being bushwhacked?"

Range shrugged. "You're an important man around here. Figured you knew just about everything."

Garth looked back over Candace's shoulder. "He need the doctor?"

She shook her head. "I don't think so."

Twenty minutes later Candace was still sitting on the edge of Brandon's bed, but now she was alone. Garth had gone back to the barn to finish whatever it was he'd been doing in there, and Range had gone, she assumed, to the bunkhouse.

"He saved my life," Brandon whispered softly.

Candace, jerked from the jumble of thoughts that had
been crowding about in her mind, turned to him. "What?"

"He saved my life," Brandon said again. "Connor.
Pulled me to safety."

"What were you doing?" Candace asked, bending close
to him. "Where were you?"

"Out past . . ." Brandon grimaced as pain evidently shot
through his head. "Out past the west field, in a canyon."

"Why? What was there?"

A long hiss slipped from Brandon's lips. "I don't know,"
he said softly. "An . . . an old prospector."

Candace stared down at her brother in confusion. An
old prospector? What did that mean? He'd been with
Range, not an old prospector. Was Brandon hallucinating?
She started to question him further, but it was obvious he
needed to sleep and was in no condition to answer her
questions. Candace rose and, leaving her brother's room,
locked his door behind her, slipping the key into her
pocket. If anyone else wanted to get into his room, they'd
either have to break down the door or break in the room's
lone window. Leaving the house, she headed straight for
the bunkhouse.

Lights were on inside, and several wranglers were still
sitting around a table just finishing their dinner.

But Range wasn't one of them.

J. D. Sharp looked up from his place at the table and
saw her standing in the open doorway. "Men went into
town for a little heehawing, Miss Candace." He rose and
walked toward her. "Something I can do for ya?"

She shook her head. "No, thanks, J. D."

The look on his face as he stared at her was a one of
concern and curiosity. Then he smiled. "You need anything, you just holler, ya hear?"

She nodded and turned away. A light was on in the barn.
She started for it, then paused. Garth and Jesse were most

likely still in there, unless they'd gone into town, too? Candace sighed. She wasn't in the mood for Jesse's sarcasm, and she was even less in the mood for Garth's gruffness, but there was only one way to find out if Range was in there, or if he had gone into town. She stepped from the porch of the bunkhouse and walked to the barn.

When she first entered she didn't hear anything. Then Range's voice, snapping with rage and challenge, whipped out from the back regions of the large building.

Chapter 20

"You murdered her, Murdock," Range growled. "You cold-bloodedly murdered her."

Candace stopped, fear instantly seizing her heart and nearly stopping it. Garth had killed Brianne? The thought momentarily paralyzed her. A groan of despair ripped from the depths of her being, but was suffocated within the airless passage of her throat.

Killed Brianne. Killed Brianne. Killed Brianne. The two words echoed mercilessly through her mind, tormenting her. Her legs threatened to buckle beneath her. Candace reached out for a nearby post to steady herself. A roaring sound, like that of an approaching tornado, drowned out the men's voices as it filled her head and blackness spun around her madly, closing in and threatening to consume her.

"No," Garth said. He shook his head. "No, I didn't. I swear."

"You murdered her."

"She ran off."

"No, she didn't," Range said softly. "I was there, remember?"

"She ran off, she did. I swear. Everyone knows. I came—" Garth paused, his mouth dropped open, and he stared at Range as his words finally sank into Garth's mind. "You were . . . there?"

"You don't recognize me." His tone was as cold as a norther's chilling bite, his words taunting.

Garth's eyes narrowed as his mind spun with the effort to make sense of Range's words, to remember where he had seen a face that was little more than a stranger's. He shook his head. "No, I . . . who are you?"

A cold smile slowly pulled at Range's mouth. He settled his hands on his guns. Readying himself for the inevitable. For what he had been waiting to do for the last twenty-four years. "Nick Landers."

Garth's brow furrowed into a frown. "Nick Landers?" he repeated dumbly.

"Nicky," Range said, prodding the man's memory. "Allison's son. Remember? I escaped through my bedroom window that night, after you'd killed my mother and were breaking down my bedroom door to come after me."

"That's a—" Garth suddenly stopped and looked past Range.

A cold chill snaked its way up Range's back. He knew instantly that someone was behind him. If he hadn't been so preoccupied with making Garth Murdock sweat, he would have known it before it was too late, which it now was.

He waited for the bullet to slam into his back. Then he saw Garth's pallor pale even more, and realized that whoever was standing in the shadows behind him was clearly not a threat to Range. At least, not at the moment. Taking several steps to the side, so that he could see whoever was behind him and still keep an eye on Garth, Range glanced in the direction Garth was staring.

Candace stood clutching a post and staring at her husband. "You murdered his mother?" she said softly. She never would have believed Garth capable of murder. Not like that. Not of killing a woman. But then, she'd never wanted to believe he had wanted Brandon dead ... yet the accidents had continued, Brandon was now in a wheelchair, and a hired gunman, Range Connor, was living at the Rolling M.

Compassion for Range's loss tangled with the relief she felt at discovering they hadn't been talking about Brianne.

Garth instantly shook himself, his gaze darting between Range and Candace. "No, I didn't kill Allison. She left me. You have to believe that."

Candace looked at Range.

"It's the truth," Garth shrieked.

"I was there," Range said softly, looking at Candace. "He beat her because she intended to leave him."

"I would never have hit Allison," Garth said, his tone stronger. "Never."

Range's cold, hate-filled eyes turned on him. "You didn't hit her, Murdock," he fairly snarled, "you *beat* her! You beat her to within an inch of her life, and somehow, God knows how, she managed to get away from you for a few minutes and send me away."

"No," Garth said. He shook his head wildly. "No, no, no. That's not right. No."

The grip Range had on his temper threatened to slip, and he struggled to hold on to it. "Do you know what it's like for a six-year-old boy to cringe in his room and listen to his mother scream while someone's hitting her, Murdock?" His fists clenched as rage rushed through him. "Do you know how helpless a six-year-old child feels then? How terrified?"

A sob broke from Candace's throat. "Oh, no, he couldn't have," she moaned, shaking her head in disbelief.

Range ignored her. "The last time I saw my mother, Murdock, her face was covered with blood and she was crying. She half-crawled, half-ran to my bedroom door, pushing me ahead of her so that you couldn't get me, too. I thought she'd come in and hide with me, hide from you. Instead, when we reached the door, she fell to the floor and died."

Tears stung the back of Range's eyes as the memory filled his mind.

"Oh, my God," Candace whispered, her hands trembling at the story Range was telling.

Range's fiery gaze held Garth's. "I knew she was dead." He paused and drew in a ragged breath. "I watched my mother die, Murdock. And then I heard you coming, stomping your way down the hall toward me. I slammed the door shut and locked it, but that didn't stop you, did it?"

Range smiled then, and Candace knew it was the coldest smile she had ever seen on a human being. A shiver snaked its way up her back and left her arms covered with goose-flesh. She knew she was deeply frightened, but whether her fear was for Garth, or for Range and what he might do, she didn't know.

"I heard the door splinter behind me," Range said, his voice deceptively calm, "but by that time I was already half out the window."

Garth shook his head again. "No, no, I didn't do that. I loved Allison. I loved her."

"You loved her so much you weren't going to let her go. Loved her so much you couldn't stand the thought that she'd leave you when she found out that my father was still alive."

Candace looked from Range to Garth, waiting for him

to say something that would convince her, convince Range,
that he hadn't killed his first wife.

"No, no, listen to me," Garth pleaded. "I—I came home
that day from a business trip, and she was gone. She left
me a note, saying her first husband wasn't dead. He'd
come back and she was returning to him. I—I still have
it, in the clock in my study."

"And you couldn't stand the thought that she'd leave
you for someone else," Range said.

"No, she was already gone when I came home."

Loathing, bitterness, and a burning need for revenge
roiled through Range. Digging into his pocket he brought
out his mother's crucifix and, holding it by the chain,
held it up so that Garth could see it. "Remember this,
Murdock?" he asked. "The crucifix she never took off."

Garth stared at it. "I remember it. She said your father
made it for her."

"It was on her body, Murdock."

Garth's eyes, full of shock, jumped to meet Range's.

"Yeah, I found her body in the mine, right where you
left it."

"The mine?" Garth echoed.

"Did you plan to put Brandon's body in there, too?"

Candace gasped softly.

"And maybe Candace's and Brianne's, once they were
of no use to you anymore? Or when they made you mad
and you beat them to death?"

Garth looked from the crucifix to Candace. "I didn't
kill her. I swear."

Horror and shock held Candace immobile.

Pain twisted Garth's face into an ugly mask of torment.
He looked from Range to Candace wildly. "You can't
believe this," he said again and again.

Range shrugged. "It's the truth."

Suddenly a keening wail, like that of a suffering animal,

broke from Garth's lips, and he dropped to his knees. Bending forward he hugged his hands to his chest and rocked back and forth. Sobs wracked his body.

Range stared down at him, assuming it was just another ploy for sympathy and belief.

Candace, overcome with compassion, took a step toward Garth, then stopped as her gaze met Range's.

"I loved her more than anything," Garth wailed.

"You're not fit to say those words," Range growled.

Garth looked at him through his tears. "She was my wife."

"And you killed her."

"No. I loved her." He looked up at Candace, his face streaked with tears, his lips quivering. "That's why I couldn't love you, Candace. That's why I couldn't really be your husband." He sobbed. "I'm so sorry. I'm sorry, but I still love Allison. I married you as a favor to your father, but not a day has gone by, not a minute passes, that I don't miss Allison. Don't think about her and wish she was here with me." He rocked back and forth. "I fooled myself into thinking our marriage could work, that's why I went through with it for your pa, and after a while, when you didn't seem to mind that I couldn't . . . I still love her." He curled in on himself again, his body wracked with sobs. "I'll always love her."

"Garth, I—" Candace stopped, not sure what it was she'd wanted to say.

A shudder whipped through his body, then he looked up at Range. "Allison was my life. I could *never* have harmed her. Never."

Range looked down at the man he'd hated for twenty-four years. For every day of that time, he'd thought of how he would wreak his vengeance against Garth Murdock. His hate had kept him going. It had fed his will to live, it had given him the strength to survive, and now, for the first time Range found himself questioning his memories, wondering if he'd spent his life hating the wrong man.

His gaze bore into Garth's. No, he decided, hesitation, uncertainty, that was exactly what Garth Murdock wanted him to feel. To get him off guard. Forgetting that Candace was there, Range closed the distance between himself and the other man, grabbed his shirt collar, and hauled him to his feet.

"Why did you hire me?" he demanded savagely, his face a contorted mask of rage.

Garth shook his head, fear now shining in his eyes. "I didn't."

"What do you *mean* you didn't? I got your wire, remember?. You wanted me to come here and kill your brother-in-law, Brandon. But is that all there was to it? Or was there a bullet waiting here for me, too? Did you find out who I was and figure better late than never?"

Candace gasped and grabbed for the post to steady her suddenly violently trembling body. "No," she whispered, staring at Garth. "No."

Garth looked at Candace, then hurriedly back at Range. "I didn't hire you. Jesse did. By the time I found out, you were already here."

Range released him with a shove. "You could have told me not to kill Brandon."

Garth staggered. "I never knew you were *supposed* to kill Brandon. I thought you were here to protect us about the water rights dispute, just like I said. ."

"You're lying."

"No, I'm not. That's what Jesse told me. He said he was afraid the other ranchers would gather against us, and he wanted us to have some protection. He admitted to forging my name on the wire, said he figured it was better the wire came from the owner of the Rolling M, and he was afraid I wouldn't do it."

"And you never suspected anything?"

Garth shrugged. "Maybe I didn't want to."

"So, why would Jesse want Brandon killed? What's in it for him?"

"I don't know," Garth said. "Maybe . . . maybe you just misunderstood. Maybe he really wanted you here just for protection."

Range dug the wire he'd gotten in Wichita from his trouser's pocket and, flipping it open, held it out to Garth. "Does this look like I misunderstood?"

Garth looked at the wire, and finally, his shoulders sagging, he shook his head. "No."

Candace grabbed the paper and looked at it. "Why?" she said, a moment later. "Why?"

Range shrugged. "You tell me. But I know one thing: it was no coincidence that he picked me." He looked back at Garth. "How would Jesse know who I really am?"

Now it was Garth's turn to shrug. "I don't know."

Range thought about the statuette that had been left on his pillow, Jesse's comments about Allison's disappearance, and the note tucked into his holster, reminding him why he was really at the Rolling M.

Then he remembered the looks he'd seen Jesse give Candace when he thought no one else was watching. The warnings he'd issued to Range to stay away from her. Now Range suspected that Jesse's warnings hadn't been admonitions to stay away from his brother's wife, but to stay away from the woman Jesse loved. The woman he had lost to his brother, but still wanted.

Everything Jesse had done had been toward one goal, Range suddenly realized. Jesse wanted it all. He'd hired Range to come to the Rolling M to kill Brandon, so that Brandon wouldn't be able to take over control of Gates End, therefore taking it away from the Murdocks. But somehow he'd known who Range really was. How? his mind screamed.

And then he remembered something Two Hawks had told him more than once. If a man wants something bad enough, there are many ways for him to get it. That could pertain to Range's identity as well.

"Jesse wants it all," Range said. "Not just Gates End. He also wants Candace, most likely always has, and he hates you for having her. And he wants the Rolling M all to himself."

"No." Garth shook his head, not wanting to believe what he was hearing, yet knowing in his heart that it was the truth.

"He didn't lure me here only to kill Brandon," Range said. "He also intended that I kill you."

Range looked at Garth Murdock. If all that was true, did that mean that Garth was telling the truth? Did that mean that Jesse—

Range turned toward the barn door, intent on finding Jesse.

"Range!" Candace suddenly screamed.

With lightning speed, Range reached for his guns as he spun back.

Jesse stood behind Garth, his gun drawn and pointed at his brother's head. "I should have known to just do it myself," he said. Madness gleamed from his eyes.

"Jesse, please," Candace said.

His gaze whipped around to meet hers. "Jesse, *please*," he mocked. "*Please* don't touch me. *Please* don't do that. *Please* don't say those things." He laughed. "Now there won't be any reason to worry about that, Candy. Not after we get rid of these two."

"Jesse, no," Candace said. "You've got to listen to me. You can't—"

"Yes, I can," he snapped. "They have to die. Then we can have it all."

Range moved slowly to his left. If he could get close enough, he might be able to—

"Stop!" Jesse screamed, swinging his gun around and taking aim at Range.

Range stopped.

Garth made a grab for Jesse's gun.

Jesse yanked his hand away, then swung back, hitting Garth in the temple with the barrel of his gun.

Garth jerked back, spun, and fell against the wall. Blood trickled from a large gash on his forehead.

Candace started for him.

"No!" Jesse yelled.

She stopped.

Range cursed under his breath. If she hadn't been there he would have hit the floor and gone for his guns, but he couldn't risk it. He wasn't sure how steady Jesse's hand was. A stray bullet could hit Candace. Even kill her.

Range would rather let Jesse put a bullet through his heart than take the chance of one finding Candace.

"I kept track of you," Jesse said, smiling as he turned back to look at Range again. "Real good track. Bet you didn't know that, did you?"

Range shook his head. "No."

"That general store clerk up in Wichita you used to get your mail from, I'd send him a few bucks, and he'd write me where you'd gone."

Range nodded. He'd never liked that man, but hadn't known why. Now he did.

"But you knew where I was before that," Range said, guessing.

"Yeah. I saw you once at Fort Weatherford, long time ago. You were still just a kid, sixteen or so, and you were with some old man. But you didn't see me, I made sure of that. I made a few inquiries, found out who the old geezer was and what name you were using. But I never told anyone what I learned." He reached out and nudged Garth's shoulder with the end of his gun. "Never told you, did I, big brother?"

"No," Garth said softly, his brow furrowed in obvious pain from the blow to his head.

"No," Jesse mocked. "Because I figured there'd come a time when I could use that information for myself." An ugly giggle broke from his lips and he nudged Garth again, harder this time. "See, big brother, and you thought I was just stupid ol' Jesse, didn't you?"

"I never thought you were stupid," Garth said.

Jesse struck Garth with the gun again, jamming it into his shoulder and nearly knocking him over. "Yes, you did. You're always calling me stupid. Telling me I'm wrong, can't do things right. But you know now, don't ya, big brother? I ain't the one who's stupid."

Range stepped forward.

Jesse swung the gun back toward him. "Tsk tsk," he said, and laughed. "You know, I knew Allison was leaving. She wrote Garth a note. Left it on his desk. I heard her tell her kid—" he looked at Range, "you, that she had to talk to Garth that night when he got home, then afterwards she said her and Nicky were going to leave and go on a trip." Jesse chuckled. "But I couldn't let her leave."

"You?" Garth said, as if he hadn't thought of that possibility before.

"Yeah, big brother," Jesse sneered. "Me. I knew she was going to leave you, and you wouldn't do a damned thing about it. Whatever made little Allison happy, that's all you cared about, even if it meant leaving you. But she would have taken all her money, and we needed that. So . . ." he shrugged.

"Her money?" Range echoed.

Jesse threw Range a disdainful glare. "Yes, her money," he snapped. "This place was nothing before Garth married her. A worthless piece of desert. But she gave him money to fix it up, buy cattle. Hell, she even paid for building the house. All we had was a damned one-room sod shack. I knew if she left she'd want her money back, or make us sell the ranch. We'd lose everything."

"So you killed her instead," Range said.

"Well," Jesse smiled slyly, "I tried to reason with her first. Tried showing her just how appreciative I could be, you know? She slapped me. Then she said she was going to tell Garth what I'd done."

"So you killed her."

"Yeah," Jesse sneered, "I killed her. And I put that stupid button from Garth's jacket in her hand when I left her out in that mine, so if anyone ever found her they'd figure she ripped it off of whoever killed her."

"Very smart move," Range said, playing for time.

Jesse preened, puffing out his chest. "I thought so, too. And since it was Garth's jacket," he poked Garth with the gun again, "one he'd shown off to lotsa people 'cause sweet little Allison had made it for him, I figured people would remember that button and blame him for killing her." He jammed the gun hard into Garth's shoulder. "Remember that jacket, big brother? Remember how you nearly beat me to death 'cause I wore it that one time?" He laughed.

"Put down the gun, Jesse," Garth said.

"Put down the gun, Jesse," he mocked. His face instantly contorted to an expression of disdain. "I should have killed you years ago, Garth. You're weak. A real spineless good-for-nothing."

* * *

J. D. stood at the barn's entry door, hidden within the shadows. He'd been on his way in to brush and bed down his horse, but had stopped short at the door upon hearing Jesse's voice and realized instantly that something was wrong. A few minutes later he'd stealthily drawn his rifle from its saddle sheath. Everything was finally coming together. All the questions were at last being answered. He gripped his gun tightly, but he couldn't get a clear shot at Jesse without taking the risk of hitting Candace.

Range watched Jesse. A wildness glistened in his eyes as he waved his gun around and boasted of what he'd done.

Garth looked like the blow to his head was leaving him barely able to maintain consciousness. No sooner did the thought register in Range's mind, than he saw the older man sway dangerously and reach for the wall.

"We'll be happy together, Candace," Jesse said. "You'll see. If your pa hadn't said no to me when I asked for your hand, I wouldn't have had to shoot him, and you'd of been married to me all this time, instead of Garth."

Candace gasped in horror. "You—you killed my father?"

"Well, he said no," Jesse whined. "And he had no right. We was in love, you and me."

"Jesse, I never—"

"Your pa saw that, too, but he didn't like me and he said no anyway. Said I wasn't good enough for you, I wouldn't amount to nothing. I knew he wouldn't change his mind, so I had to get rid of him. I figured it was the only way we could be together, like we wanted. So, I waited for him on the side of the road that night. Hid in the bushes along the road and didn't shoot 'til he went by, so it would look like a robbery or something. Course," he shrugged, "I didn't know he'd live awhile, then make you marry Garth. But I'll make it up to you, having to be married to him." He shoved his gun barrel into Garth's shoulder again.

Range looked at Candace and his heart nearly stopped. She was glaring at Jesse as if at any second she was going to throw herself at him and scratch his eyes out. He knew then that he had to do something and do it quick, because if he didn't, and soon, it would be too late.

As if knowing exactly what Range was thinking, Jesse suddenly turned his gun on him and cocked its hammer.

Chapter 21

He could make a play for Jesse and end up dead, or he could just stand there and wait—and most likely end up dead. He had nothing to lose. But at least if he tried to get Jesse first, he might save Candace.

Garth moved and Jesse swung his gun toward him.

It was the chance Range had been waiting for. His hands moved toward his guns.

But Jesse had already started to turn back toward him, saw what he was attempting to do, and pulled the trigger of his own gun.

Candace screamed as the explosion of gunfire filled the barn.

The bullet slammed into Range's thigh and knocked his leg out from beneath him.

"No," Candace screamed, rushing toward Range as he staggered back up and fought to remain on his feet.

J. D. ran forward, but made certain to stay out of Jesse's view. He cursed himself for waiting to make a move and feared the worst, but even as he neared where they stood, he could see that a clear shot at Jesse was impossible. He pressed his back to the tack room and watched, praying Jesse would move just a little to one side or the other, so that he could see past Candace and Range for a clear shot.

"Get away from him," Jesse screamed, love and hatred suddenly melding in his mind as he glared at Candace. "You love me, not him. Me! You hear? Me!"

Candace whirled on him, placing herself between Jesse and Range. "No, I don't," she screamed back. "I've never loved you. And I never will!"

Ignoring the searing pain in his leg, Range reached out to push her aside. "Don't," he said softly, fearing her rejection would only antagonize Jesse and put her in more danger than she was already in.

She slapped at his hand, evading his effort to pull her back toward him, then, as Range staggered and stepped to one side, Candace did likewise, making certain she stayed between him and Jesse.

Jesse pointed his gun at Candace's heart. "Drop your guns, Connor, or I'll kill her."

"You don't want to do that," Range said, his tone soft and deceptively suggestive. "You love her."

Jesse smiled. "Not anymore. Anyway, she doesn't love me. She ran to you." He pulled back the hammer on his gun. "Now drop your guns."

Range released the buckle of his holster, then reached down to pull his thigh ties loose. Holding the buckle, he let the holster's other end swing loose, then dropped it to the ground. "Okay, Jesse," he said, "now let Candace go."

"Let her go?" Jesse repeated. He laughed. "She has to die now. Just like you."

"Jesse," Garth yelled. "Don't."

"Don't," Jesse mimicked, swinging his gun on Garth.

His eyes narrowed. "I don't need any of you. But especially not her."

He turned the gun on Candace again.

Garth pushed himself away from the wall and lunged at his brother.

Seeing Garth's attempt out of the corner of his eye, Jesse stepped back quickly, swung his gun around, and fired.

The bullet struck Garth's chest and stopped him in his tracks. A look of disbelief swept over his face, and then he slumped to the floor.

Candace screamed.

Jesse laughed, then looked back up at Candace. "He should have known better," he said gleefully. "I always was faster than him."

Range reached out and, grabbing Candace by the forearm, pulled her back and forced her behind him. He could feel the blood seeping from the wound in his thigh. Worse, he could feel his head getting light, his senses threatening to leave him; he fought with all he had in him to ward off the hovering blackness. He couldn't pass out. If he did, there would be no one to protect Candace, and there was no telling what Jesse would do to her now that she'd spurned him.

He swayed slightly, and Candace clutched his arm.

As if in answer to Range's speculation, hatred emanated from Jesse. "We need to go to the house," he said, waving his gun in the direction of the barn door. "I think we're going to have us a little accidental fire. You two, and that good-for-nothing in the wheelchair."

"Jesse, please," Candace said.

He grinned. *"Jesse, please, Jesse, please.* Too late, Candy. I don't love you anymore." He waved the gun at them again and laughed madly. "Now move, or I'll just shoot you right here and drag you both to the house."

* * *

J. D. backed away from the barn's entry, knowing he was going to have to get a better vantage point if he wanted to take Jesse without Candace and Range getting shot in the process. A little help wouldn't hurt either.

He ran to the bunkhouse, burst through the door, and cussed. It was empty. He looked around dumbly, then remembered that today had been payday. The boys had all gone into town.

Moving to the window, he knelt on a chair and, resting his rifle's barrel on the thick adobe windowsill, waited.

Candace exited the barn first.

J. D. spit the wad of tobacco he'd been chewing into the spitoon that sat on the floor near his feet, and slowly pulled back on the rifle's hammer.

Range appeared next, his hands held up in the air.

J. D. bent and placed his face next to the rifle's stock, closing one eye to peer with the other down the rifle's scope. His finger curled around the trigger.

Then, just before Jesse stepped into view, J. D. saw the gun barrel pressed to the small of Range's back.

Jesse came into view.

J. D. cursed softly and straightened. There was no way he could fire now without taking the risk that the minute his bullet hit Jesse, the finger Jesse held on the trigger of his gun would contract during a death throe. If that happened, Range was a dead man, and J. D. hadn't waited all these years just to see that take place.

But he might get a clear shot yet. J. D. bent down again, getting into position to fire, just in case. He took careful aim.

Suddenly Range stopped.

Jesse yelled at him to move.

Instead, Range turned and faced him.

J. D.'s finger held to the trigger, waiting for an opportunity.

"Let her go," Range said. "Your brother's dead. Kill me, but let her go."

"No," Candace said.

Jesse laughed. "Sorry, Connor, but I don't want her anymore. And she knows too much now. She'd tell."

"No, she wouldn't," Range said, throwing Candace a look that was clearly meant as a warning for her to remain silent.

"Yes, I would," she contradicted, glaring at Jesse. "I'd tell everybody."

Range sighed in frustration. If they managed to get out of this somehow, he was going to have to remember to wring her neck. Of course, that would be after he dragged her up against him and ravaged her lips, just as a way to reassure himself they were still alive.

J. D. wiped his brow.

"Get movin', Connor," Jesse yelled.

Range started to turn toward the house.

The sun reflected off something around his neck. The bright flash of light shot out and nearly blinded J. D. for a split second.

He jerked back and cursed, then unconsciously touched the silver cross that had hung around his own neck, for the past thirty-three years. A gift from the woman he'd loved.

Range led the way up the front steps of the house. Candace followed alongside of Jesse, who had his gun pressed to Range's back again and held Candace's forearm tightly with his free hand.

"Brianne will know what you've done when she gets back," Candace said, in an effort to dissuade him.

Jesse laughed. "Brianne's dead. Garth sent your gunman out to see to that."

Range heard Candace's gasp.

"But I didn't do it," Range said.

"I don't believe you."

They neared the door.

Candace prayed Brandon had overheard them or seen them from the window, and had his gun drawn, ready for Jesse.

"It's true," Range said. "I caught up with them, then let them go. I even covered up their tracks so you and Garth, or whoever else he sent out there, couldn't follow them."

"You're a hired gun," Jesse said. "You wouldn't do that."

Range chuckled. "Haven't you ever heard, Jesse? Hired gunmen do just about anything they want."

"Then I'll just have to kill her, too, and that worthless piece of nothing she ran off with. Who'll care? No one will be left around here to miss them."

Range unlatched the door.

Jesse shoved him in the back, pushing him inside.

He dragged Candace in after him.

J. D. ran to the side of the house. For twenty-two years he's been working on the Rolling M, hating Garth Murdock and trying to find out what the man had done to Allison and Nicky. Staying there, at the last place Allison and Nicky had been known to be, had been the only way he could think of to try and uncover the truth. For years he'd prayed she'd come back, while at the same time he'd known she never would have voluntarily left, not without him. He'd waited for Garth to slip, to give something away about what had happened that night, but he never had.

J. D. had almost given up hope of ever uncovering the truth. Demanding answers of Garth would have been, he'd always known, futile. Then Range Connor had ridden onto the ranch, and the moment J. D. had seen him, the pieces of the puzzle had instantly started to fall into place.

Jedidiah Dellos Landers had never seen his son. He'd been at sea when Nicholaus had been born, but he'd only needed to take one look at Range Connor to know that he was looking at Nicky.

And that first night, when he'd caught a glimpse of the cross around the gunman's neck, he'd known all his instincts had been right. That's why he'd left the figurine on Range's pillow. He hadn't dared come out and say anything, for fear someone would overhear or that he would put his own son in danger, but he'd wanted Range to know that someone else was there that knew the truth, and would help him if need be.

Climbing onto the gallery, J. D. moved to a window on the side of the parlor. He would most likely only have one shot at Jesse, but he'd already lost his wife to a Murdock, and had lost his son for thirty years. He wasn't about to let a Murdock kill Nicky now that he'd finally found him, therefore that one shot had to be perfect.

"Where's the cripple?" Jesse said, as they entered the house.

"Upstairs," Candace said. "In bed."

Jesse smiled. "Well, go get him."

Candace turned.

"No," Jesse snapped, looking toward the corner. "Looks like there ain't no need."

Candace saw Brandon sitting in his wheelchair, obviously having just awakened from a nap, and she nearly groaned. How had he gotten downstairs?

Jesse pointed his gun at Candace's head. "Drop that gun you got hidden under that lap blanket, kid, or I'll kill her."

Brandon glared at him.

"I said drop it!"

Brandon's gun hit the floor.

Jesse smiled. "Good."

He looked at Candace. "You know, if he'd have just fallen off that horse the way he was supposed to, he woulda broke his neck and be dead already."

Brandon suddenly pushed on the wheels of his chair and shot across the room toward Jesse. But he wasn't fast enough. Jesse spun and, throwing out the hand that gripped his gun, slammed it into Brandon's face.

The impact sent Brandon jerking back. His chair toppled and Brandon lay sprawled on the floor.

"Brandon!" Candace screamed, starting forward.

"No," Jesse said, stopping her. He threw a disdaining look at Brandon. "Stupid kid."

"Jesse, please, don't do this," Candace said.

He whirled on her. "Please don't do this? *Please don't do this?*" he mocked. "This is all your fault, Candy! You ruined everything, you know? And after I worked so hard to make it all perfect for you. For us. We could have been together, like we were supposed to be. We'd have had it all, Candace. The Rolling M, Gates End, everything. But you ruined it."

"I . . . I'm sorry, Jesse, really," she said, trying to buy them time. "I didn't know."

"Yes, you did, but you didn't care," he snapped back, sounding like an angry child. "You knew all along what I was doing, I know you did."

"No, I—"

Range stepped behind Candace. If he could block Jesse's view of his hands by standing behind her skirts, he might be able to get to the knife hidden in his boot.

"You did!" Jesse yelled. "You knew I killed Allison. And you knew I shot your Pa and cut the strap on Brandon's saddle so he'd fall and die. You knew!"

Fury swept through Candace and made her blind to

caution. "I'll kill you," she screamed, and lunged toward him.

Range moved fast and grabbed her. "No," he said softly.

The room suddenly spun around him. Pain filled his leg and groin. He tried to lift his leg in order to reach his boot without bending. The room tilted. Range fought to stay on his feet, but couldn't help but sway.

Candace felt him falter and whirled about, fear for him filling her and causing her to momentarily forget about Jesse.

"Range," she said, "are you all right?" She gripped his shoulders.

He held on to the back of a chair.

"Who cares if he's all right?" Jesse screamed. "He's gonna die."

Candace ignored him.

Candace and Range stood between J. D. at the window and Jesse, preventing J. D. from getting a clear shot.

"Candace, come here," Jesse ordered.

"You've lost a lot of blood," Candace said, looking down at Range's leg.

"And he's going to lose a hell of a lot more right now, Candace," Jesse yelled, "if you don't come here."

She spun around, her eyes burning with hatred at her former brother-in-law. "How could you do this?" she demanded.

He grinned. "Well, I started off doing it for us."

"You're an animal."

"And you're a slut."

She took a step forward. "How could you murder all those people, Jesse?" she said softly. "Your own brother?"

He laughed, and the maniacal sound sent a chill up her spine.

Range reached out and grabbed her arm. "Don't," he whispered.

Suddenly the room's shadows began to close in on him and, as if it couldn't stand his weight any longer, his injured leg buckled beneath him and he dropped to one knee.

J. D.'s finger tightened slightly on the trigger of his rifle, but Candace was still standing in his way.

Furious, Jesse paced hurriedly about the room. "Come here," he screamed at Candace. "Come here right now."

Range fought off the dizziness. If he succumbed, there would be no waking up, no tomorrow. It would be all over . . . forever.

He didn't care so much for himself, but he couldn't let that happen to Candace. Trying to move without drawing Jesse's attention, Range reached down into his boot. His fingers searched for the knife, but as he found its blood-covered handle and his fingers curled around it, he tried to pull it out and it slipped from his grasp.

"I wouldn't come to you if you were the last man on earth," Candace said, glaring defiantly at Jesse. She started to take a step forward.

Range stopped her. "Be still," he whispered urgently.

"What happened to you, Jesse?" Candace taunted, hoping she could buy enough time so that whatever Range was attempting to do behind her would work. "Didn't your mother love you as much as Garth? Did your father beat you? What happened to turn you into an animal, Jesse?"

"Stop it," he screamed. "Stop it." Throwing his arms around wildly, he knocked over a table, a vase, and finally a lamp. Its etched glass shade shattered instantly. Shards and splinters of glass flew everywhere. The lamp's brass base fell over and hit floor.

Oil flew from the base, soaking the rug and splashing onto the simmering embers in the fireplace. Flames instantly exploded in the grate and shot out of the fireplace like hungry, scalding, menacing tongues.

Candace screamed.

Fire touched the dried flowers on the mantel and they burst into flame. It reached out and caught the edge of the drapes that covered a nearby window. Within seconds the entire window was surrounded by flame.

Jesse laughed. "This is perfect," he crowed.

Candace glanced frantically toward where Brandon lay unconscious, and tried to jerk away from Range. "We've got to—"

"No," he snarled under his breath, and held her firm. He tried to grab for his knife again.

Before she knew what was happening, Jesse closed the distance between them and grabbed her, jerking her free of Range's grasp. "I've waited so long, Candace, maybe before you die you should at least share your favors with me, huh? Don't you think?"

She struggled against him.

"I mean," he laughed, "after all, I've waited long enough and done enough to earn them, you know?"

"Never," she said, trying to jerk away. "I'll die first."

He laughed. "Oh, you'll die all right, but not first."

"Drop your gun, Jesse," J. D. said.

Jesse whirled around and looked straight into the barrel of J. D.'s rifle. "This ain't none of your business, old man," Jesse sneered.

"Yes, it is."

Jesse laughed. "You can't even put a horse with a broken leg out of his misery, you old coot," Jesse sneered, "so I doubt you've got the courage to pull that trigger on me."

"Don't count on that, Jess," J. D. said over the sounds of flames crackling behind them and spreading up the wall.

Jesse's eyes narrowed.

"Allison was my wife," J. D. said.

Range's startled gaze shot to J. D.'s.

"And Nick there is my son."

"Nick?" Jesse echoed.

J. D. smiled. "Range."

Candace coughed on the smoke that had started to fill the room.

Jesse jerked Candace to him. "Get back, old man, or I'll kill her." He swung his gun back and forth between Range and J. D.

"Your killing days are over," J. D. said.

Jesse aimed at J. D.'s chest.

Candace yanked away and slapped at Jesse's hand.

"You bitch." He pushed her away and fired.

The bullet pierced J. D.'s shoulder. At that same moment he pulled the trigger on his rifle, but as he was thrown back from the impact of the bullet, his own went awry, slamming into the ceiling.

Range lunged at Jesse, his knife gripped tightly in his blood-covered hand.

Jesse whirled, ready to fire again.

Suddenly another shot exploded within the small room.

Jesse's eyes bulged, and a shriek ripped from his lips. He staggered forward a step, then fell.

Shocked, everyone turned to see Karalynn standing in the doorway, Brandon's gun in her hand.

Smoke swirled around them, but for several moments no one moved.

Karalynn stared down at Jesse's prone body. "He swore he loved me," she said softly. "And he lied."

Candace coughed. "The fire," she said, choking and waving a hand in front of her face. "It's spreading."

"Get out," J. D. yelled, then ran to help Range.

"I'm okay, help the women." Turning, Range limped to where Candace was kneeling, trying to drag her brother toward the door. "Go," he said, and pulled her aside.

J. D. grabbed Candace's arm and urged her toward the door.

Range hauled Brandon up and, grimacing against his own pain, slung the younger man over his shoulder. Candace ran beside him as he crossed the yard toward the bunkhouse, then dropped to one knee, and let Brandon slip to the ground.

She looked at her brother. "Is he . . . ?"

"He's all right," Range said, after checking him. "His jaw might be broken, but that'll mend."

Candace looked at Range. "I thought Jesse was going to kill you," she said softly.

"So did I."

With tears filling her eyes, Candace slipped into his arms, pressing herself against him.

Range held her tight, closing his eyes and wishing the moment could last forever. But he was no fool. She had touched a part of him that no other human being had ever come close to even finding. She had made him feel again, made him want to live, made him want things he knew he could never have. He had fallen in love with her, but he couldn't pretend that there was a future for them, because he knew there wasn't.

He was a hired gun. A killer. A man who had nothing to offer. A man who every young buck in the country wanted to challenge and bring down in order to make a name for himself. That would never end. There would always be somebody with a gun hunting him, daring him, forcing him to fight or die.

That was all he had to offer her, and Candace deserved better.

Garth Murdock hadn't been able to love her, but he'd given her a home and, until now, security.

Range could offer her love, but he had no home, and he'd never have security.

Pulling away, he looked down into her eyes. "Are you all right?" he asked softly.

She nodded.

"Then I guess we'd better tend to Brandon and get you two into town, find someplace to stay."

"No, we can go to Gates End," Candace said. "We've kept the house up, and the outbuildings. We can all stay there."

There was nothing wrong with the bunkhouse, no reason for her to have included him in that comment. He looked at her sharply, and Candace knew he was thinking the same thing. But a moment ago, where there had been softness and warmth in his eyes, the chilling hardness had slowly begun to return.

Range shook his head. "No," he said. "Someone has to ride into town and tell the sheriff what happened here."

But it doesn't have to be you, she wanted to cry, suddenly afraid that if he went, if she didn't stop him somehow, she would never see him again. It was a gut instinct, and it frightened her more than anything she'd experienced to this point in her life.

He was going to leave her.

"I can send one of the wranglers," Candace said softly, forcing the words past her dry throat. "Or J. D."

"No," Range said, glancing back at the still burning house. It had gone up quickly. If they hadn't gotten out when they did, they might not have gotten out at all. He stared at the flames, dancing hungrily, devouring every board and post within its grasp, leaping out through every crevice of the house where his mother had died, as if reaching out for more wood, more lives. Maybe it would have been better if he hadn't gotten out. He'd cheated death twenty-four years ago in that house. And he'd cheated it dozens of times since in so many towns across the prairie he couldn't even remember them all, or even the faces of the men he'd faced down. Maybe it would have been better if, this time, he had lost.

Range looked back at Candace, at the only woman who had ever managed to touch his heart, who had made him feel things he had never felt, had never thought to feel. Dying would have been easier than leaving her was going to be.

But he had a feeling that now, since he'd satisfied the need for revenge that had been his mainstay for so long, his reason for fighting to survive, forever wasn't really going to be that long for him. And that was all right, because he knew that the feelings she had awakened within him, the image of her that he would carry in his mind, the love and loss he would carry in his heart, would be a slow torment he could do without.

"Wh . . . what happened?" Brandon said, pushing himself up from the floor.

J. D. looked down at him. "You ran into Jesse's gun."

Brandon flexed his jaw.

Range continued to look down at Candace, ignoring the pain in his leg, the lightness in his head, and imprinting the image of her face in his mind and heart.

Tears shimmered in her eyes as she held his.

She knew he was going to leave. He could see the acknowledgement in the blue depths, behind the glistening veil of tears. Range swallowed hard, wanting to take the hurt from her eyes, but knowing he would cause even more to be there if he relented and stayed.

Agony tore at his soul, but he refused to change his mind. He couldn't, because he knew that eventually, sooner or later, he would only bring her trouble and heartache.

The roof of the house suddenly caved in with a loud crash. Brandon jerked his head up. "Damn," he muttered, staring at the fire consuming the house. He turned to his sister. "Like I said, what the heck happened?"

Candace tore her gaze reluctantly from Range's. She wanted to throw herself back into his arms, to hold him to her and never let him go. She wanted to plead with him to stay, because she feared she was right, and he was going to leave. Instead, she turned to Brandon. "I'll tell you later," she said, reaching out to touch his already discoloring jaw. A sad smile pulled at her lips. "Are you up to riding home?"

Chapter 22

"Thought I'd go on out to California," Range said. He stared down into his cup and inhaled the aroma of the strong, dark coffee, then swirled it around. "New land, new opportunities," Range continued. "I hear there's still plenty of places out there where a man can lose himself forever, then start over."

He took a drink of the coffee, put his cup on the table, and stretched his injured leg. The bullet had missed his bone, but had managed to rip up a couple of muscles. He swung the leg out and back again, then pressed his foot on the floor, testing the level of pain the gesture sent up his leg.

It had been three days since Jesse's and Garth's deaths. The sheriff had wrapped up his investigation and was satisfied that no one had been murdered. At least no one this time. The story of Allison Landers Murdock's long-ago fate was something else again. That had undoubtedly shocked the sheriff, and Range had no doubt the news had spread through Tombstone and probably beyond like locusts over a prairie crop. J. D. had taken on overseeing the ranch operations, and the wranglers had started rounding up the cattle for branding.

But Range hadn't seen Candace. She was at Gates End, and he had figured it was best he stay away from her. But the impact of not seeing her, not being near her, was more profound than he'd expected. It tore him up inside, and sometimes he felt certain it hurt worse than if a bullet had ripped into his gut, but he would live with it . . . because he had to.

J. D. sat with his chair balanced on its rear legs, one booted foot propped on the edge of the table, and stared silently at the son he'd been waiting over thirty years to meet. He had Allison's eyes. Those deep blue, almost mid-night black eyes that were as infinite as forever, and the expression of every feeling in the heart that went along with them. J. D. felt a stab of the old pain creep back over him at the thought of his wife. In all the years since she'd disappeared, there had never been anyone else for him. He'd known she was dead. That night she was supposed to meet him and didn't show up, he'd felt it, and something in him had died, too. But he'd tried to ignore it, reason the feeling away, reassure himself that he was merely imagining things because he was nervous. The next afternoon, how-ever, when he heard the first stirrings of rumor rippling through town about Garth Murdock's wife running off with a peddler, he'd known the feeling had been right. But all of his searches led nowhere. He'd stayed around Tombstone for a while, then finally got a job at the Rolling M, hoping that one day Garth Murdock would give himself away, and J. D. would discover the truth of what happened to his wife and son.

He had hoped . . . J. D. paused in his thinking, looked at his grown son, and suddenly realized that he wasn't

Nicholaus Landers. Nicholaus was a name on a letter Allison had sent him telling of the birth of their son, who had been given the name they'd chosen in case the child was a boy. Elizabeth was the name they had agreed upon if the child was a girl.

But, since father and son had never met until just recently, Nicholaus Landers was merely an image in J. D.'s mind, not a memory. Range Connor, however, was real. He was a hired gunman, a bounty hunter, and a wanted man, but he was also J. D.'s son. And he was a man J. D. liked and respected, which was saying a lot, since J. D. could just about count on the fingers of one hand how many people he'd come to like and respect over the last thirty-four years.

Range wouldn't stay at the Rolling M. He wouldn't even stay in Arizona, but deep down J. D. couldn't deny that he had also known that Range's staying was impossible. There were too many men out there looking for "the gunman who was as fast as Wyatt Earp." Some of those hunting him were after the various bounties on his head. Some wanted to hire him to kill someone. And still others wanted nothing more than to call him out, draw him down, and make a name for themselves.

It was a life with very little promise, and no future except death.

As he had been doing for days, J. D. cursed the heavens and whoever was up there controlling things. If he hadn't gone to France all those years ago, if he hadn't stood up for that barmaid when the Duke slapped her for spilling his drink, if he hadn't called the judge at his trial a pompous fool, he would have been there to save his wife . . . to raise his son . . . to keep them safe.

But hindsight never did anyone any good. And now he was going to lose his son again.

Range looked at J. D. "Thought maybe you'd like to

come along. We could get to know one another." Range turned away and looked out the bunkhouse's window at the charred remains of the ranch house. "If you want," he added.

J. D. took a swallow of his coffee, then slowly shook his head. "Much as I'd like to, I'm afraid I can't leave here," he said. "Leastways, not just now."

Range looked back at the older man and nodded thoughtfully. "What will you do?"

J. D. removed his foot from the table and let his chair settle back onto all four legs. "Brandon's going to be going up to Boston to see if the doctors there can help him walk again. Ol' Doc Swaydon was out at Gates End this morning to check on that wallop the kid took on the head. Doc told Candace about some experiments he heard were taking place up north that might help Brandon."

"You're going to Boston with him?"

J. D. smiled and shook his head. "Nah. Wade Hawkins wired the sheriff the other day. After hearing what happened, they're coming back, so they'll probably go with Brandon. Either that, or Candace will go." He watched Range closely for a reaction, but when he got none, J. D. went on. "I'm gonna be staying here. Candace needs someone to run the ranches for her, at least until either Brandon comes back and can do it or—"

He knew how Candace and Range felt about each other, even if they didn't, and wondered for the hundredth time if there wasn't some way things could work out. "Or she finds herself a husband," he finished.

Nodding, Range stood. Everything in him wanted to stay, screamed at him to stay, urged him to stay, but he knew he couldn't. All he would be doing was bringing trouble onto the people he cared about, and he wasn't going to do that. "Then I guess there's no reason for me to stay any longer."

J. D. stood, the old, unsettling sense of loss washing over him anew. "You're leaving now?"

Range looked at his father. They'd been cheated out of a lot, but they had shared at least two things: an unquenchable need to know the truth and see justice done, and love for a woman remembered, but long gone. In the short time they'd known each other, Range had come to realize that J. D. Landers had more guts and courage than any man Range had ever met. He was going to regret not being able to better know this man whose blood flowed through his own veins. But maybe someday they'd meet again. "No. I'll get a good night's sleep, and leave first thing in the morning."

"I'll be over at the ranch house," J. D. said. "Gates End. Come by before you leave, and I'll have some supplies ready for you."

Range shook his head and turned to walk to the window. The acrid smell of burnt wood still hung heavy on the air. "I don't think that's a good idea."

J. D. stared at his son's back. He knew the pain Range was in, even if he didn't want to admit it. He knew, because he'd gone through it. Losing the woman you loved was about the hardest thing a man had to go through, but when he was willingly leaving her . . . J. D. sighed. That had to be an even deeper pain, knowing you could have her, but you can't. He took a deep breath. "You have to say goodbye to her, Range. You owe her that much. And you owe it to yourself."

Range didn't answer.

"I didn't get to say goodbye to your mother," J. D. said. His voice broke and he paused to clear his throat.

Range turned to look at him.

"Don't make that mistake with Candace," J. D. continued. "At least say goodbye."

"It would be better if we didn't see each other again."
J. D. shook his head. "You're wrong."

Range was up and ready to go long before dawn broke
over the horizon. But after mounting Satan, instead of
heading west, or even to Gates End, he rode out to the
mine where the old prospector had led him to Allison
Landers's remains, and died for his trouble. He didn't go
inside, however. There was nothing left in there. Instead,
Range walked to the top of a nearby hill, hunkered down,
and waited for the sun to rise above the distant mountains.

Its light silhouetted the mountain peaks long before it
turned the black sky blue and chased away the stars. Memories filled his mind, like an ever changing kaleidoscope of
images and scenes, all crowding together, each demanding
to be seen and heard.

Good times and bad, happy times and some so sad they
nearly brought tears to his eyes, were all there to be seen
and remembered. Times with his mother. Times with Two
Hawks and Range's Indian mother, Little Dove, and times
with Old Connor, the scout. They had all taught him something different, contributing to the man that he was today.
Each had given him the best part of themselves, but he'd
taken their gifts and buried them deep within himself,
hiding them from the world, even from himself, and had
allowed his need for revenge to take over his life.

None of them would be proud of what he'd become.

Range threw down the pebble he'd been rolling about
between his fingers and shot to his feet. No one would be
proud of what he'd become.

He paced the hilltop. He had come here to say a final
goodbye to his mother, figuring it was as good a place as
any. Instead, he was sitting here reliving the past. All of it.
And that was something he didn't want to do. Something

he'd never before allowed himself to even consider. Yet today it served a purpose. Painful as it was, it kept thoughts of Candace at bay, kept the pain that gnawed at his gut—whenever he thought of never seeing her again—at a tolerable level.

Range looked up at the sun peeking over the mountains in the distance, its brilliant glow like a burst of gold on the horizon. How many sunrises had he watched alone? How many more would he experience? Once that last question had been important to him. Now it wasn't. He didn't care. There was no purpose to his tomorrows anymore.

He stood and walked back down the hill to where Satan stood waiting. It was time to say goodbye.

Thirty minutes later he rode through the gate leading to Gates End. The drive was long, but the house at its end was clearly visible. It had been built of adobe rather than clapboard, and its walls were the color of the desert, so it resembled a hacienda. Its windows had green shutters, drawn back, and the house stood two stories, with verandas visible through large, arched pillars.

J. D. was standing in front of the house, watching him approach.

Range tried to ignore the knot coiling hot and tight in the pit of his stomach. In the next few minutes he would say goodbye to everything he wanted: his father, a home, a normal life. But most of all he'd say goodbye to the woman he knew he would love forever. He would say goodbye, turn his back, and ride away. Because he had no choice.

The knot tightened.

"I'm glad you came," J. D. said. "I have to admit, I was afraid you wouldn't."

Range looked down at him. He suddenly felt empty. "When you get done here . . ."

"I'll come to California," J. D. said.

"When I light somewhere, I'll let you know."

J. D. nodded, then placed a hand on Range's thigh. "How's the leg?"

"I'll live."

J. D. nodded again and turned away. "Take care, son," he said softly.

"Pa?"

J. D. turned back, a smile pulling at his lips as tears filled his eyes. He shook his head. "You know how long I've waited to hear that word?"

Range returned the smile. "About as long as I've waited to say it, I guess."

J. D. nodded.

"Soon as I put down somewhere, I'll wire you," Range said.

J. D. turned back toward the porch. "I'll be here."

"Tell her I said goodbye," Range said.

"Tell her yourself," Candace said coolly.

Range jerked around.

Candace felt herself nearly sway from her feet as his gaze swept around to find hers. It was only by the sheerest thread of self-control that she held herself together. One wrong word from him, one wrong move or look, and she knew she would crumble. She would fall to her knees, spill a thousand tears, and beg him to stay.

She twisted the stem of the tiny wildflower she held in her hands. Everything in her urged her to plead with him to stay, but she couldn't do that, because she knew it would be the same as killing him. She hadn't wanted to admit that to herself, but she'd finally had no choice. If she asked him to stay and he did, she might as well kill him herself, because she would be the one responsible for his death even if she didn't pull the trigger. Word would get around that he'd stayed in Tombstone, that he'd settled down, and men would start coming after him. Bounty hunters, or men looking to heighten their reputation by taking down Range Connor. Ruthless men who wouldn't care how they cut him down, as long as they did.

Someday, if he stayed, he would end up getting killed, and it would be her fault. That was why she would not ask him to stay, why she would not tell him that she loved him. And that was why she would not cry. He had aroused feelings within her that she had never thought to feel. He had stolen her heart, and she had no desire to even try to get it back. Range Connor was the man she had been waiting her whole life to love, the man she would dream about for the rest of her life, the man she would cry over when the loneliness became too much to bear. But those were her secrets, because she would rather he ride out of her life and live, than stay and end up dead.

Range looked into her eyes and felt his heart reach out to her, even as he staunchly held his arms rigid at his sides and fought to keep the emotion churning within him from appearing on his face.

"J. D. said you're going to California," Candace said softly, forcing the words past the dryness constricting her throat. Tears threatened to fill her eyes, but she fought them back. She clasped her hands together beneath the folds of her skirt, hiding their trembling from his view.

Range shrugged. "Getting a little too crowded out here for me."

Candace nodded, as if understanding, when in reality she hadn't even heard him. There was too much noise in her head, a roaring of voices, all screaming at her to make him stay, stop him from leaving, tell him she loved him, stop him from riding away.

J. D. moved to the corner of the gallery, taking himself out of their view, but not moving so far that he couldn't see them, or hear what they said.

Range knew he should go. All he had to do was nudge Satan into movement, lay his reins across the animal's neck, and the huge horse would turn and canter back down the long drive. But he did nothing. His hands remained settled one over the other on top of the saddle horn. His legs and feet remained still in the stirrups, and his eyes continued to hold hers, blue delving into blue, trying to draw away and holding tight instead, saying good-bye, but not leaving, clasping the reins in which she held his heart, intending to jerk them from her grasp, and finding he had neither the strength nor the will.

"I wanted to thank you," Candace said after the silence that hung between them seemed without end, "for everything you've done."

Range nodded. It was time to go, time to end this self-torment. He tore his gaze from hers and raised his reins to go.

Candace's heart lurched in panic. "Range—"

He paused and, though it was as if a dozen knives were suddenly slicing up his insides, he forced himself to look back at her, back into those fathomless blue eyes that held everything he wanted in life, and everything he couldn't have.

She clenched her hands together tightly, fighting the urge to fly from the gallery and fling herself at him. "I'll never forget you," she said softly.

It was more than he could bear. Swinging his leg over his horse, Range dismounted and, in only a couple of long strides, moved to where Candace stood and swept her into his arms.

Just one more time, he told himself. He could not leave without holding her again, without crushing her lips to his and tasting the honeyed sweetness of her kiss, imprinting it on his mind to remember for all time, but especially during those long nights when he was going to lie awake aching for her, wishing her beside him, and enduring the knot that was, even now, threatening to consume him in its torment.

One more kiss, he told himself, one more feeling of her body pressed to his, her arms around his neck, holding him . . . then he could ride away and not look back. Then he could be satisfied with his memories.

His lips descended on hers with all the demanding possessiveness of a man desperately in love. Until that very moment he hadn't realized, hadn't let himself admit just how deeply he really did love her. But now he knew. She was his heart, his soul, the only woman who could ever fill the caverns the past had left within him, the only woman who could light the dark places and make him feel whole again. He loved her, and that was why he had to leave her.

His lips cajoled and teased, titillated and seduced, while his arms held her tightly pressed against him, his body enveloping hers and drawing it into him, as if wanting to hide her there within the shadow of his length, to keep her safe, or just to keep her.

Although it was less than Candace had hoped for, it was more than she'd expected. Her entire body responded to him in a flash of instant fire. Her arms slipped around his neck, her lips opened to welcome the thrust of his tongue, her breasts hardened and pressed into his chest.

The caress of her tongue to his was like velvet flame raging through his senses, inciting them, teasing them, while the feel of her in his arms, when he knew it was for the last time, when he knew he had to let her go, was almost more than he was able to bear.

Loneliness lay behind and ahead of him, but at least this time it would be different, this time he would have the memory of Candace to console him . . . or maybe torment him.

A moan of desperate desire escaped from his throat,

and Range tore himself away from her, knowing if he didn't do it then, he never would, and he couldn't allow that.

Her arms, like the future she knew stretched ahead bereft and solitary, suddenly seemed so empty. What was there without him to share it with?

Range held his shoulders stiff and walked down the steps. He grabbed Satan's reins.

"Don't go," Candace said softly, doing exactly what she'd promised herself she would not do.

He turned and looked back at her. It would be so easy to do as she asked, so easy to throw caution to the wind and say yes. But he couldn't. If anything ever happened to her because of him, he wouldn't be able to stand it.

Someday someone would come looking for Range Connor, looking to take him down and steal his reputation, and they might use her to get to him. He wasn't about to take that chance. He shook his head. "I can't. I have nothing to offer, not even a good name. All I have is trouble, and you don't need that. You've had enough."

Candace moved down the steps on wooden legs. She had meant to let him go with no pleading, no begging words for him to stay, but she couldn't. Slipping her arms around his neck, she pressed herself against him. "I don't need a good name," she said, her voice little more than a whisper, "I only need you, Range. I only need your love."

Calling on every ounce of willpower he had, Range forced her arms from around his neck and stepped away from her. He loved her, that was more than he'd ever thought he could feel. But he loved her more than life, and because of that, because he wanted her to go on with her life, find someone else, and give herself a chance to love and be loved by the right kind of man, he knew what he had to do. "I don't love you, Candace," he said harshly. "I came here to seek revenge for what was done to my mother years ago, and we . . ." he shrugged nonchalantly, "had a few good moments together. Don't make it out to be anything more than it was."

J. D. knew what Range was doing and was suddenly filled with a battling mixture of anger that his son was too stubborn to reach out and take the love that was being offered to him; compassion because he knew that Range desperately wanted to stay; and pride because he also knew that no matter how much he wanted Range to stay, he knew his son was doing what he thought he had to do to protect the woman he loved.

"I don't care what you say, Range Connor," Candace said as he slipped his foot into his stirrup and mounted Satan, "I love you, and I know you love me."

He stared at her long and hard before answering. "Even if that was true, lady, and it's not, I can't hide from my reputation. Someday some young buck would show up on the doorstep and demand that I face him, that I draw on him. And when I said no, maybe he'd figure out a way to force my hand, like using my wife against me, holding her, or even kidnapping her, to make me draw against him."

Candace opened her mouth to protest, but he kept talking.

"And his only reason would be so that he could say he'd killed me, that he'd outdrawn Range Connor, and now he was the fastest gun around." He shook his head. "I'm not waiting around for that to happen."

Nudging Satan, the big horse started to turn away.

"Range Connor may be a man without a future," J. D. said loudly, drawing Range's and Candace's attention as he suddenly moved into view, "he may be a hired gun that every young fool with an iron tied to his thigh wants to take down, every bounty hunter wants to bring in, and every man with a grudge wants to hire to kill his enemy, but Nick Landers isn't."

Range shook his head, ready to discount his father's

words, then paused as they penetrated the resistance he'd built up against any argument about his leaving.

Candace watched nervously, her hands clutched tightly together, her heart pounding madly, as silence hung heavily on the air.

Range stared down at the ground, J. D.'s words hanging on the morning air like jewels of hope thrust unexpectedly within Range's grasp. His first reaction was to disregard them, to deny that what J. D. was suggesting was even feasible.

But when he turned to look at Candace, he couldn't deny the hope he saw in her eyes and felt in his heart. All of the reasons he'd had for leaving, all of his arguments against staying, could be argued away with J. D.'s suggestion. And wasn't that what he wanted . . . to stay with Candace? To spend his life loving her, waking up next to her every morning, going to sleep with her beside him every night?

With Garth's and Jesse's deaths, Range's old way of life—the motivating factor that had turned him into the kind of man he'd been—was over.

"What if it doesn't work?" he said softly, his gaze holding Candace's.

"We'll make it work," she said, tears shimmering in her eyes.

"Someone could find out, come after me, demand I face them down."

"And maybe no one will ever come."

"But if they do . . ."

"We'll face them together."

Range continued to stare at her for a long moment in which his entire life swept through his mind in a succession of images. There had been touches of love here and there, but mostly there had been emptiness . . . an emptiness that he hadn't been feeling since he'd met Candace. And it was something he knew he never wanted to feel again. Not if there was a chance he didn't have to.

He tried once more, for both their sakes. "It'd be too dangerous."

Candace smiled. "It'd be more dangerous if I had to come after you, and I will if you leave."

He was lost, but then he'd known that from the first moment he'd looked in her eyes all those days ago. Dropping Satan's reins, Range swung off his saddle and took the steps to where Candace stood two at a time. Dragging her into his arms, he pulled her close. "Are you sure?" he asked, his voice husky with the pent-up emotion smoldering within his veins, his dark eyes riveted upon her own.

Her heart sang. He was everything she had ever wanted, and he was going to stay. There weren't going to be any lonely days and nights ahead, she wouldn't have to cry herself to sleep for want of him, or wonder where he was, or even if he was still alive. He loved her, and he was going to stay.

His gaze darkened, and a frown furrowed his brow as he continued to look into her eyes. "Are you sure?" he said again, when she didn't answer.

Candace reached up and touched her fingers to his cheek. "More than I've ever been about anything in my life," she said softly.

"I don't know anything about being a rancher," Range said.

"J. D. will teach you."

Both looked toward J. D., still standing a few yards away, and he smiled and nodded.

Range turned back to Candace. "I've pretty much always been alone," he said. "I don't know if I can—"

"We'll manage."

"I'm not a man of many words, Candace. I can't—"

She pressed a finger to his mouth. "Do you love me?" she asked softly.

"Yes."

She smiled. "That's all you have to say."

"I love you," Range said, as his mouth came down on hers.

The sun was hanging low on the horizon when Range and J. D. lifted the unusually light coffin off the bed of the buckboard and carried it up a grass-covered knoll to the small gravesite Range had dug earlier

"This is nice," J. D. said, straightening after he and Range had lowered Allison's coffin into the earth. He looked down at the river that meandered through the property of Gates End. Its slowly moving water glistened in reflection of the setting sun, like a river of gold moving ever southward. "She would have liked this spot."

"Yes," Range agreed, "I think she would have." He picked up the shovel he'd left there earlier and began filling in the grave. Minutes later, Range pounded a small white cross at the head of his mother's grave and lay a bouquet of yellow roses at its base.

J. D. looked down at the cross and the words he'd engraved across its face.

Allison Landers, Always Loved, Never Forgotten.

The tears he had denied himself for so long slipped down his craggy, weather-beaten face.

Range wrapped an arm around his father's shaking shoulders and let his own tears flow. It was the first time, in longer than he could remember, that he'd cried.

Chapter 23

"Yesterday two local residents, Garth Murdock and his younger brother Jesse, died in a gunfight with Range Connor, a gunman they'd hired to protect their property, the Rolling M ranch, in a water rights dispute they were engaged in with their neighbors.

"Range Connor, whose reputation as a hired gun rivaled that of Wyatt Earp, Bat Masterson and Doc Holliday, was also killed in the confrontation."

J. D. looked up from the newspaper he was reading aloud from and smiled. "What do you think, Nick? Sounds pretty good, don't you think?"

"Yeah," Range said, still unable to totally think of himself as Nick Landers. He was getting used to hearing the name, he just wasn't used to answering to it. "If people believe it."

Candace stepped into the parlor. "They will," she said, and smiled. "And if they don't, so what?"

"They'll come looking for me," Range growled. "That's so what."

She walked to him and took his hand. "Some people think President Lincoln is still alive, and Jesse James, Johnny Ringo, and Curly Bill Brocious. Some people believe in fairy tales, and others believe in mythology. It doesn't matter," she said. "The only thing that does is that I love you."

Range smiled. "And I love you."

Candace stood on tiptoe and brushed her lips across his. "Good. Then let's go, we have a funeral to attend."

She slipped her arm around his crooked one, but as she started for the door, Range held back. Candace looked up at him, puzzled.

"Maybe I shouldn't be there," Range said. "What if there's someone there who knows me? Who might recognize my face? I mean, I did talk to quite a few people around here, and I didn't make any secret of who I was."

J. D. moved past and opened the door. "You're Nick Landers," he said solemnly, "my son, and you always have been. Range Connor is dead."

Range nodded. "Okay, then let's go bury him."

An hour later they stood in the small town cemetery located in the foothills just outside of Tombstone, as several townsmen helped to lower three coffins into the grave, two with bodies inside, one holding nothing but stones. When they were done, a preacher said a few words.

Candace looked around from behind the black veil that hung from her hat and covered her face. A few townspeople had come to pay their respects, but most had stayed away.

She looked back at the grave sites as the preacher finishd his short eulogy.

The three grave markers held nothing but the men's

names. Garth Murdock, Jesse Murdock, and Range Connor.

A few people approached Candace and offered their sympathies, said hello to J. D., and were introduced to J. D.'s son, Nick, who had just arrived in town that morning.

One man, a neighboring rancher who Range had questioned in regards to his mother, looked at Range with an expression that was clearly disbelief.

"Funny," he said slowly, "you look exactly like that gunman who stopped by my place a few days ago. The one Murdock hired."

"Really?" Range said, and smiled. "Well, maybe we ought to dig him up and see if I had a twin brother I never knew about."

"That wasn't funny," Candace whispered, the minute the man walked away. "What if he'd taken you up on that?"

Range looked at her and smiled. "Sweetheart, he might have been curious. He might even have figured out the truth, but the man's a rancher not a gunman, so I doubt he has any desire to face down Range Connor."

She screwed up her face in a frown of admonishment. "Well, please do me a favor and refrain from doing that again, unless you want to make a nervous wreck out of me."

"Yes, ma'am," he said lightly.

"Mr. Landers?"

Both Nick and J. D. turned.

John Donnelly held his hand out to Nick. "I just wanted to welcome you to Tombstone."

Range stared at the man for a long moment before accepting his hand. They'd shared a bottle in the saloon, Donnelly had told him all about Candace's father, his murder, and how she'd come to marry Garth. There was no way John Donnelly could not know what was happening.

They shook hands.

Donnelly smiled. "Too bad about Connor, though," he said, glancing toward the freshly dug graves. "I liked him." Tipping his hat, he said goodbye and walked away.

Before they made it out of the cemetery, two more people stopped Range and Candace and commented on the fact that Nick Landers looked like the gunman the Murdocks had hired.

That night a man dressed totally in black paid a midnight visit to three ranches situated near the Rolling M. Making certain to stay just out of the light of the lamps the ranches' occupants held when they opened the door to the summons of their unknown visitor, the rider issued a warning: "Range Connor is dead. Let him rest in peace." Its meaning was all the more threatening for the man in black's softly hushed tone.

Epilogue

"Nick Landers, if you so much as knock on this door again, I swear I'm going to cut off your nose," Brianne said, glaring at him with fists propped on her hips.

Nick laughed. That was one threat he'd never heard before. "Okay, okay," he said, backing away from the small door of the church's anteroom. "I just wanted to know what was taking so long."

Brianne smiled. "A woman wants to look perfect on the day she gets married."

"Candace would look perfect in a burlap sack," Nick said. It had been two weeks since the funeral ceremony. Two weeks since *The Tombstone Epitaph* had announced to whoever wanted to know that Range Connor was dead. He hadn't been sure it would ever happen, but he was finally starting to get used to being called Nick.

J. D. moved up beside him and wrapped an arm around his shoulder. They walked outside, and J. D. struggled to keep a smile from his face, but the pride and joy shining from his eyes was there for all to see. The desert sun beat down on them mercilessly as they paused beside the doorway of the large old cathedral several miles ouside of Tucson.

Other than the fact that Candace loved St. Xavier's, whose twin towers rose high above the desert floor and thick adobe walls offered a cool sanctuary inside, they'd chosen to marry there in order to stay out of the way of the town busybodies who inhabited Tombstone. It wouldn't inhibit their wagging tongues any, but at least they wouldn't get a personal look at the ceremony.

"You okay?" J. D. asked quietly.

Nick turned to his father and frowned.

"You're not having second thoughts?" J. D. said, noticing the look on his son's face.

Range shook his head. "Never," he said softly, glancing over his shoulder at the anteroom. "No, but there's been something I've been wanting to say to you."

The older man remained silent.

"Thanks for not letting me leave."

J. D. smiled and, for the second time in two weeks, tears filled his eyes. "I lost you once son, I wasn't going to lose you again if I could help it." He reached out and drew Range into his arms.

At that very moment organ music filled the church.

J. D. released Nick. "Well, I guess she's finally ready," he said, and laughed.

Moments later Nick watched Candace walk toward him. Swirls of white lace surrounded her body, flounced and draped over her satin skirt, hugged her bodice, and flowed down the back of her gown to trail behind her on the floor, while her long blond hair shimmered upon her shoulders like strands of gold.

But it was her eyes that drew and held his: pools of misty

blue that shone with happiness and quietly promised a lifetime of tomorrows and an eternity of love.

As she neared where he stood at the altar, Candace reached out to him, her hand nearly becoming lost in his as his fingers wrapped around hers tenderly and drew her close.

The organist continued to play softly, and the priest spoke, but neither Nick or Candace really heard.

Candace looked up at him, her heart so full of love and happiness she was almost afraid to breathe, lest the dream shatter and cause him to disappear before her eyes.

But then the pressure of his warm hand wrapped around hers penetrated her consciousness, and she knew the moment was real.

"I now pronounce you man and wife," the priest said.

Tears of happiness filled Candace's eyes as she turned to Nick.

He pulled her into his arms, and just before his lips covered hers, she heard him whisper . . . "Forever".

TALES OF LOVE FROM MEAGAN MCKINNEY

GENTLE FROM THE NIGHT*   (0-8217-5803-$5.99/$7.50)
In late nineteenth century England, destitute after her father's
death, Alexandra Benjamin takes John Damien Newell up on his
offer and becomes governess of his castle. She soon discovers she
has entered a haunted house. Alexandra struggles to dispel the
dark secrets of the castle and of the heart of her master.
    *Also available in hardcover (1-577566-136-5, $21.95/$27.95)

A MAN TO SLAY DRAGONS   (0-8217-5345-2, $5.99/$6.99)
Manhattan attorney Claire Green goes to New Orleans bent on
avenging her twin sister's death and to clear her name. FBI agent
Liam Jameson enters Claire's world by duty, but is soon bound
by desire. In the midst of the Mardi Gras festivities, they unravel
dark and deadly secrets surrounding the horrifying truth.

MY WICKED ENCHANTRESS   (0-8217-5661-3, $5.99/$7.50)
Kayleigh Mhor lived happily with her sister at their Scottish es-
tate, Mhor Castle, until her sister was murdered and Kayleigh had
to run for her life. It is 1746, a year later, and she is re-established
in New Orleans as Kestrel. When her path crosses the mysterious
St. Bride Ferringer, she finds her salvation. Or is he really the
enemy haunting her?

AND IN HARDCOVER . . .
THE FORTUNE HUNTER   (1-57566-262-0, $23.00/$29.00)
In 1881 New York spiritual séances were commonplace. The mysterious Countess Lovaenya was the favored spiritualist in Manhattan.
When she agrees to enter the world of Edward Stuyvesant-French,
she is lead into an obscure realm, where wicked spirits interfere with
his life. Reminiscent of the painful past when she was an orphan
named Lavinia Murphy, she sees a life filled with animosity that
longs for acceptance and love. The bond that they share finally leads
them to a life filled with happiness.

ROMANCE FROM JO BEVERLY

DANGEROUS JOY (0-8217-5129-8, $5.99)

FORBIDDEN (0-8217-4488-7, $4.99)

THE SHATTERED ROSE (0-8217-5310-X, $5.99)

TEMPTING FORTUNE (0-8217-4858-0, $4.99)